BLOOD ON THE STONE

About the Author

Jake Lynch divides his time between Australia, where he is Associate Professor of Peace and Conflict Studies at the University of Sydney, and Oxford, where he acts in amateur theatricals and runs a local book group. Previously, Jake enjoyed a twenty-year career in journalism, with spells as a political correspondent for Sky News and the Sydney correspondent for the *Independent*, culminating in a role as a BBC World presenter. For his work in peace journalism research, training and development, he was honoured with the 2017 Luxembourg Peace Prize, awarded by the Schengen Peace Foundation. In 2020, he will be a Leverhulme Visiting Professor at Coventry University. Jake holds a BA in English and a Diploma in Journalism from Cardiff University, and a PhD from City University, London.

BLOOD ON THE STONE

JAKE LYNCH

unbound

This edition first published in 2019

Unbound

6th Floor Mutual House, 70 Conduit Street, London W1S 2GF

www.unbound.com

This book is a work of fiction and, except in the case of historical fact,
any resemblance to actual persons, living or dead, is purely
coincidental.

ISBN (eBook): 978-1-78352-790-8
ISBN (Paperback): 978-1-78352-791-5

Cover design by Mecob

Printed and bound in Great Britain by Clays Ltd, Elcograf S.p.A.

To Annabel and Finn, as ever

Super Patrons

Zainab Abdulnabi
Clariza Denise Ablaza
Nitasha Akerman
Lyn Aldridge
Patricia Aliño
Dan Anlezark
Vanessa Bassil
Ignasius Loyola Adhi Bhaskara
Madeline Brennan
Polixeni Brennan
Birgit Brock-Utne
Michael Brown Woliver
Laura Cairns
Nico Candelario
Leigh Cholakos
Peggy Craddock
Hilmi Dabbagh
Lyn Dickens
Fred Dubee
Saskia Gem Lear
James Godfrey
Vicki Hansen
Annie Herro
Amanda Hickey
Laura Holbach
Brami Jegan
Nimalan Karthikeyan
Dan Kieran
Dong JIn Kim

Robert Kinnane
Simon Lynch
Melissa McCullough
John Mitchinson
Diane Moore
Mark Norman
Biannca Pace
Scott Pack
Andrea Pagella
Erik Paul
Justin Pollard
Richard Powell
Jon Rail
Gobie Rajalingam
Nick Riemer
Senthan Selvarajah
Ahmad Shboul
Antonio Carlos Silva Rosa
Peter Slezak
Tedla Tedla Desta
Lauren Thackray
Leon Thapa
Heather Watkins
Sandra Whitehead
Leanne Wilson
Wei Zhu

Contents

Prologue

Monday 17 March, 1681

Captain Edwin Sandys was still a furlong short of the column's vanguard when a loud bang and bright flash cut through the gloaming. A gunshot – and, judging by the size of the flame, a backfire. Quickening to a canter, he noticed several of the Guards drawing steel as he rode past. Colonel de Vere would be mystified. Moments earlier, the commanding officer's carriage window had burst open with an irritable clatter, as Sandys bent down to brief him.

'Well, Captain?' he snapped.

'Slight hold-up, sir. Should soon be on our way.'

'Papists?' The question was accompanied by a raised eyebrow.

'No, sir – cattle.'

As the London road narrowed on its final descent through Shotover Woods, the Blues had run into a herd of milking cows, being taken in for the night. Frozen in panic, the animals formed a stubborn barrier. The news was received with a groan. In the order of conveyance, the Royal party itself travelled directly behind the regimental command, and the King was not known for his patience. Sandys remembered the men's unease at receiving orders to escort His Majesty to Oxford for the forthcoming session of Parliament. He shared the Colonel's scepticism at the popular notion of a 'Popish Plot' against the Crown. But what if it was right after all, and they were now coming under attack?

As the captain approached the front of the convoy, it was clear the shot was a false alarm. The Guards were moving again. One, dismounted by the path-side, had flung off his coat and was now stamping out a smouldering mess of fabric and embers. On the ground by his side lay a flintlock pistol, its hammer down. An irascible countenance, with a Cavalier's T-shaped moustache and beard, turned in Sandys' direction: Trooper George Gregory. He'd be in trouble. Discharging a firearm except in battle was deemed conduct prejudicial to military order and discipline.

'What d'you think you're doing, soldier?'

'Clearing the King's highway for His Majesty.' The shot had caused a stampede, and the terrified beasts were trampling through the straggly bushes bordering the laneway.

'Well, you should clean your weapon properly. Give it here.'

A quick examination of the gun showed the errant Guardsman was lucky. Sure enough, the mechanism was caked with residues he had not bothered to scrape off. But the extent of blowback through the touch-hole had been small, mostly diverted sideways by the frizzen, with the rest baffled by his tunic's thick upturned cuff. Looking around for a fellow officer as he returned the firearm to its owner, Sandys' gaze settled on the most junior of his colleagues, Captain Thomas Lucy.

'Kindly keep your company in order, sir! That shot would've been heard in the Royal carriage.'

'Sorry, Captain Sandys. Won't happen again,' the younger man replied, whey-faced.

The last of the cattle were disappearing up a slope on the far side of the hedgerow, and Sandys felt a pang of concern on seeing the young woman who'd been tending them set off in forlorn pursuit. If the herd should come to any harm, it would risk turning the countryside against the Royal party before they had even reached their destination. But his qualms were cut short by an urgent call from behind.

'Colonel's orders – make haste: Old Rowley is furious!' (Old Rowley was the King's nickname, after one of his stallions – a backhanded compliment to his sexual appetite. On this occasion the Royal party included not one but two of his mistresses.)

So the column pressed on towards their muster point on the meadow of Christ Church College. There, His Majesty would find succour, as his father had before him, during the Civil War; the Guards would be allocated their billets, stable their horses, and disperse for the night.

Chapter 1
Parliament Comes to Oxford

It had been one of those Oxford mornings when mist seems to percolate from scholastic limestone and half-dissolve the domes and spires, as though they had been dreamt into existence overnight and were about to fade away. By noon, however, the vapour had nearly all burnt off. The pale, unflattering daylight picked out the brown builder's dust filming the windows of The Unicorn and Jacob's Well, a tavern just opened on Fish Street, opposite Christ Church.

Luke Sandys, Chief Officer of the Oxford Bailiffs, had already made two calls to chase up the unpaid licence fee, and now his patience was at an end. As they emerged from the Guildhall, Robshaw, his deputy, was squinting and rubbing his eyes.

'I still don't see why we have to call again.'

'That's because you're hung over, Robshaw – or still drunk.'

'Why, if a man gets paid in ale for an early shift, what's he to do?'

'While you're a constable, you're supposed to be on a break from the brewery.'

'Aye, but malt still needs turning. They got me to come in special, like. Big order on, see, what with them political folk coming to town. 'Tis reckoned they'll be thirsty, from all that talking.'

Luke stopped, turned to face him, and sighed. Through their bushy-browed, bloodshot defiance, the other man's eyes glinted with native intelligence, beneath furrows of vexation deepened by a shapeless black hat pulled down tight over unruly blond locks.

'Yes, normally we would be content to wait for the licensee to pay up. But these are not normal times.' He was rewarded with an indeterminate grunt. 'That tavern is just across from the chambers that will house the King and Queen.'

'King and mistresses, more like.'

'Be that as it may. I'm not having the City exposed. If anything untoward goes on in those premises, and they turn out to be unlicensed, it'll come back on us.' With that, Luke turned and strode off down the slope in the direction of Christ Church. Robshaw dug his hands further into his pockets, set his shoulders, and plodded along behind.

The door opened on a rowdy scene, with as many as two dozen drinkers already well into their cups. Luke marched across to the counter.

'Unsworth, how's this? You're not to entertain customers till your licence is paid in full, you know that.'

A crafty gleam in his eye, the landlord replied: 'Why, Master Sandys, you see, these gentlemen ain't customers, they're guests. This here's a private dinner.'

'A liquid one!' a loud voice exclaimed from the back of the room, to general merriment.

Luke made no move to leave, and a tall, aquiline character approached them, whereupon the din lowered appreciably.

'I'm sure you'll find whatever outstanding debt may remain will be paid with due despatch.' A sidelong glare at the innkeeper added an undertone of menace to the otherwise emollient voice. 'We are a bona fide political society, sir, and we are holding a meeting here.' Greying temples only served to accentuate the speaker's air of calm authority.

'Aye – and lifting the cloven foot of Popery off the throats of freeborn Englishmen,' came a growl from a thickset, hard-looking character at the end of the bar, whose intervention was greeted by noisy approval. The senior man hushed them by lifting a hand.

'That will do, Hawkins. William Harbord Esquire, Member of Parliament for Thetford, Norfolk, at your service, sirs.'

'Luke Sandys, sir. Chief Bailiff's Officer.' Somewhere close behind him, Robshaw grunted again.

'I'm sure neither you nor the City would want to interfere with our liberties,' Harbord continued. In an oddity Luke had overlooked on entering, every man wore a small green ribbon. He knew about the blue ribbons of the Whigs, or Country Party, and the Tories' red, but this was new.

'Why, we just turned away a gentleman, Luke, as wanted to come in,' Unsworth wheedled. 'We're not open for business, not really.'

'That "gentleman" was not a member of this club,' Harbord said frostily.

'Very well, sirs. Finish your meeting, but this must be the last alcohol served on these premises before the fee is fully paid.' Luke quit the inn with Robshaw in tow, and resolved to ask his brother Edwin that evening – assuming he arrived in time for supper – about the green ribbons.

Next on their list of jobs was to advise on arrangements for royal security at the Bodleian Library, where the King would open the parliamentary session in the Convocation House. A red-coated military officer consulted a sheet of paper, pegged to a board of wood, as they approached.

'Sandys?'

'At your service, sir.' Robshaw emitted yet another grunt.

'Captain Sutherland. Foot Guards.' He turned abruptly to a

newly fitted door in the medieval Divinity School, opposite the back entrance of the Sheldonian Theatre.

'This won't do, Sandys. 'Tis a weak point. His Majesty will pass through right behind this door.'

Luke ran his hand over the timber. It seemed substantial enough. But the twitching of Sutherland's ginger moustache was matched by his officious tone.

'You'll have to station constables outside at all times, is that clear?'

'Crystal,' Luke mouthed absently, but the deputy, roused at last from his stupor, cut loudly across him:

'Daft idea!'

Sutherland turned on him at once, seething.

'You will obey orders, damn you!'

But Robshaw merely planted his feet wider apart, hooked his thumbs in the belt that stretched across his ample waist, and returned the officer's glare.

'Not yours, I won't.'

'Robshaw!' Luke warned.

'Well, it don't make no sense, do it? We should be out keeping an eye on troublemakers, not standing around behind the Sheldonian.'

Luke was suddenly aware of a tension that had been building up behind his brow. With an effort, he redoubled his concentration on the situation in hand.

'He has a point, Captain. Surely the best contribution we can make to the King's security in Oxford is by drawing on our local knowledge.' Sutherland looked back to Luke and released the hilt of his sword – only after a moment of clenched fury.

'I suppose you have a list of all the Papists hereabouts?' The initial plosive 'P' was spat out with contempt.

'We know where they are.'

'Very well. But I shall want your men on duty here from daybreak on the first morning of Parliament.' With that, Sutherland turned on his heel and bade Luke a curt good-day.

'Looks like he's got a sword stuck up his arse, that one,' Robshaw said, as the officer marched stiffly away.

As they left, Luke glanced up at the Sheldonian's smooth grey curvature. The building had made the reputation of Christopher Wren, a hero from his student days. The door that upset Sutherland was installed at the architect's behest, to allow graduands to robe up in the Divinity School before walking across the narrow gap between the two buildings to reach their graduation ceremonies. Now his own son, Sam, was a bound apprentice in Wren's London practice, working on the new St Paul's Cathedral. But the boy had left a gap in the Sandys household when they'd waved him off, months earlier; and the gap, Luke realised, was starting to ache. Then, he'd had to suppress a wave of nausea, to go with his throbbing head, at the Captain's menacing reference to 'Papists'. There was one Roman Catholic household he routinely missed off any such incriminating list – but not even Robshaw knew about that, he was certain.

A sharp 'clack' sounded a discordant note amid the tinkling bells attached to the frame of Simon Gibson's door as Luke pushed it open. The apothecary seemed to put something down in a hurry behind the counter, rubbing his mouth on his sleeve as he mumbled a greeting: 'Why, Master Sandys, sir! Good day to you – good day indeed.'

'Good day, Gibson,' Luke said, suddenly on his guard. 'Anything I should know about?' he enquired, nodding towards the hidden shelf. A faint sickly-sweet undercurrent joined the familiar waft of herbal and floral scents that filled the shaded interior.

'Why nay, sir, 'twas just some of that new tonic – laudanum, they call it.' The man lifted an empty cup on to the surface to show his customer.

'Laudanum – worthy of praise,' Luke quickly translated.

''Tis surely that, sir. Strange thing is, once a man's tried it, he always comes back for more. Maybe I can interest you...?'

'Nay, one of your milder remedies should suffice. 'Tis only a headache.'

'As you wish. Some of this wood betony perhaps? Picked fresh this morning, from Wytham.' He produced a vase of greenery from a ledge at the back of the shop. 'Just wants making up into a nice hot drink, with a pinch of salt and a touch of honey.'

'Aye, that'll do. Thank you kindly.' Luke handed the man a coin, and took his leave.

Chapter 2
Brotherly Reunion

A draught of the infusion, and a lie down, eased Luke's physical ailments at least. The family home on Magpie Lane presented a deceptively modest frontage to the world at large. Behind lay a capacious interior, which tended these days to an almost sepulchral quiet, the daytime hubbub of the nearby High Street muffled by its thick stone walls. The children's pattering footsteps and excitedly raised voices, enlivening the sombre rooms and corridors, were now a fading memory. Today, even Luke's prized possession – one of the new pendulum clocks, accurate to within fifteen seconds a day, and obtained at great expense from a London merchant – brought him no consolation. From its niche in the hallway, its loud 'tick-tock' seemed to build up, layer on layer, into a jarring resonance.

Luke had begun the long-overdue job of restoring order to his study, but found he tended to clutch at any opportunity for distraction. He leafed through one of his father's favourite books, retrieved from the back of a shelf: *The Practice of Piety*, by a Puritan, Lewis Bayly. Its doctrine of predestination was theological poison these days, as Anglican orthodoxy was prosecuted with ever greater official zeal. Better keep it out of sight. Still, Samuel Sandys had never let his nonconformist convictions get in the way of worldly advancement. Success in his trade of fine joinery had paid for Luke's university place, and Edwin's commission in the Royal Horse Guards. 'Keep your shop,' he would say, 'and your shop will keep you.' Fingering the intricate oak decorations on the arms of his favourite chair,

Luke remembered helping the old man to carve it: a lucrative commission from a college Fellow who found himself embarrassed when it came to pay. So, they decided to use it themselves. A rare occasion when his father indulged in a bit of luxury – a comfortable seat on which to pore over his accounts.

The clattering from the kitchen that cut through Luke's reverie, as his wife supervised culinary arrangements for their guest, signalled her need for his attention. He'd wed Elizabeth in haste, after they 'got carried away', as it was said, and she fell pregnant with Jane. Now their daughter was herself safely married off, and Sam gone, her nest was empty. Much as he might roll his eyes and shake his head at her summons, sheer force of habit carried his feet downstairs.

'All well, my dear?'

'Well, husband, thank you. If, praise God, Edwin ever gets here. We must hope he's not too long delayed on the road.' Mistress Sandys impatiently seized a dish from Joan, the cook-maid, and took over the job of whipping cream for a posset, to be set to cool for pudding, while the servant went and sulked in the corner over a plate of dried fruit.

'He shouldn't be too long. I heard they met the Lord Lieutenant's party at Wheatley earlier.'

'Build up the fire in the hall then, Luke, and light some more candles,' she said, vigorously agitating the mixture. 'If he's had to wait around outside this evening, he'll be chilled to the marrow.'

'The Green Ribbon Club?' Captain Edwin Sandys – Ed, now he was back in his old home – helped himself to another portion of rabbit pie. The family did not stand on ceremony while dining in private: the Sandys' retainers were now so old and infirm that their presence at table was less a help than a hindrance. 'They're convinced we're all about to be murdered in our beds, on direct orders from the Vatican.'

'We met their leader today – a Member of Parliament, William Harbord.'

'Aye, Harbord's a hammer of Rome, all right,' Ed reported, with a grimace. 'Never backward in accusing men of treachery, either.'

'Are they dangerous?' Luke recalled the sense of menace in the air at The Unicorn and Jacob's Well.

'They would be, given half a chance. They can't make any real trouble here, with so many Guards around. But of course they're fanatical about the Exclusion. They'll be trying to put pressure on the Lords to pass it.'

'Why, 'tis wrong to make the King cut off his own brother!' Elizabeth said.

''Tis politics! James was outed by the Test Act. That's when he had to step down from the Admiralty. He could have been a Papist in private – but in public?' Ed gave a wry shake of the head. 'The real problems will start when he accedes.'

Luke got up to put another log on the fire. 'The Green Ribbon men are loyal to Charles, though?'

'Well – they'd rather have someone keener on persecuting Catholics. There's Monmouth, of course. If they do manage to exclude James, he'd be favourite for the succession.'

'Your old commander?'

'Indeed. Though I haven't seen him since the Anglo-Dutch Brigade at Saint-Denis – three years ago, now.'

'Is he still in exile?' Luke had not kept up with recent developments as well as he should, he now realised.

'They sent him away? How come?' his wife asked. ''Tis no way to treat a man who fought bravely for King and country!'

'Made him too popular, I'm afraid. Started up all that business again, over his birth.' Luke made a quizzical expression. 'Was

Charles secretly married to his mother, is he the rightful heir after all?' Ed explained. 'No, England has to have time to forget his derring-do, then he can come back when he's no longer a threat.'

''Twill be the doing of that damn Frenchwoman, no doubt – the King's mistress,' Elizabeth said, in distaste. Luke looked at his wife askance: it was rare for anything to move her to curse out loud, even with only close family for company. 'Duchess of Portsmouth, they call her. Power behind the throne, 'tis said. She's probably here now, is she, Ed?'

'Louise de Kérouaille? Yes, she's come to Oxford, she travelled in the Royal Carriage.'

Elizabeth shook her head and sighed.

'Anyway, shouldn't you be persecuting Catholics, Luke?' Ed wondered. 'Orders are being sent down from the Privy Council all the time. I presume they reach you here?'

'Latest is, we're supposed to give lists of "recusants" to the magistrates, who have them brought to court and make them take the oaths in public.'

'What if they don't?'

'Then we're to collect their fines, and lock them up if they won't pay – or can't.'

'And do you?' Luke paused, wondering how to put it.

'It doesn't really get that much of anyone's time or attention.'

'Ah, then you'd fall foul of the Green Ribbons. For showing insufficient zeal against the Popish Plot.'

'You're not going to get in trouble, are you, Luke?' Elizabeth asked nervously.

'Nay, wife! And surely,' he said, turning to Ed, 'that nonsense can't go on for much longer?'

'Now, that would get you in trouble, Luke, if you said it out loud in the wrong company.'

'I just can't believe the Catholics in Oxford are involved in some Jesuit conspiracy to seize the crown.'

Ed finished chewing a mouthful of the pie, then took a deep draught of wine.

'Between ourselves, of course, I agree with you. But – well, 'tis as the Earl of Halifax put it: "We must all act as though the Plot is true, whether we believe it or not."'

'But what's the evidence? A moth-eaten list of names, found by some reprobate in a closet, or so 'tis said? And men have been sent to the gallows for it.'

'Politics doesn't work like one of your Wadham experiments, Luke. Circumstances alter cases: something is evidence if enough men say it is.' Luke had become attached to scientific methods at meetings of the Natural Philosophy club, run by the Warden of Wadham College, John Wilkins, during his student days.

'The true method of experience first lights the candle,' he said now, as he replenished his cup. '*Adaequatio intellectus nostri cum re* – let our minds conform to the facts. That's how I've always tried to work. At least then we don't hang the wrong man. Well, not very often.'

Joan brought in the posset and dried fruits.

'Jis, but there's a sharp chill out now,' she mumbled ill-humouredly. 'I could freeze my bubbies off, going out there in this weather, to be sure!'

'Joan!'

'Beggin' your pardon Mistress: but 'tis just the boys – and they know me too well, I can't change my ways at my time of life, so I can't.'

'Their father would've whipped you for insolence! Maybe they'll do likewise.'

'Thank you Joan, we'll manage from now on,' Luke said, stifling a grin. 'Perhaps you should turn in for the night, and leave tidying up till the morning.'

'Very well then, Master. I'll be off to bed, soon as I've finished my cup of sack.'

Elizabeth exhaled audibly and shook her head at the maid's departing back.

'Still the same Joan, then,' Ed said, smiling, when she had gone.

'Aye – more's the pity,' Elizabeth replied. 'Though how much longer she'll be able to get up and down those stairs…'

'If she stopped working, I don't know what she'd do, or where she'd go,' Luke mused. 'She's got no relatives that we know of.' Joan's Irish labourer father, and her mother, a freed African slave girl, were both long dead, and her siblings scattered to the four winds; so the Sandys were her only family.

Ed returned to the subject.

'So, apart from rounding up recusants, how are things at the Guildhall these days?'

'At least that prating ninnycock Robert Pawling's left off being mayor,' Elizabeth cut in. 'He gave more troubles than all the knaves in Oxford!'

Luke discreetly moved the jug of canary out of his wife's immediate reach.

'Yes, we don't have to look after Pawling on night watch any more. He's gone back to farming, over at Headington.' As incumbent mayor, the previous year, the farmer had sent constables out on night patrol, and regularly joined them in person; thus antagonising the University, whose proctors were in sole charge of law and order while the city was asleep.

'Men still paying to get out of serving as constables?' Ed asked. Luke's term in the office now stretched over several years, as other freemen decided they could not afford to take time off their trade or craft to fulfil the historic duty.

'Aye, still plenty of them.'

'And you still wouldn't stand for one of the elected offices?'

'I think not,' he replied. From the corner of his eye, he glanced at his wife as she raised her cup. In quiet moments alone, Luke still raked over the series of misunderstandings that had brought him to her door when she was alone in the house; and their rashness in sitting together unchaperoned on that fateful afternoon, nearly twenty-five years earlier. Her pitiable expression, when she later came to confide that she was with child, had jolted him into the right, indeed the only responsible course of action. Of that, he remained certain. But these days he felt, if anything, ever more keenly what he had lost. His chance of a college Fellowship – a position reserved for single men – for one. And even now, people referred to their union as a 'knob-stick wedding'. He was sure it was held against him. Luke was proud of the bachelor's degree he did manage to achieve, but University connections were not seen these days as a political asset, at least not in the City's eyes; let alone lingering memories of their father's suspect religious allegiances. All would risk being dredged up if ever he put himself forward for an elected office as a bailiff or councillor.

'Nay,' he told his brother. 'Better to grow the oak than seek the laurel.'

Chapter 3
A Body Politic

Elizabeth had not long gone up to bed, declaring that she had 'a-boused and bolled enough for one night' – more than enough, Luke thought – when there came a thunderous knock at the door.

'Sorry to disturb, sirs.' A great dark cloak made Robshaw's outline in the candlelight even more bearlike than usual.

'What is it, Robshaw?'

'A body, sir. Night watch found it, a short while ago, on the doorstep of that there new tavern, where we was earlier.'

'Have you seen it?'

'Not yet – one of the proctors knocked me up and I came straight here. 'Tis said he's been stabbed.' Luke felt a twist of dread: the political atmosphere already contained enough tension, as their supper conversation had affirmed. An act of violence, as MPs and their hangers-on converged on the city, smelt of trouble.

'You did right. Very well, let's go.'

The grey of the once-distinguished temples seemed to have drained through the face, washing out the vitality, as Luke peered down at the still, beaky face and splayed figure of the man who had introduced himself to them earlier as William Harbord, MP. Steady luminescence from the clear night sky mingled with the guttering light of Robshaw's lantern as he held it above the body.

'There's the wound,' the deputy pointed out unnecessarily, as the two light sources refracted in the congealed surface of a pool of blood emanating from Harbord's abdomen.

'Where's the weapon?' One of the University proctors, who had stood guard over the scene, piped up in reply.

'Can't be found, sir.'

'Well, hasn't been found, anyway. We'll have to take a proper look in daylight.'

'I'll need to clean up this here step, sirs.' Unsworth had pulled on coat and boots over his vest and canions, against the chill, and was now shifting agitatedly from foot to foot, a grimace of dismay etched on his features. The innkeeper had been held back from the murder scene by the watchmen, who looked a question in Luke's direction. He nodded.

'May as well move it now, we can't learn anything else here for the moment. Robshaw, put the body in my parlour.' The 'parlour' was in fact a wide stone landing at the head of a staircase down to a small cellar, behind Sandys' office at the back of the Guildhall, a little further up Fish Street. Robshaw jingled his bunch of keys at the men to fetch the low cart they used to scoop up the dead and the dead drunk alike from the city streets.

Turning to the innkeeper, Luke asked: 'So he was lodging, as well as drinking, in your unlicensed premises?' Unsworth's voice and manner assumed their default attitude of obsequious wheedling.

'That he was, Master Sandys sir, though he was ever such a proper gentleman, sir.'

'That's beside the point, Unsworth, as well you know. You told the night watch that you heard and saw nothing of this... incident? No altercation, no raised voices?'

Unsworth made as if to say something, then glumly shook his head.

'Very well. I shall want to talk to you further tomorrow. Make sure you're here, or if you must go out, don't go far.'

'Yessir,' he nodded, relieved.

Luke held open the door at the back of the Guildhall, off the stable yard. Harbord's corpse was manhandled in and through to the chamber at the back of the office, laid on a trestle table and covered with a length of muslin. Then he bade his deputy goodnight, locked up, and walked slowly back along Fish Street, towards the river. Unsworth was, sure enough, swabbing the threshold of The Unicorn and Jacob's Well, too preoccupied to notice him passing by on the other side. The imposing limestone of Christ Church formed an apparently impenetrable barrier. Surely the King would be safe here? Though, on second thoughts, men still talked of the nine-pound shell fired by the New Model Army during the siege of Oxford in the time of His Majesty's father, Charles I, which had thudded against the wall of the college dining hall.

The great wooden doors, long since bolted for the night, were just a stone's throw from the murder scene. He would have to interview the porters to find out if they had seen anything amiss. That would mean approaching the dean of the college, Bishop Fell, for permission to speak to them. Fell was an old friend, but would doubtless want something in return. Luke sighed. They had already been braced for a busy week – and now there was this.

Turning homewards, Luke reached the junction of Blue Boar Street. He could take the short cut to the back end of Magpie Lane – but, on second thoughts, decided to go the long way round. With time now to plumb his memory, he recalled seeing Harbord's name mentioned in one of the newsletters, or 'mercuries', that carried reports of parliamentary proceedings. Jane occasionally sent them to him from London. The Member for Thetford had been a great agitator of the Popish Plot, telling the House of Commons that 'I profess I never go to bed, but I expect the next morning to hear of the King's being killed.'

In a few short hours, news of his own death would be bruited abroad on the streets of Oxford.

As he passed The Mitre, a large coaching inn on the High Street, a faint light was snuffed out somewhere inside. Someone must have been tidying up, and was now retiring to bed. Luke's pulse quickened as he realised it might be her – Cate Napper, the landlord's daughter, and the person in Oxford whom he was most anxious to protect. He turned to walk on, though more slowly now, delaying his return. As he trod the moonlit pavement, he stepped in his mind's eye into the bright future he imagined with Cate. Her faith seldom intruded into the vision, but now it loomed large as a potential hazard – for the Nappers were devotees of the old religion.

Luke turned up the collar of his coat as a chill breeze blew in from the east and wrenched his attention back to the present. Harbord was not short of friends or allies, and their chief preoccupation seemed to be – as Ed put it – persecuting Catholics. Wouldn't they immediately blame the MP's murder on 'Papists'? How would they react, if they found out about the Catholic family who ran one of the city's most frequented drinking establishments? Was there any way they could know what Luke himself knew – that Romish rites and sacraments were secretly administered in The Mitre's generously proportioned vaults? He shook his head impatiently. No point vexing himself with conjecture. On the morrow, he would have to begin taking practical steps to solve the murder – hopefully before it had time to ratchet up the political tension still further. Home now, he turned the key, let himself in, lit a candle, and quietly climbed the stairs to bed.

Chapter 4
Blood on the Stone

If Captain Edwin Sandys soon forgot about the brief hiatus in the Royal progress, for Emily Hopkins the shot that frightened her cattle signalled the start of a traumatic evening. Earlier, Richard Bourke, her betrothed lover, had met her on his way back from work in Oxford as an apprentice stonemason. A few precious minutes alone together in the afternoon sunshine had turned into an hour. They felt the gentle swelling of her belly, hidden by the farm smock she wore for her duties, as the milchers cropped the season's first growth. But a glance at the rapidly darkening horizon told her that she had tarried too long in the field. With a start, she shooed him on his way, and hurriedly summoned the beasts for the trudge back to Magdalen Farm.

The only pasture fit to be grazed this early in spring lay on a south-facing slope, at the far side of the London road – which they must therefore cross on the way home. In her haste, Emily realised too late that the herd did not have the route to themselves. Suddenly, on a narrow bend, cavalrymen in blue-and-red uniforms were shouting and angrily motioning at her to let them pass. But the kine had other ideas. A dozen in number, they stopped abruptly, glazed-eyed and fretful, their ears twitching.

'Please sirs, let me round the front of them,' Emily begged, in vain. 'They'll come quietly, if they see me leading them, sirs!' The road widened out up ahead, with plenty of space for them to pass, if only the Guardsmen would make way. But they were not listening.

'Damn your impudence, girl!' one barked.

'This'll get them going,' his companion said in a grating north-country accent, brandishing his flintlock. Emily would later remember seeing the soldier's finger pause on the trigger, as if frozen in time. Then, for an instant, the world turned white, as the weapon discharged.

She blinked through the shock of incandescence and the sudden report, followed immediately by a loud and violent curse from the shooter. It seemed as though the man's wrist was on fire, though as he dropped his weapon and shrugged off his jacket she could see it was actually the lower part of the sleeve. The gunshot echoed through the bare branches of Shotover Woods behind, where a flock of half a dozen magpies sought sanctuary, scolding 'chack-chack-chack' as they flapped away. But the terrified bellowing of her beasts drew her attention back to them – they were lumbering off, trampling down the undergrowth abutting the roadway.

Emily plucked up her skirts and followed the cattle as best she could through the gap they had made in the hedgerow. Her heart sank: she was now venturing on to land newly enclosed on behalf of the young Baron Headington, King Charles's illegitimate son by Nell Gwynn. Any livestock found on the baronial estate could be forfeit. After a few minutes she crested a blind summit, a natural fold in the escarpment, and looked down on a derelict chapel – its stones being plundered for other buildings, now the enclosure had cut off public access to worship. Her apprehension turned to horror as the dreadful truth revealed itself. Two of the animals lay prone below her, having evidently lost their footing on the steep bank as they ran, and tumbled down among the ruins.

With a gasp, she noticed that Daisy's foreleg was protruding at an odd angle, and a groaning sound filled her ears. But Cassie's plight was even worse. The demolition crew had left behind a large pickaxe, wedged among the stones, and its pointed blade had pierced the milcher's flank like a spear. The creature had rolled off the spike in trying to right herself. But now, from the wound, her life's blood issued in rhythm with each labouring breath, dribbling out with a hiss on to the cold, smooth surface beneath. Before long, the beast keeled over with a final sigh as her half-full udder lolled, a forlorn appendage to her still, stark form. The low seething of Daisy next to her told Emily she could not give way to self-pity. She would have to strike out for home, her parents' cottage by the barton at Magdalen, and get help. The other cattle, she would have to trust would make their own way back. And – Lord-a-Lord! – what would Farmer Pawling say?

Reaching the farm at last, she paused shivering on the threshold, and looked out over the Cherwell meads, the ancient landscape impassive under the starry firmament. As she entered, the cheery greeting froze on her mother's lips, and the batlet she had been using to smooth the linens dropped from her fingers. She listened in anguish as Emily's tale dribbled out between sobs. When the men had set off in their horse-drawn cart, with rope and tackle to bring back the stricken beasts, Mistress Hopkins found a tub of balsam and dabbed it on the worst of her scratches by the insipid glow of a tallow flame.

'Daze my eyes, missy! We must hope your father don't catch it too hard from Farmer Pawling. You mind how he takes on sometimes.'

'I couldn't stop them, Ma. Not once that cavalryman fired his gun.'

'I know you couldn't, petal. I feel for you, I do. God's body, you've had some cruel luck, going out into the wide world.'

Emily shifted closer to her mother, her hand involuntarily resting on her abdomen.

'Why, it feels like five minutes since you'd be in here of a Monday, helping with the wash-tub, and getting under my feet,' the mother said tenderly. 'And now look at you, set to be a married woman and have a littl'un yourself, one of these fine days.' And she placed her own hand, reddened as it was from a day's laundering, on her daughter's. They sat for a moment, looking at the glowing logs in the fireplace.

'I'm scared, Ma.'

'I know you are, sweet. But 'twill all be for the best in the end, if it do please God.'

Later, Jacob Hopkins roused her from the chair by the hearth, with John Davies, the farrier, in tow – but his twinkle, which Emily remembered from Christmases when he would invite them in for mulled wine, was now replaced by a grave expression. Trotting to keep up with the long strides of the men, Emily crossed the yard and into the farmhouse, then up a dimly lit staircase, where Jacob knocked on the door of Robert Pawling's study. A deep, clear voice answered, 'Come!' Seated behind a heavy mahogany desk, the farmer looked up from his accounts book, an ominous frown etched deeply on his brow by shadows from a sconce of thick wax candles.

'Ah, Davies. How was it with the beasts?'

'Well as can be expected, sir. The one was still alive, so we knocked her on the head with the hammer. No point making her suffer.' Emily winced as she thought of poor Daisy. 'The other was long gone. We'll take the carcases next door, first thing.' Next door meant to Caskey's, where one of the farm sheds was set up as a small local slaughterhouse. A place she'd avoided since childhood.

'Well, that'll have cost me, then. They'll be no better than a pair of beeves. Might fetch a few shillings, I suppose.'

Then he turned to her.

'Now, Emily, you'd better tell me exactly what happened.' She gulped and reddened – this was the bit she'd been dreading.

'W–why sir, 'twas all so sudden! Them soldiers, sir, I never seen the like! Must have been hundreds of them.'

'What colour were their uniforms?' It seemed a strange question. Why did he want to know that? Hesitatingly, she pressed on.

'Why, blue, sir: blue with bits of red. And they...' but Pawling cut in, his voice rising.

'Guardsmen! I knew it! The Royal procession! Bunch of rogues!' The farmer tapped on the dark wood with the handle of a small brass paperknife as Emily continued.

'I asked them to let me past, sir, so I could lead the cattle away, but there was too many of them, coming up from behind, like. Then one of them, he took out his gun, and fired it! Made such a big flash and a bang, as proper spooked the beasts, sir – they was off, straight away.'

At this, Pawling lurched to his feet and flung the implement across the room, where it clanged against the grate and skittered over the bare boards.

'Damn their guns and damn their King! Coming here, with his debauchery and lewdness. And now they've murdered two of my prime milchers!'

Emily shrank back, trembling, and her father interposed himself between them.

'You could tell Luke Sandys about it, sir – he'd know if there was aught to be done in the matter.'

'Aye, Hopkins, aye. You're speaking sense there,' the farmer replied, gripping the back of the chair as he struggled to calm himself. 'And you'll come with me,' he continued, with hardening resolve. 'We'll ride into Oxford in the morning.'

Turning back to Emily, he asked suddenly: 'The gun made a flash, you say, as well as a bang?'

'Aye, sir, 'twas nearly blinding!'

'And what happened then?'

'Why, the soldier, sir, as shot the gun, his wrist was on fire!' she said, wide eyed at the recollection. 'So he got off his horse, threw down his coat, and started stamping on it, by the road.'

'Gun must have backfired, and set light to his cuff,' Pawling murmured.

Chapter 5
A Doctor Calls

Just a few minutes' walk from Magpie Lane, in a cosy tavern off Holywell Street, Dr John Radcliffe was on his feet.

'So this bishop notices the young curate, eyeing up the shapely housekeeper, and giving him the odd quizzical look.' The rapt audience kept their eyes fixed on the physician, as bar staff at The Spotted Cow moved among them, clearing up blood and feathers from the cock-fighting earlier.

'And he says, "I know what you're thinking. But I can assure you, my relationships with my domestic staff are entirely proper."'

More came over to listen. Radcliffe's gift for a salty anecdote was well known, and – who knew? – some of his tales might even be true.

'So anyway,' he continued, 'a week later, the housekeeper comes to the bishop, and she says, "Your Grace, ever since that young curate came to supper, I've been unable to find the silver soup ladle. You don't suppose he took it?" "I'm sure he didn't," the bishop replies, "but I'll ask." So, he writes to the curate: "Sir – I'm not saying you did take my silver soup ladle, but since you were here for supper, it cannot be found. Would you care to explain?"'

Little noticed by the assembled throng, a chill blast momentarily dimmed the candles as the outside door opened to reveal a burly figure in a blue-and-red military uniform. Radcliffe went on:

'Well, a few days later, the bishop hears back from the curate. "Your Grace, I'm not saying you are sleeping with your housekeeper; but, if you slept in your own bed, you'd have found that soup ladle by now!"'

Through the gales of laughter, the newcomer rasped:

'Is there a Dr Radcliffe here?' Eyes turned towards the man of medicine. 'My Colonel sent me to fetch you, sir.'

'Why, man, 'tis too late now. Can't you see I'm in company?'

'Sir,' the soldier said, 'my orders are to bring you.'

Quite how it was accomplished, no one at the bar that night could say, in retrospect, but suddenly Radcliffe's arm was pinioned behind his back, with the military man's hand clamped firmly on the nape of his neck. And, before the astonished doctor could take leave of his companions, he was being marched off into the night. The pair traversed narrow lanes, sporadically illuminated when a shaft of moonlight found a gap in the high limestone walls, as the chimes of Great Tom, the bell of St Frideswide's in Christ Church cathedral, sounded the nine o'clock student curfew.

Presently, they arrived at the back door of a tall, thin house in a grimy alleyway.

'What the Devil's this?' Radcliffe demanded. 'Your colonel doesn't live here?'

'Nay,' said his military captor. 'My colonel don't live here, but my comrade does, and he's worth two of the colonel, so, by God, doctor, if you don't do your best for him, it'll be the worse for you.' Only when they had mounted the narrow staircase did the powerful grip relax, and the two men entered a room whose dingy fug was pierced by a single rushlight.

Wordlessly, the moustachioed 'comrade' presented his hand and wrist, which – even in the semi-darkness – Radcliffe could immediately see were mottled with powder burns.

'Ah – have a backfire, did you?' He'd seen such several times before. The scorched skin would need carefully washing, but the men had prepared a basin of water for the purpose.

'Good job for you I had time to grab my budget before your friend here spirited me away,' the doctor said and, delving in the bag, he found suitable salves and dressings. The soldiers watched intently as Radcliffe deftly completed the procedures, before a gruff 'thank ye' and a silver sixpence sent him on his way. Relieved at having, apparently, fulfilled the function expected of him, the doctor clambered back down the narrow stairs. He shut the door quietly behind him and walked – rather more quickly than was his wont, and suddenly feeling very sober – the short distance back to his college rooms for the night.

Chapter 6
Morning, and a Warning

Ed was already in the kitchen when Luke rose the next day.

'You'd have to be up early to catch a military man still abed,' he said as he accepted a portion of the previous night's pie from Joan. The last one, Luke noted in disappointment. No wonder the servant avoided catching his eye.

'Aye, well, 'twas a long night,' he replied, warming himself by the meagre fire.

'Of course – your dead body. Any news?'

'Someone you know, actually. The MP, William Harbord.'

Ed hurriedly put down his piece of crust, and sucked air in through his teeth.

'Damn me, Luke, that'll cause a stir. How did he die?'

'Found on the step of The Unicorn and Jacob's Well, the tavern where we met him earlier. Big stab wound, here.' Luke indicated the spot where Harbord had been skewered. 'I assume the Green Ribbon men will blame it on "Papists"?'

'Not half, they will. God's teeth! As if the build-up to Parliament were not tense already. I shall have to tell the Colonel. And he'll tell the Foot Guards.'

'They were nervous enough yesterday, as it was – we had to meet Captain Sutherland at the Bodleian.'

'Hugh Sutherland? Ginger whiskers?' Luke nodded. 'Yes, I've met him before. He's a nervous type. Still, it can't make their job any easier.'

The brothers sat in silence, Ed slowly munching his breakfast as Luke suppressed an urge to tap his foot. The captain was delaying his departure, obviously not relishing the job of bearing bad news.

'That's a pretty thing,' he remarked, pointing out the clock in the hall as he got up to go at last. 'I noticed it last night when Robshaw knocked us up. I've never seen one before, with a pendulum that long.'

'Aye, and it cost a pretty penny.'

'Made by William Clement, London,' Ed read from the clock face.

'Ah, but it's a Dutch design. So you see, your Maastricht enemy was not just a nation of cheesemongers after all.' This allusion to the Dutch war was greeted by his brother with a wry smile.

'Not the enemy now,' he replied. 'The politicians decided to undo all our good deeds. Handed Maastricht back to William a couple of years ago, in the Treaty of Nijmegen.'

'William?'

'Stadtholder of the Netherlands, they call him.'

'I hadn't heard about the treaty.'

'Well, you wouldn't, unless you took the trouble to find out. No-one here wanted to make a song and dance of it.'

Alone at last, Luke quit the house, and retraced his steps of the previous night. As he crossed the threshold of The Mitre, big Jim Napper caught his glance from behind the counter, lifted an index finger in acknowledgement, and disappeared round the corner. Moments later, she emerged: the landlord's twenty-one-year-old daughter, wiping her hands on her lap as she left off baking in the kitchen. Removing her apron, Cate signalled with her eyes that they should take their usual table in the corner. Trade would thicken up through the morning – for the moment, at this early hour, they had the place to themselves.

'How are things in the city then, Luke?' she asked, once Jim had brought their coffee, with a caraway cake for him.

'Taken a turn for the worse.' Those blue eyes now widened to beguiling effect, studying him with concern. 'An MP was murdered last night: William Harbord, who I'm afraid was very prejudiced against... your people.' She reached for the sugar, as if to sweeten the bitter news as they swallowed the dark fluid swirling in their cups.

'So we'll get the blame, I suppose?' The tone was flat, as though in resignation at the seemingly unrelenting tide of troubles, shared in these, Luke's semi-regular briefings on events in the wider world. When they started, it was Jim who would sit in conclave, while Cate brought the drinks. But the daughter proved quick on the uptake, if only while listening to snatches of the conversation. Soon, Luke found it easier to get his message across to her. And the innkeeper evidently felt no need to chaperone his daughter too closely in the company of the Chief Officer of Bailiffs: as they sipped, he busied himself in a far corner of the room.

'You should ask your father to send word to the priests not to come for a while, at least till Parliament opens and we have a chance to see how things develop.' He watched as Cate fingered the crucifix under the kerchief about her neck. 'And what about you, Cate? Would you not be safer back at Hanage House?'

'I've no friends there, Luke.' She bit her lip, as if to suppress the vehemence of her reaction, cupped her chin in one hand and momentarily turned her face away from him. Pausing to calm herself, she went on: 'Marcus was the second son, remember. The estate was never destined for him. It was his family home, but we'd already started to think about moving out, when...'

'Of course.' Luke cut in quickly to obviate any account of

Cate's tragedy: the loss of her husband just a few weeks into their marriage.

Feeling Cate's anxiety, Luke was seized with an almost irresistible instinct to envelop her in his arms, and console her with soft words and kisses: the very instinct he'd struggled to suppress, in fact, throughout the investigation into Marcus Weston's death. She looked up beseechingly into his face, hungry for even the smallest crumb of reassurance.

'No one knows anything, do they?' she asked. 'I mean, that they shouldn't? 'Tis one thing for men to come up from London with prejudice and hatred in their hearts…'

Luke held his breath for a second, trying to keep his hands and voice steady.

'I've no reason to think so. Look out for anyone hanging around or asking questions.' He swigged the rest of the coffee. 'And let's pray to God we soon find Harbord's killer, and the murder turns out to have no connection with any of these political intrigues.'

As he closed the door of the inn behind him, Luke was accosted by a pamphlet seller.

'Master Settle's latest, sir? Vindication of the Character of a Popish Successor. New out in time for Parliament.' Luke handed over a sixpence, and folded back the cover as he strolled along the High Street towards the Guildhall. The opening seemed exceptional in its hyperbolic rage, even by the standards of the day: 'Truly, when tho' by the permission or aid of any English King, Popery, Superstition, Idolatry and Cruelty, are ent'ring our gates, and are ready to butcher our Protestant Ministers at their Divine Worship, make Human Smithfield Sacrifice of us, our Wives and Children; we justly may resist the invading Tyrannick Power of Rome.' He closed it again with a grimace. If Harbord's murder was to be blamed on the baleful influence of 'Rome', then that kind of rhetoric – on sale at every street corner – could only encourage someone to seek out targets to strike back, as an act of 'just resistance'. It had seemed unnecessary to go into detail with Cate about the Green Ribbon club and their anti-Catholic agitation. But he had sounded, he now realised, less worried than he felt.

Chapter 7
Confession in the Vaults

Cate watched Luke's retreating back as he quit The Mitre, then quickly scanned the room to make sure she was not observed, took up and lit a candle, and trod softly round behind the counter, there lifting aside a heavy curtain and passing through. Reaching into the pocket of her apron, she fished out a large iron key and turned it noiselessly in the lock of a thick oaken door: the door to the staircase that led down to the vaults.

'How was your breakfast, Father?' she asked, as she reached the subterranean level. Father Morris grunted and twitched awake. He'd set off very early to arrive before dawn.

'Fine, thank you,' he replied. She came and sat by him. Should she pass on the warning she'd received? It was all very well for Luke Sandys to advise that priests should stay away, but the need for spiritual solace and guidance in these fraught and troubled times was especially acute.

'There are strangers in town, Father. And many more on the way, 'tis said – for the Parliament.'

'Oh, aye?'

She paused, watching the dust drift in the shafts of light from the gratings at street-side.

'There could be danger.'

'We must pray for the Lord's protection.'

'Perhaps you could make sure 'tis fully dark before you leave this week, Father?' The elderly priest would sometimes cause consternation by walking out of the inn's front door in daylight, impatient to reach his bed after a long day. 'And could you come in plain dress – that is, not in your cassock?'

'Why, child, God's raiment is the only clothes I own. But I'll take extra care, don't you worry.'

'Thank you, Father.'

She stacked the breakfast things on the tray, and laid it on the bottom step, ready to take up into the kitchen; then turned back.

'Will you hear my confession now, Father?'

'Of course, dear Cate.' He rose with visible effort, placed his biretta upon his sparse silver locks, and walked stiffly across to the cubicle they'd installed in a corner of the cellar. She took the seat outside it as he drew the curtain behind him, and lit a candle.

'*In nomine Patris et Filii et Spiritus Sancti,*' Father Morris intoned. 'Yes, my child?'

'Bless me, Father, for I have sinned. 'Tis a week since my last confession.'

'What is it you wish to confess?'

Now she was here, how should she put it?

''Tis over a year since Marcus died, Father.' She paused. 'I… I am still a young woman.'

'And the Lord did not see fit to bless your union with child.'

It was an unpromising start, but she resolved to press on.

'There is another man, Father.'

'And what do you know of this man?'

'Why, he is a good man. And well respected.' And – she was surprised to find this rising to the tip of her tongue, before she thrust it firmly back down – still a fine figure of a man.

'Is he of our own religion?'

'Nay. Nay, he is not.'

The priest drew a long sigh.

'Do you love him?'

Did she? Well, she would have to say something.

'I admire him, Father.'

'And does he love you?'

She recalled Luke's struggle to contain his intense reaction when they sat down over coffee.

'I believe so.'

'You believe so? He has not spoken of it, then?'

Now for the difficult part.

'He is not... in a position to speak of it, Father.'

There was another pause while the old man caught the drift of her words. 'He's not a married man?'

Cate gulped.

'He is, Father.'

'Well, then, what you have mistaken for love is a mortal sin!' The priest's tone had grown harsh. But she cut in quickly with the question she'd been preparing, to forestall his tirade.

'If he were to divorce...?'

'Marriage in our Church is a lifelong bond, in the eyes of God,' Father Morris snapped. 'And in any case, I doubt whether he could afford a divorce. Very few men could. Say three Hail Marys. And let's hear no more about this man. Do I make myself clear? You must forget about him!'

Cate dug her nails into her palms to suppress her rising anger at the seeming finality of the priest's words.

'What if I can't forget?' she asked, her tone more defiant than she had intended.

'Why... why, then, we must look to more drastic measures. You must consider your immortal soul, child!' His manner was gentler now, but still adamant. 'There are convents in France. We can make arrangements for you to enter one. But it would be much better if you were to overcome this temptation.'

Cate rubbed vinegar-and-water into the kitchen tabletop with more than her usual vigour. The thought of being banished to a French convent served only to compound her annoyance at Luke Sandys' suggestion of a return to Hanage House. That she could never feel at home there was confirmed, early in the marriage, in a confidential interview with the elder Lady Weston, who intercepted her as she returned from a walk in the grounds with Marcus. As he attended to some business in the stables, Cate was treated to a piece of the dowager's mind.

'You will be aware that my grandson has stooped to marry an innkeeper's daughter, only because there are so few suitable Catholic girls hereabouts, in these Godforsaken times,' she had begun portentously.

As she wrung out the cloth, Cate recalled the terrible feeling, on hearing these words, of shrinking in her very shoes. Still, they did not come as a complete surprise. The lady had already fixed her with several withering looks, when she thought no one would notice. Being, to some extent, prepared, Cate had at least managed to speak up for herself.

'I believe he does love me, your ladyship,' she had said, albeit tremulously.

'Love? Pah!' had come the immediate reply. 'You will carry yourself with due gratitude! And see that you breed successfully. Your duty is to bear sons and daughters who will carry on the one true faith.' But Marcus had gone as they were still trying to conceive, so there was no role and no place for her at West Hanage. There had been no demurral from the family at her plans to return to Oxford. She surveyed the fireplace, the implements hanging from the beams, and the now-gleaming wooden board. This was her home now, modest as it was; and no warnings of sectarian strife, nor even care for her immortal soul, would drive her out of it.

Chapter 8
A Tale of Two Mayors

By the time Luke reached the Guildhall, the place was in a state of upheaval as dignitaries of the city prepared for the official parade of welcome for the King and Queen. His daydreams of raven-haired Cate were rudely dispelled as Robshaw appeared at the office door.

'Old Night-Mayor's back,' he pronounced without ceremony. 'Tying up his horse in the yard, with Jacob Hopkins.'

In the early days of Farmer Pawling's term in office, Luke discouraged the irreverent nickname that Robshaw had now revived. However, tidying up after the man's blundering, if well-meaning interference in the work of his constables became so wearisome that before long he was forced to admit its aptness to the case.

'What does he want?' he asked, suppressing a groan.

'He wants to see you, Master Sandys.' The words were those of Pawling himself, uninvitedly pushing open the door and striding in for all the world as though he were still incumbent, as Hopkins tagged along behind, nervously fingering his hat.

'I should say, Master Pawling, you've picked a very busy day to call. It's the Royal procession as you know, and to cap it all we had a murder last night.'

Pawling pricked up his ears as the men sat down.

'Anyone we know?'

'A Member of Parliament, newly arrived in the city. William Harbord, from Norfolk.'

'Can't say I've heard of him. Cadaver in the parlour yonder, Luke, as usual?'

'Indeed it is.'

'You've not looked at it yet, then?' the farmer persisted.

'Not yet. Now, sirs, what can I do for you?' Luke listened to the tale of the flintlock, its backfire and the ill-fated kine, interrupting only to enquire sharply of Hopkins: 'Emily's not hurt?'

'Only in spirit, sir, only in spirit.'

'Dick Bourke's due in for a shift later,' Robshaw reminded him. The apprentice would earn extra coin by standing in for constables who had to skip their duty from time to time.

'Aye, well, I think we can let him off that. He should be with Emily. Will you see him, Jacob?' The man nodded.

'I'll tell him.'

'The shooter should be easy to pick out,' Pawling added. 'His coat cuff'll be all singed and shredded, from where he stamped on it to put out the smouldering. And he'll have had to get those burns seen to.'

The door opened and a head appeared around the side of it, at a level surprisingly lower than seemed feasible. Its owner, Paul Calvert, was a 'pint-sized pipsqueak', as Robshaw memorably put it, who ran errands for the current mayor, John Bowell.

'Sandys, Robshaw?' he trilled. 'Mayor wants to see you urgently. You're to come with me.'

'We'll wait here,' Pawling said immediately. 'No rush, Luke.' So they had no choice but to leave their visitors in the office unattended, with a promise to return as soon as practicable.

'We'll need to get the Mayor to calm down, so let's not mention Pawling,' Luke hissed as they climbed the Guildhall stairs, a few paces behind Calvert. Robshaw nodded agreement. Bowell's predecessor had steered the city towards some treacherous political waters, causing queasiness among the aldermen. Freedom of the City had been granted to both Titus Oates, accuser-in-chief of the Popish Plot, and James, Duke of Monmouth.

'The Worshipful Mayor first his Grace did Salute, And welcomed his Highness most kindly to Town,' Robshaw recited. Calvert shot a reproachful look over his shoulder. 'Then gave way to Squire White, retired, and was mute!' the deputy continued, unabashed. The lines were from a satirical verse, circulated anonymously following the latter occasion, which caused merriment among the constables as it punctured Pawling's pretensions. Those who could not read learned bits of it by heart. Feeling himself slighted, he had rounded off his year in office with a valedictory speech, harshly criticising several prominent persons, before departing to concentrate on his farm, to widespread relief.

'What is to be done, Sandys?' Bowell demanded tremulously, as they entered. He wrung his ceremonial robe in his hands: a garment mysteriously shrunken, he had discovered this morning, since the last municipal banquet. 'We've Whiggish mobs, Tory mobs, Guardsmen all over the place. Now there's this here MP been murdered.'

'I'm sure we'll get whoever did it, sir.'

But the mayor's florid bulk was positively quivering with fear, rage and indignation.

''Tis a political killing, man – this could set everything off! Paynton's brought me this.' Pointing to his desk, he indicated yet another of the pamphlets that seemed to have been conveyed to Oxford in large quantities.

'The town clerk is full of doom and gloom, sir...' Luke began.

'That bit there – read it!' the Mayor demanded, jabbing a pudgy finger at a passage he'd underlined in evident alarm.

Luke looked at this new publication, which seemed to be of the opposite persuasion from the one proffered on the High Street: purportedly an exchange of views between the pilot of an Oxford riverboat and two of his London counterparts. The words put in the mouth of this supposed 'everyman' supported the rights of the King's brother, James, Duke of York – the 'Popish Successor' – as heir apparent, and presaged trouble if he was thwarted.

Luke read aloud: 'The Scholars of Oxford are thought, by many, will be as unmannerly as the Prentices in London.'

'It'll be Scholastica's all over again!' Bowell fulminated. 'If students start taking to the streets as them City apprentices do, why, we'll have mayhem!' The Saint Scholastica's Day Riot had taken place fully three centuries earlier, but was still notorious as a nadir in relations between townsfolk and scholars, over sixty of whom perished in three days of pitched battles. 'You're a University man – you'll have to see the Chancellor, and get him to keep them undergraduates under lock and key.'

'I could approach the Provost, sir,' Luke said reluctantly. Another errand to add to his list. 'Perhaps he could put some of his proctors on duty during the day, as a precaution.' It was just about enough to get them away from Bowell's chamber.

'That true, then – we're to have town set against gown, all on account of this here Parliament?' Robshaw wondered, as they trotted back down the stairs.

'Well, they've brought the King to Oxford because he's guaranteed a warm welcome, at least by the University. The pamphlet's right, the students support the Duke of York, and oppose the Exclusion. But...' Luke tailed off meaningfully, and the deputy finished the sentence.

'But Old Rowley has no friends among common folk.'

'Mm. That's why he travels with hundreds of armed guards.'

Back at Sandys' own office, Pawling was emphatic:

'That Guardsman is a rogue and a rascal, Luke, who needs bringing to justice. Why, when I think of what happened to them cattle, 'tis tantamount to murder!'

'Well, not quite…'

But the farmer cut him off.

'Your brother's in the Guards ain't he? You can get him to find out who fired that shot, and have him bang to rights.'

'Well, aye, I could ask Ed if he knows aught about it. But it's not one for the magistrates; he'd be under military discipline – unless he'd committed a felony. Now, frightening cattle is ill usage, indeed, but I've never heard of anyone coming before the assizes for it.'

Pawling leaned back in his chair, apparently sensing there was no point in pressing the matter further for the moment.

'Very well. You'll let me know, then, what happens?' Luke nodded assent. 'And be sure you take a good close look at that dead body.'

'As always, Master Pawling. Good day to you; and to you, Jacob.'

Robshaw rose to see the men out of the Guildhall, as if to satisfy himself that the ex-Mayor really was leaving the premises.

Luke stepped into the back parlour, looked down at Harbord's body with a sigh, and straightened the cloth. There would be time to examine it later – but they would have to spend the rest of the day trying to pick up the trail of his killer, before it had a chance to go cold. He recalled the day when Marcus Weston had lain there. Cate's husband was killed when trying to calm a quarrel in the queue at Bacon's Tower, to enter Oxford from the south. One of the protagonists drew a knife, and instinctively whirled round at Weston's touch on his shoulder. The blade severed the brachial artery under the would-be peacemaker's raised arm. Luke rode out several times to West Hanage, the family seat in Berkshire, to report progress in the investigation, as the knifeman was tried then hanged for voluntary manslaughter.

A well-known heavy tread brought Luke back into the main office, where he found his deputy grinning and shaking his head.

'What ails you, man?'

'Oh but that is good, Master Sandys, 'tis good indeed.'

'I know I'm going to regret this Robshaw, but what's "good"?'

'Well – supposing you was to say to I, "Guess what's today's news? Dick Bourke's Emily has lost her spotted cow." Well then, I should say, "That ain't no news – I thought everybody knew!"' He chortled at his own joke as Luke wondered whether to feign ignorance. He knew the country euphemism for a girl losing her virginity, but it stuck in his craw to acknowledge it to his arrant deputy.

'Robshaw,' he replied at length, 'you are grotesque.'

'Yessir!'

Chapter 9
Pomp and Circumstance

A scarlet tide ebbed and flowed its way down Oxford High Street. Not the bloodshed of Mayor Bowell's fevered imaginings, but the regalia of fully four-and-twenty dignitaries of the City: aldermen and bailiffs, all in fur-trimmed red robes, each mounted on horseback in solemn procession, two by two. Liverymen walked alongside, ready to grasp the reins if any of the animals broke rank. Encompassing this garish contingent were the sober colours deemed suitable for those clinging to the lower rungs of civic flummery: sixty or so black-robed members of the common council, bringing up the rear.

From his position in the foremost – though least auspicious – part of the parade, Luke glanced round at his men, the other twenty constables, as they preceded the four sergeants at mace and Paynton, the town clerk, with his silver chain. They all had the same powers of arrest, and the same basic responsibility: to keep the King's peace. The others followed his directions because, it was commonly agreed, 'Master Sandys knows what he's about.' How far, he wondered, could this miscellany of butchers, bakers and candlestick-makers, stepping out of their trades and crafts for six months or a year at a time, hold the line against the political plots and intrigues now entwining their city in tentacular embrace? Far enough, perhaps, if the city itself was on their side – though the issues dividing Parliament also divided Oxford; or at least, the University from the general populace. And expectations of them seemed to be growing alarmingly. Already that day he had been urged to cross jurisdictions to arrest a serving member of His Majesty's Horse Guards, and to forestall a riot by students. He would put his faith, as ever he did, in the principles of evidence and deduction he had learned in his own student days. But it did not stop him from uttering a silent prayer, that all would somehow turn out for the best.

A stertorous breath at his shoulder announced Robshaw's presence. Together, they watched Mayor Bowell lower his pendulous person to kneel down on a mat placed by the Royal coach, and offer up his gestamen of authority.

'Wouldn't think he was up such a height just an hour ago,' the deputy said. Luke, too, was impressed at the dignified bearing the man had managed to cultivate in the time since they left him in a state of agitation at his office.

'Aye, he plays his part well.' The King and Queen received gifts from the City – a pair of gloves each, fashioned of finest sable with fringes of gold braid.

'Won't have to dirty his hands with the likes of us now, will he, Charles?' Robshaw quipped.

'Or with Parliament for much longer, probably,' Luke replied.

'How come?'

'Why, given half a chance, he'd take all the money paid in taxes and duties from the whole country, and spend it as he saw fit. Or so 'tis said.'

Frowning, Robshaw smoothed his whiskers down with his fingers, scattering crumbs from his breakfast as he did so.

'And they won't let him, them politicians?'

'Not on your life! That's what the civil war was about. But he's forever scheming to find a way round them.'

Presently, the Royal carriage was ready to move off, and the mayor rose and shouldered the five-foot-long silver mace. Their Majesties entered the city, to loud cheers from the loyal portion of Oxford opinion, with Captain Sutherland's Foot Guards lining the route and watching for any signs of dissent.

Chapter 10
Morning at Magdalen Farm

Emily sat on her three-legged milking stool and rested her cheek against the warm roan flank of one of the ten remaining cows. They had indeed made their own way home, and overnight, it seemed, munched sporadically on the winter fodder she had drawn from the small remaining supply. Suffused with relief at their appearance before her summons to the farmhouse, she had bitterly resolved never to dawdle over her duties again.

'Good 'cess with them milchers, girl,' Liza, her mother, said as she slipped out that morning. 'Knowing your luck, they'll have gone dry.' But no, the milk squirted out as her fingers worked the teats, albeit not in great quantity.

If only she had set off earlier to bring the beasts home! She had replayed the scene, over and over, through the night. Every time, in her mind's eye, they quit the road just before the arrival of the cavalrymen. The late meeting with Farmer Pawling had left her in a state of righteous indignation at the rough treatment she and her charges had received. So, when she went to bed, sleep came intermittently at best. The cow she was milking stamped in protest and rolled her big eyes backwards as Emily, riled all over again as she thought about the gunshot, squeezed harder on the udder.

'Sorry, my pet,' she soothed. 'Cush-cush-cush! There, now,' – and the flow of milk resumed.

She had been wide awake at first light, in her cot by the window, watching Mistress Blackbird swooping down for beakfuls of nesting materials, when she spotted Pawling's familiar figure.

Hunched in the saddle and hat pulled down against the morning chill, he was leaving the farm on his great dappled gelding. She frowned. Wasn't her father supposed to be going to town with him? And surely it was too early to find anyone up and about? At the time, she dismissed the thought as quickly as it arrived, and turned over in search of more sleep.

Anyway, she had made a mistake. The farmer had not apparently been departing for Oxford, for now she could hear him, back already. She broke off from her task and came to the door of the dairy to watch.

'Fetch us a slice and a cup of small beer,' he demanded of the serving girl, as his horse sidled off to a clump of long grass, and Pawling sat himself down on the low wall around the chicken coop.

'Everything ready, Hopkins?' he enquired through a mouthful of bread.

Emily's father hurried to saddle up the piebald nag to accompany him as arranged.

The cattle were to be kept in for a few days, to get over their ordeal. So, by mid-morning, Emily was set to help her mother to make soap for washing themselves and their clothes, and scrubbing the iron-hooped wooden pails she used to collect the milk. They would start with bits of the dead cattle, which Caskey, the slaughterer, had returned to the farm first thing that morning.

'Them there's the kidneys, and them's the livers,' Liza said, removing the cloth that was covering the pile of reddish-brown offal. The daughter swallowed hard, and looked away. Still, at least it meant poor Daisy and Cassie would do them one last service. 'We'll each take one at a time. Pick up that other knife, look, and do as I do.' Emily watched as she deftly cut the fat from around one of the large, yielding organs, and haltingly followed suit.

'You've to grab it good and hard!' the mother exclaimed, when a liver slipped from the younger woman's grasp and slithered off the wooden board.

As they removed the yellow tissue, they placed it in a metal pot, which Mistress Hopkins then suspended over a low flame to melt.

'Go and stack the leaching barrel then,' she instructed. Emily took up the pail of ash from the previous night's fire and sprinkled it between layers of straw in the downward-tapered structure which stood in a corner of the farmyard, tongue protruding slightly from the corner of her mouth in concentration. When she had finished, it was time to strain the melted fat through a cheesecloth to collect the tallow. Kneeling by the fire, she held the fabric tight over another pot as her mother poured it, little by little, pressing it through with the back of a wooden spoon.

Presently, the women were distracted by the sound of hoofbeats approaching, and went out to meet them.

'Did you see the King and Queen?' Liza wondered.

'Nay! Load of fuss and bother,' Pawling replied. The piebald horse, breathing heavily from the attempt to keep pace with the farmer's larger mount as they trotted up the slope, slowed in relief as they reached the head of the path.

'Now then, my girl,' Emily's father said kindly as the riders dismounted. 'We've been to see Luke Sandys, and he said he'll look into the matter of them poor cattle. That there Guardsman with his gun has done us a wrong, and no mistake.'

'Aye, and with what I've given Sandys, that rascal won't have much longer to do any more wrongs in this world, I can tell you,' Pawling thundered as he stalked off into the farmyard. 'Come, Hopkins, stable the horses and let's set about us. Busy day.'

'Right away, sir,' the other replied, exchanging sympathetic looks with his daughter.

Emily wore a puzzled frown as she returned to the leaching barrel. Had she heard aright? She half-heartedly shooed away old Jack, the farmyard donkey, who was taking too close an interest in the straw she'd carefully laid in. The placid creature had been both a childhood pet and a beast of burden, carrying baskets of stuff between field and farm – though now he was too frail and rheumaticky for work.

'Can you understand it, Jack?' she asked him, as the animal tilted long, threadbare ears alternately forward and back. 'What could Farmer Pawling have given Master Sandys? And why should the shooter not be long for this world?'

Taking up another pot from the fire, Emily trickled its contents of hot water down through the barrel, carefully positioning a large wooden bowl underneath to catch the lye, which they would then mix with the tallow.

'Surely he didn't mean to say he'd hang for it? We wouldn't want that, would we, old lad?' But Jack merely chewed his cud, with rhythmic, circular movements of his jaw, and gazed back at her. 'Richard would call us soft-hearted, Jack, worrying about what's to happen to that there cavalryman. But enough lives have been taken already, I reckon.'

'Emily! Where's that lye?' her mother called from inside the cottage – and, switching her attention to the work, Emily gave Jack's ears a fondle, and set the matter to one side.

Chapter 11
The Green Ribbon Club

The mayor, bailiffs and councillors were tucking in to their banquet with the King and Queen, but, to Elizabeth's chagrin, the invitation had not been extended to constables, let alone their spouses. In reality, Luke could have pressed to be added to the guest list, and perhaps even swung a place for his wife; but he cared little for such occasions, and now – with an investigation to begin in earnest – he was relieved not to have set arrangements in train that would have kept him from making headway. Raucous laughter guided him to where his deputy was loitering with some of his cronies in a corner of the Guild-hall stable yard. As Luke caught his eye, the burly constable picked up the corner of pastry he had been munching, pushed it into his mouth, wiped his hands on his breeches, and came to join him.

'Where do we start, then?' he asked. ''Twas a political killing, Bowell reckoned?'

'Let's hope not,' Luke replied. 'We could do without faction fighting on the streets of Oxford.'

Robshaw nodded as he swallowed the last of his mouthful.

'Them Green Ribbon fellers seemed dead fierce on Popery. Even more than the usual.'

'Indeed. Ed told me, they're wanting us to crack down harder, what with the Popish Plot, and such.'

'Don't make no sense to me. Left-footers round here knows their place. Not that there's many of them left, these days.'

'If we don't find Harbord's killer, they'll take the blame. I'm sure the Green Ribbon men have already started.'

'Step's clean,' the deputy remarked, as the pair once again crossed the threshold of The Unicorn and Jacob's Well. The crowd was thinner, and the conversation of a harsher tone than the previous day.

'Good day to you, sirs,' Unsworth said. 'Licence all paid for now, Master Sandys.'

'Yes, can I have a word, gentlemen, please,' Luke said, holding up his hand for quiet in an unconscious echo of Harbord's own gesture. 'We are investigating the murder of Master Harbord and we need to ask you a few questions.'

'That fine gentleman was martyred, sir,' one of the Green Ribbons immediately piped up. 'This place should be a shrine to righteousness!' There was a buzz of acclaim.

'You should be out, rounding up all the Papists in the city,' a thin, ratty-looking character called out from his position on a bench at the back of the room, where Luke immediately noticed a rare sight indeed: the speaker's neighbour was a black man, an African, or 'blackamoor'. The Sandys' old cook-maid, Joan, had long been known as 'the only blackamoor in Oxford'. Well, no longer, it seemed.

'Unsworth, you said a caller came by yesterday asking for Master Harbord,' Luke began, before the din rose too high to make himself heard. 'Did you see or hear the conversation between them? From what he said, Harbord didn't seem to welcome the call.'

'Well, sir, he sent him away with a flea in his ear, it seemed,' the innkeeper volunteered, before being quieted by a frown from the first speaker, who had evidently taken on the mantle of group leadership from his late colleague.

'Such a man as Bill Harbord will have no end of callers petitioning and pestering for notice or favours of all kinds. 'Tis the burden of being a public figure.'

'And you are...?' Luke enquired.

'Edward Norton, MP, of Westbury in the county of Wiltshire, at your service. It's abundantly clear, sir, surely, that this evil is yet another Popish act of roguery?'

'Popery, superstition, idolatry and cruelty are entering our gates,' the thin man declaimed, reading from a pamphlet spread out on his knees – the same pamphlet, Luke straight away realised, that he'd bought earlier, 'and are ready to butcher our Protestant Ministers at their Divine Worship, and make Human Smithfield Sacrifice of us, our Wives and Children.'

'Allow me to present our learned pamphleteer, Elkanah Settle Esquire,' Norton said, as the general growl of approval at the inflammatory words died down, 'the author of that and many other truths that our rulers will heed, sir, or 'twill be their ruin.'

'My information, sir, is that very few Papists have been sent down by Oxford magistrates of late,' Settle intoned nasally, as the room fell quiet. 'Are they failing in their duty to prosecute, or are the bailiffs and constables neglecting their duty to inform? It can only be one or the other.'

'You watch your mouth,' Robshaw growled, feeling for his heavy wooden stave. In a fluid motion, Settle's dark-skinned neighbour reached under the table and drew out a dagger, which he set down in front of him. Luke sensed that he must quickly take back control of the conversation.

'Does anyone here have any actual evidence of any Roman Catholics threatening the life of Master Harbord?' The question was greeted with an angry murmur, but no one came forward to reply.

'In that case, let us all keep an open mind.' He turned once again to the innkeeper. 'This man who called for Harbord, what did he look like?'

'He was mature in years, sir, and shabby, like, but he'd seen better days, if you get my meaning.'

'What sort of terms did they part on?' Robshaw asked.

'It seemed to me the man gave Master Harbord something. He was putting a paper in his pocket, like a letter, when he came back to the bar.' As Norton made to quieten him again, Unsworth hastily added: 'But I was busy sirs, drawing ale for these gentlemen, so I may have been mistaken.'

Chapter 12
The Parliamentary Clerks

'We shall have to look for that piece of paper when we get round to examining the body,' Sandys said, as the pair quit the highly charged atmosphere of the tavern.

'Office locked up?' Robshaw asked. Luke had, through many cases, convinced him of the importance of preserving physical evidence intact, as far as possible.

'Yes, I turned the key before we came out.' The clouds chasing each other across the Oxford sky had gradually turned greyer, and a damp squall suddenly sent the foot traffic scurrying for cover. The constables made their way back up Fish Street, and now headed for shelter at the Cornmarket, where the roof had been restored with tiles after the lead of the original was melted down for bullets in the Civil War.

'They seemed excited. Too much so, for my liking. What did you make of them?' Luke asked, as they watched the rain drumming on the cobbles outside.

'I was more worried about that there blackamoor,' Robshaw replied. 'I ain't never seen one. Apart from your Joan, of course.'

'Hired muscle, no doubt, in case the speeches are not persuasive enough by themselves.'

'They know something they're not telling,' was Robshaw's considered verdict, and Luke was inclined to agree.

The brief shower abating, they cut along Brasenose Lane, between Exeter and Lincoln Colleges, and emerged presently at the back gate into the quadrangle of the Bodleian Library. Immediately, two heavily armed Royal Foot Guards challenged them to state their business.

'We've an appointment with the Commons Clerks,' Luke said, as he presented their letters of office. Earlier, he had sent a messenger from the Guildhall with a request for records of Harbord's activities as an MP. The parliamentary administration services had decamped to Oxford for the duration, and were in the process of being settled into their temporary home in the Bodleian. The stenographers would have to come and go between there and the Convocation House, where the King would attend the opening of Parliament, so strict security measures were in place.

'Ah,' one of the Guards replied with a grin. 'You want Bob Tim and Bob Sim.'

'Bob Tim and Bob Sim?'

'You'll see.'

Parliament's arrival in Oxford represented a commercial bonanza. For those charged with actually running the City and the University, however, it meant extra work, bother and disruption. Obliged to follow instructions to accommodate the business of state, some officials nevertheless found or contrived covert ways to signal their disgruntlement. Staff of the Bodleian were no exception, and, when it came to allocating a room for the parliamentary clerks, the only convenient space turned out to be a chamber normally reserved for the storage of bookbinding and restoration materials, and cleaning supplies.

Sandys and Robshaw climbed the stone steps to these cramped quarters, only to find the landing partially blocked with stacks of files.

'Hulloo?' Robshaw called out. From behind the stacks, a head popped out, the pink plumpish face bearing a determinedly jolly expression, surmounted by a grey periwig.

'Robert Timpson, sirs, at your service.' At this, a second face, thinner and comparatively sallow, though under an identical wig, just as suddenly materialised in the gap on the opposite side of the tallest stack from the first.

'Robert Simkins, at your service, sirs,' this one said.

'Good day to you gentlemen,' Luke replied, presenting their credentials once again. 'We are interested in any records you may have pertaining to the late William Harbord, MP. We're investigating his murder, last night here in Oxford.'

'Yes sir, we received your note...' Timpson began, but Simkins cut in to finish his sentence:

'...and we've been hunting high and low ever since.' Luke began to realise why the Guards had chuckled at the mention of the two clerks.

'Yes, we're just settling in to our new office...'

'...but it's rather small. If we didn't know better we'd say this was some kind of...'

'Cleaners' cupboard!' Bob Tim and Bob Sim cried in unison.

'Well, I daresay it was the best that could be done in the circumstances,' Luke said. 'Now, if you'd be good enough to let me have that file on Harbord...'

'Yes, we've found it, sir,' Bob Tim said perkily.

'Ah, good.' Luke waited, but nothing happened.

'There's just one problem.'

'A problem, sir,' Bob Sim concurred. 'When they moved us in here, the files were all brought up by the Bodleian porters.'

'Great, big, tall men sir,' Bob Tim added helpfully. 'And the member files, sir – are up there...'

'...on that shelf.' Bob Sim once more completed the sentence.

Only now he had picked his way into the room did Luke notice that the Bobs were standing on either end of a long wooden box marked Committees, T-Z, 1679. As they stepped down to point out the high shelf, they revealed themselves to be not only attired in identical grey suits, but also both around the five-foot mark in height. All eyes turned to the strapping Robshaw, who pulled a chair over to the wall beneath the shelf, mounted it with a grunt and – under the Bobs' direction – located and took down the file on William Harbord MP.

'Educated at Leiden, it says here,' Luke remarked as he started to read.

'The University of Leiden, sir, yes,' Bob Tim confirmed.

'In Holland, sir,' his colleague added. The Bobs, Luke realised, were not going to let him peruse the file in peace, but instead stood vigilant, heads slightly tilted like mistle-thrushes sighting a worm, ready to enlighten him on any point of parliamentary procedure. The further he read, the longer the list grew of men whom Harbord had attacked or antagonised.

'Served on the committee to impeach Danby, I see.'

'Lord Danby, yes sir.'

'In '79, sir,' the Bobs chorused. Luke turned the next page.

'Danby was Treasurer, wasn't he? It says here that he was trying to get MPs to approve public spending for a standing army...'

'Ah, but what did he want it for, sir?' Bob Tim interrupted.

'There were those letters, sir,' Bob Sim continued, reaching out to turn the page again. 'Letters sent in secret but then read out loud to the House...'

'...proving he was trying to make a peace deal with Louis, on the King's orders,' Bob Tim completed the story.

'So if his army was not intended for war with France, what was it for?' Luke wondered.

'Why, sir, to do away with Parliament altogether, and enforce absolute rule from the Palace,' Bob Sim explained. 'Or, so 'twas said.'

'Of course, Danby didn't help himself, sir,' Bob Tim chimed in. 'Didn't believe in the Popish Plot.'

'Many don't, you know sir, in private – but Danby never bothered to hide it,' Bob Sim added.

'In the Tower of London now, sir,' Bob Tim informed them, dolefully.

Then, Luke saw as he read further in the file, Harbord was named as the source of allegations in Parliament that Samuel Pepys, an MP and senior Admiralty clerk, had conspired to sell naval secrets to the French. He remembered the episode as one that occasioned some disquiet in the Sandys household, since Pepys was in charge of the department where their son-in-law, Roger, was employed. They'd been relieved when it appeared to blow over.

'Well, our man certainly seems to have made plenty of enemies,' he said at last, closing the file and handing it back.

Chapter 13
A Rabble is Roused

Taking their leave of the Bobs – 'Do come back, sirs... If you need any more help, sirs' – Sandys and Robshaw made their way down Queen's Lane. This brought them out on the unofficial 'Tory end' of the High Street. In search of another perspective on Harbord and his manoeuvrings, they entered Tillyard's coffeehouse on the corner. Ignoring the traditional greeting of 'What news?' as they stood in the doorway, Luke peered through the tobacco smoke for any familiar faces, alighting on a company of apparently well-to-do characters seated around a table at the far side. 'Excuse me, sir – is it Richard Jones?' he asked, as they approached.

The man seated by the window was dressed and bewigged in Cavalier fashion, and wore an expression that somehow combined elements of both smirk and sneer.

'Guilty as charged,' he drawled. 'Do we know each other?'

'Slightly, sir. Luke Sandys – we met when attending demonstrations by Robert Boyle, when he was in Oxford. Pressure of gas and air.'

'So we did!' Jones replied. 'Student days,' he explained briefly to his companions.

'You were engaged to Boyle's sister, I seem to recall?'

'That's right. She's Lady Ranelagh now, of course, since I came into the title.'

'Oh! I beg your pardon, my Lord.'

'Think nothing of it, dear boy. So – how may I be of service?'

'It's about William Harbord, my Lord. He was killed last

night outside a tavern opposite Christ Church, where the Royal party is staying.'

'Yes, I heard about that. Can't say I see him as a great loss to Parliament. And it comes to be your business how, exactly?'

'We're investigating the murder, my Lord – we're constables of the Oxford Bailiffs.'

'How madly interesting for you. And you want to know if I can think of anyone from our side of politics who might have – how shall I put it? – eased Harbord from this vale of tears?'

'Quite so, my Lord.'

While Robshaw took a seat on a neighbouring table with some of his cronies, taking a mug of ale and the chance of a pull on his pipe, Luke drew up a chair to join Lord Ranelagh's party.

'What brings you to Oxford, my Lord, may I ask?'

'I rode down with the King, from Windsor. My estate lies over that way.'

'I thought you were something in Ireland now?'

'Why yes, you could say I am something,' he replied, amused. 'Treasurer in His Majesty's government, to be precise. Trying to bring some semblance of civilisation to that benighted place.'

'And the Parliament here?' Luke wondered. The peer's eyes grew cold, and his hand shifted to the hilt of his sword.

'Let's just say I've come to Oxford to see fair play.'

'How so?' At this, one of his cronies, who was listening to the conversation, joined in.

'What we have here, sir, is an attempt to impose rule by the mob. It must not stand. It will not stand!' The others around the table murmured agreement.

Luke sensed that, beneath their show of nonchalance, these men had been badly rattled by the dispute between Crown and Parliament.

'The mob can be turned on anyone, these days, sir,' one of them was saying. 'Look at what happened to poor Pepys.'

'Samuel Pepys is a good man,' Ranelagh said, leaning in. 'But he's spent the past two years in Parliament fending off unfounded allegations from Harbord and his gang, that he sold secrets to the French, when in fact his only "crime" has been to impose some order on the Admiralty.'

'No easy task,' his companion chipped in. 'No wonder he didn't stand again for election.'

'Ah, so Pepys is not in Oxford,' Luke thought aloud. 'What about the other men Harbord targeted? Lord Danby is not here either, I think… could one of his friends have sought revenge?'

'Unlikely,' Ranelagh returned crisply. 'Danby never had many friends.'

'None at all now he's in the Tower,' the other speaker added.

As the constables left Queen's Lane and strode westward towards the Guildhall, progress slowed and the crowd palpably thickened.

''Tis our "friend" from the Green Ribbon Club,' Robshaw said, as the unmistakable tones of political speech-making made themselves audible.

'Good people of Oxford! Well you know the cruelties of Popery. Well you remember brave Bishop Latimer, and valiant Bishop Ridley. Traduced, and wronged! Bound and incarcerated, in the Bocardo, the very prison at the north gate of your fine city!'

Sure enough, Edward Norton MP stood out above the mass of faces, from his vantage point atop a portable set of wooden steps, and set about the task of whipping up the crowd to fever pitch.

'They stood for the one true faith! They stood against heresy, infamy and treason!' At each ringing phrase, the cheers grew louder. 'And you remember Archbishop Cranmer. They tortured him. They made him sign away his faith, and his honour.'

There were groans at this reminder of the most famous of the Oxford Martyrs, burned at the stake under 'Bloody Mary', Queen Mary Tudor who had reigned over a century earlier, England's last Roman Catholic sovereign.

'But they could never break his spirit. He came back at the last to the true Church, and plunged his hand into the flames – the unworthy hand that wrote his false confessions!'

'I don't like this,' Robshaw said. 'Don't do no good getting folks all het up.'

'Agreed,' Luke said. 'And I'm afraid I know what's coming next.'

Sure enough, Norton now switched tack to bring his narrative up to date.

'And today, we have another martyr. Another martyr in the righteous struggle against Popery. William Harbord – a true man of the people. A Member of Parliament, here to take up that struggle for King and country. Martyred here in Oxford, on your very doorstep!'

''Twas The Unicorn's doorstep, jackanapes,' Robshaw growled. But Norton was out of earshot, and his audience was rapt.

'Martyred – yea, murdered, last night, while good folk were safe in their beds! And some of our men of government still want to put the Crown of England back on the head of a Popish King.'

Now the shouts of anger were accompanied by weapons being brought out, and waved above their heads by the mob – sticks and staves, a pitchfork or two, but also the flash of an occasional edged blade.

'Right, that's enough,' Luke said. He and Robshaw drew their staves, and began to push their way through the press to where Norton was standing.

'Even a Mahometan would be preferable on the throne of England!' he was proclaiming. 'We know the bands of nature, morality and honour have been sacred even unto Heathens, but never to Papists!'

'I think that's a suitable climax to your speech,' Luke shouted, while Robshaw positioned himself in front of the portable steps. The blackamoor from The Unicorn and Jacob's Well was now revealed as a tall, imposing figure, whose well-cut coat in a plum colour hugged his broad shoulders and tapering upper body. He made as though to defend the speaker, but several other constables had now appeared from behind; evidently alarmed, as Sandys and Robshaw had been, at the turn events had taken. Even Norton seemed somewhat startled at the animated response to his words, and decided to finish while he was ahead. He stepped down.

'I'd be obliged, sir, if you would take your men back to The Unicorn, and wait there till this all calms down,' Luke yelled, above the tumult.

'I will be heard, sir,' Norton shot back querulously. 'I have a right to be heard. Never interfere with our liberties.'

'I respect your liberties, sir, but I hope you also wish to help us in keeping the King's peace here.'

At this, Norton faltered.

'Very well sir, we shall do as you ask. Come along, gentlemen.' To Luke's relief, the meeting began to break up and the Green Ribbons headed back towards Fish Street, apparently satisfied with their day's work.

'You was too soft on him,' Robshaw said. 'Never mind helping us keep the peace, you should've had him up for breach of the peace.'

Luke leant on his stave and let out a deep breath. 'Modus vivendi, Robshaw. Modus vivendi.'

'Whatever you say, Master Sandys.'

Chapter 14
The Colonel in his Cups

Behind the opposite side of the High Street from where Luke and Robshaw were interviewing Lord Ranelagh, Captain Edwin Sandys was at that moment presenting himself to the Porter's Lodge at Merton College.

'Here to see the Colonel.'

'The Colonel?'

'Yes – the Earl of Oxford,' he said, realising his commanding officer might not now be in regimental colours. The porter on duty suddenly craned forward from behind the desk to peer at him from beneath a pair of bushy grey eyebrows.

'Don't I recognise you, young sir? From the time that there table got brought in, for the Warden?'

As young fellows, Ed and Luke had joined their father in a major logistical exercise. The Warden of Merton, Thomas Clayton, had ordered a dining table, which he insisted should be fashioned from a single piece of oak. When it came to be delivered, however, it proved too big to be taken up the stairs to his dining hall. So, the brothers helped as old Samuel Sandys rigged up an ingenious arrangement with poles, some rope, and a block and tackle, to bring it in over the balcony instead.

'You might very well,' Ed smiled. 'Is he here now, then, Master Clayton? I would pay my respects.'

'Don't want to be doing that, sir,' the old man shook his head. 'He ain't a respectable gentleman. Anyhow, he's away on his estate, down in Wiltshire. Loaned out his apartments to the Court.' Even as a youth, Ed now recalled, he had been dimly aware of Clayton's reputation for debauchery, with particular emphasis on what his father always called 'the devil's nectar'.

'That there table has seen some terrible things, sir, I can tell thee,' the old man continued. 'Number of wine bottles coming through that dining room, when Master Clayton was in residence, why, 'twould make your hair stand on end.'

Finally managing to disentangle himself from the reminiscences at the porter's lodge, Ed found the famous oaken board in service once again. A group of courtiers had evidently repaired to the lodgings to carry on the party after the official banquet at the Guildhall to welcome His Majesty to the city. Ed clenched his teeth at the strong aroma of drink and tobacco smoke as he picked his way among card tables and empty bottles to the corner where the Colonel – Aubrey de Vere, 20th Earl of Oxford – sat among his political cronies.

'Sandys! Good man, good man. Have a drink.'

'Sir, I felt it right to alert you; a Member of Parliament's been murdered, here in Oxford, last night – shortly after we arrived.'

'May God preserve his soul,' the Earl pronounced distinctly. 'Anyone we know?'

'Not really, Colonel, a man of Whiggish sympathies – William Harbord of Thetford, in Norfolk. Could be trouble – he was with the Green Ribbon Club.'

'Hmph – Shaftesbury's bastards,' the Colonel grunted, his eyes narrowing. 'Banging on about this wretched Popish Plot.'

'Knavish Plot, more like,' one of his companions snorted.

'A plot by knaves, sir, to harry and persecute their betters,' another chimed in. 'Some men will only be satisfied when the whole House sinks to their own level of mediocrity.'

Ed's arrival had now caught the attention of the assembled company. A louche character, dressed in Cavalier fashion, draped his lace-cuffed hand over the back of a chair next to the Colonel and leered at Sandys.

'And who's this f-fine young f-fellow?' he slurred.

'William Harbord,' another chimed in.

'No sir, that's the man who's been killed,' Ed replied.

'It's the end of Harbord! No more Harbord,' the first courtier teased, affecting a melodramatic tone.

'You'll have to shteer the shhhh-ip of shhh-tate hard-a-port, de Vere,' another brayed.

'Why so, my Lord?' asked a heavily made-up young woman, in coquettish, faux-naïf style, from her place next to him on a plush satin sofa. The foppish-looking speaker waited till all eyes were on him.

'Becaush there'sh no more hard-a-shtarboard!' he finished triumphantly – at which the entire company burst into uproarious laughter at the weak joke, amid cries of 'more ale!' and 'pass the canary!'

Surmising that he was unlikely to derive much sense from his commanding officer while in his cups, Captain Sandys withdrew.

'Thank you, dear boy,' was the Colonel's only further comment on the situation – but at least he'd been informed, and would no doubt, when sober, feed the information into his shrewdly calculating strategic mind. The Blues were not directly responsible for the King's security: their job had been to get him safely to Oxford, whereupon the onus had passed to the red-coated Foot Guards. But Ed had gauged enough of his brother's concern over the potential of Harbord's death to cause trouble in the city to leave Merton College with a nagging conviction that he had not heard the last of the matter.

Chapter 15
At The Mitre

As Luke watched the mob gradually disperse on the High, Robshaw suddenly turned and said, with a meaningful look at his master:

'I'm in need of vittles.'

'Very well,' he replied. It was now well past noon, after all, and, as The Mitre was the nearest inn, he glanced towards its welcoming portals and said: 'Shall we?' Was it fancy or did Robshaw study him momentarily before replying, and was there a faint quizzical echo in his voice, when he did? Even he could not indefinitely fail to notice Luke's preference for this one tavern, and wonder at the reason for it.

'As you wish,' the deputy said, simply.

They took a confidential corner table, overlooking Turl Street – the same table, in fact, where he'd met Cate for coffee earlier. Once again, it was the licensee himself who took their order.

'Two bowls of the ordinary please, Jim.'

'Very good, Master Sandys.'

'And a jug of ale,' Robshaw added; to which Luke assented with a slight nod.

'Doesn't seem to me that we've got very far,' he mused, as the pair took sips of the beer. 'Harbord had a call from a man who might have given him some kind of letter... and they might have had a row.'

'We ought to get that Unsworth round the back of his tavern and box his ears till he tells us the whole truth.'

Ignoring this suggestion, Luke went on: 'I came away from the Bobs convinced we were on to something, but then we saw

Jones at the coffeehouse and it all seemed to fall flat. Plenty of people in politics hated Harbord but they're not in Oxford – and anyway, would they kill him?'

'Perhaps it was Papists after all.' His deputy was, in Luke's experience, disinclined to be swayed towards snap judgements: one reason why they worked well together. And yet here he was, echoing conspiracy theories from the Green Ribbon Club.

'Well – you said yourself, there are not many Catholics in Oxford, and they don't get involved in politics.'

'Aye, but what about out-of-towners?'

Their exchange was cut short by Cate's arrival with the pottage.

'Upper crust for you, Master Luke,' she said, smiling as she set down the bread. Handed the bigger, darker underside of the loaf, Robshaw issued an appreciative grunt, muttering: 'Stomach thought my throat had been cut.'

Luke looked up, but she turned her gaze modestly downwards as she placed the bowls on the table. So he contented himself with watching her hands instead; hands that had, no doubt, kneaded the very bread that now sat on the plate in front of him. He remembered the quiet day when she had come out of the kitchen in search of help to dislodge the oven door – a wooden board with a handle, shaped to the opening in the brick-built cavity and soaked with water so it would expand to a tight fit. So tight, in fact, that on the occasion in question it had wedged fast, as the cooling air contracted and pulled it inwards. Luke had managed to free it, and stayed to help relight the oven for the next batch. It was as he held the faggot, and she ignited the 'pimp' – the small bundle of twigs that would act as a taper – that their eyes had met, and a spark of mutual realisation had passed between them.

'Did you hear any of that?' he asked, before she could turn to go.

'Of what?'

'Why, I suppose you could call it a political meeting, taking place outside – a rowdy one, to be sure.'

'Ah well, I heard something, but the kitchen's not on the facing side.' Turning from Cate's retreating figure, Luke tore off a piece of the fresh bread and lowered it into the warm, slightly glutinous liquid, watching the doughy tendrils around the edge soften and dissolve into the swirling soup. Distracted from the day's disquiets, his mind ranged back over the time he'd lost in declaring his true feelings for her. He stirred absently with his spoon, replaying the latest missed opportunity that very morning, when they'd met over coffee. Which was more difficult: to suppress his longing with silence, or to speak his mind, and face the consequences? There was Elizabeth to consider, of course: though, now the children had both left... Then again, his minister, the Reverend Richard Duckworth of St Martin's, would surely warn him of the danger to his immortal soul, as he wrestled with temptation.

Robshaw broke in on his reverie.

'If you don't want that soup, I'll have it.' Luke found he had little appetite. As the deputy finished off his second helping, the pot-boy brought the bill and Luke put down a handful of coins.

Outside, the streets were still crowded, with knots of angry-looking men congregating in doorways.

'That there's where it all kicked off, they say, on Scholastica's,' Robshaw said, nodding at The Mermaid tavern, on the corner of Queen Street, where quite a few from the original mob were now loitering.

'That's right. It was called The Swindlestock back in those days. But Bowell's exaggerating, surely – we're not going to see another battle of town and gown?'

'You'd hope not.'

Chapter 16
Under the Microscope

'So, we can take a look at the cadaver at last,' Robshaw said as they neared the Guildhall. 'Might find that letter, what he got given at The Unicorn.' The 'parlour' behind Luke's room was illuminated by a window that faced south-west, so the present hour – in late afternoon – often afforded the best light for inspecting a body, especially on a day such as this, with the sky now clear. Luke turned the key in the lock and they went in.

Dust particles drifted in shafts of sunlight as Robshaw pegged back the curtain that separated the space from the main office. Luke unclasped the leather case containing his collection of medical forceps, scissors and tweezers, and took his microscope from its wooden box. The instrument came from a London master craftsman, Richard Reeve, to a design by Robert Hooke. Hooke was one of many eminent scientists to have forged a career from his involvement with the natural philosophy circle based at Wadham College during Luke's days as an undergraduate. Ostensibly, his own studies had been dominated by the classics, but Luke soon came to regard this group as by far the most stimulating part of his university education. He had watched in wonderment as one discovery after another, revealing the laws and complexities of the natural world, had been unveiled.

Hooke, now Secretary of the Royal Society in London, made his reputation at Oxford by designing and engineering precision equipment to enable deductions by such innovators as Robert Boyle, the physical chemist, to be brought to elegant life. The simplicity and harmony of their measurements, showing – with a long glass tube bent into a 'J' shape, a rack and pinion pump and a phial of mercury – that the volume of air halved as the pressure on it doubled, was a presentation Luke had witnessed in person, and one that left a lasting impression. Boyle and Hooke set up their laboratory on the High, just round the corner from the Sandys' house, adding to the young man's sense of personal involvement in the exciting intellectual ferment.

Luke still did his best to keep in touch with new developments and, thanks chiefly to the wealth accumulated by his father, found himself in the fortunate position of being able to indulge his interests. He'd treated himself to a Reeve microscope when his son, Sam, obtained his apprenticeship. The instrument had not yet been used in the course of an actual case but – he was sure – its time would come. He had been bitten by a bug: having witnessed mysteries being unravelled by human ingenuity, making deductions from evidence that could be seen and demonstrated, he saw no reason why his own inquiries into crimes in Oxford should not be tackled by applying the same principles.

The two men carefully pulled back the length of muslin they had used to cover Harbord's now-stiffened body. The distinctive aquiline features jutted slightly backwards, as though the MP's last dying act had been to avert his gaze, perhaps in search of mercy from God. Removing the wig revealed a close-cropped pate, whose sparse grey hairs matched his skin and toned with a sober ensemble of jacket and waistcoat – the only interruptions to this drab colour scheme being the green ribbon on his lapel, and the large brown stain that spread from his abdomen and picked out runnels down the front of his breeches. His belt was undone, as if he'd tried to ease the pressure on his innards as they became engorged with blood. Luke gingerly lifted the outer garment by the lapel and inserted his fingers in the inside pockets. Nothing in the first. In the other, Harbord's left, sure enough, his fingers closed around a folded sheet of paper, which he extracted and passed to Robshaw to open out. On it, in an untidy cursive, was written a short message. Luke read aloud:

'The Old House. Friday at dusk. M.F.'

Underneath this single line of text was a stylised image of four crudely drawn black and white birds, arranged in diamond formation.

'Magpies,' the deputy grunted. 'As you know well, Master Sandys.'

'From Magpie Lane, you mean?'

'It wasn't always called that,' Robshaw murmured, continuing to peruse the letter.

'Yes, I'm well aware of that Robshaw, since you take every opportunity to mention it.' Luke felt a surge of irritation. Centuries ago, the narrow thoroughfare had been known for its association with prostitutes, by a name that would, he knew, have sounded merely matter of fact to contemporaries. In the context of modern manners, however, 'Gropecunt Lane' carried an obscenely comic effect that Robshaw never failed to find amusing.

'So what's it mean?' the deputy asked as he peered at the paper.

'Could be a political symbol. Looks almost heraldic in that configuration, like a coat of arms on a shield.'

'What about them words?'

'Well – the House, in political terms, would be the House of Commons, I'll warrant. Probably not from any mystery caller at The Unicorn, then – more likely to have come with him from Westminster. Wonder why he kept it.'

'Is there a new House and an old House then, in Westminster?' Robshaw wondered. But this particular form of words had them flummoxed.

'The initials, I suppose, would be those of the sender. "M.F." – could be anyone,' Luke thought aloud. They searched Harbord's pockets again but found no sign of any other written communication. The only account of his having received a letter in Oxford had come from Unsworth, who could scarcely be regarded as a reliable source. Perhaps Robshaw was right – they would have to go back and lean on the innkeeper, though Luke was confident there would be no need for violence. A none-too-subtle hint about revoking that newly acquired liquor licence should loosen his tongue.

Sandys and Robshaw turned their attention to the wound.

'We don't have the weapon, so let's try to see from this what kind of blade the killer used,' Luke said, turning to the pump he'd had connected from here to the Hinksey water pipe, and finding a can to fill with water.

'Hold on a minute.' Robshaw was looking more closely at Harbord's stricken abdomen. 'There's something you should look at, before you clean it off.' Luke peered down the line of Robshaw's thick finger as it pointed to the centre of the stab mark. 'Bits of something in there what don't match. Blue, I'd say.' Sure enough, he could just about make out a few small shreds of what looked like blue cloth in among the brown-stained grey mess of Harbord's waistcoat front.

With mounting excitement, Luke reached for a pair of tweezers and his magnifying glass from the open leather case. Steadying his hand, he slowly eased the steel prong under the edge of the tiny object; he prised it loose, held it up to the light and squinted through the lens.

'By God, Robshaw, you're right. 'Tis a piece of blue cloth.'

'How'd that get there, then? Our man here favoured grey, not blue.'

'Well, it could have come from the killer. Could be our first real clue! Let's take a closer look.'

This was the moment Luke had been waiting for. He delicately opened the paper wrapper from around a clean slide and, with the tweezers, lifted the shred of cloth on to its smooth surface. He put the slide on the platform of the microscope and secured it in place with a metal side clamp. Applying his eye to the eyepiece, Luke slowly twisted the focusing knob on the side of the viewing column, and then – suddenly and as if by magic – the distinctive latticework structure of closely woven fabric came clearly into view. Shifting the instrument so the maximum amount of light fell upon it, he satisfied himself that the colour of the swatch was indeed different from any of Harbord's own garments.

Flushed with success, Sandys was inclined to be generous.

'D'you want to see?' he asked Robshaw. He had reckoned without the man's clumsiness, however – or perhaps the volume of alcohol he'd consumed earlier. In moving around the table, Robshaw stubbed his toe on one of the trestles and caused everything on it – corpse and microscope included – to wobble alarmingly.

'Careful, man!' Luke cried, steadying his prized possession. Good thing the slide was clamped on. A few incoherent but apparently sincere noises of apology having passed between them, Robshaw duly crouched over the gleaming instrument, a wary look on his face.

'A bit of it's black,' he said, straightening up after a long examination of the material.

'What d'you mean, a bit of it's black?'

'It looks burnt, like,' the deputy said, a faraway light of comprehension beginning to dawn in his eyes. Luke looked into the microscope again. Robshaw's inadvertent nudge had apparently displaced the slide sideways, and, sure enough, he was now looking, not at the middle of the sample as before but a portion of the fabric edge. It was, beyond doubt, burnt and blackened. Eagerly, Luke removed the slide, then with the tweezers placed the shred of material in an envelope. There would be time to label and store it later. He returned to the body and, from amid the congealed blood surrounding the wound, picked out several other fragments of about the same size. Even to the naked eye, it was plain – now he knew what to look for – that these, too, were fibres of the same blue woollen cloth, singed at the edge like the first. He went through the same procedure, confirming the impression through the powerful lenses of the Reeve microscope.

The two men looked at each other with matching expressions of consternation.

'If those burnt bits of blue stuff are not from Harbord's own clothes...' Luke began slowly.

'Then they must have come from someone else's,' the deputy reasoned.

'And we've just heard about someone who was wearing a blue uniform – one that was singed and shredded around the wrist.'

'That story of Pawling's. That there Guardsman what spooked Emily's cattle.' They sat down, and went back over the vivid account they'd received from the ex-Mayor that morning.

'He's reckoned to have had a backfire from his flintlock – and he was obviously blest by good fortune, as the powder was mostly caught by his coat cuff.'

'And that'd shred and burn the wool?'

'Certainly – it would be ablaze when it came out so it would stick on the cloth and burn through it like a hot knife through butter.'

'That'll be why he had to stamp it out, like – 'twas still smouldering.' They paused as this insight and its implications sank in.

'So some partially burnt fragments would have been left on his sleeve,' Luke continued, before Robshaw completed the thought:

'And if he'd stabbed Harbord, they could have got rubbed off when he stuck the knife in.' Now their expressions were of mounting excitement.

'When we find that Guardsman, Robshaw my friend, it looks as though we'll have found our murderer as well!'

Luke had pushed Pawling's complaint to the back of his mind. He'd promised to raise the matter with Ed – probably that evening – but it had scarcely seemed important in context. Now, that conversation took on a wholly different complexion. As he'd indicated to Pawling, the most the offending Guardsman could expect to face by way of consequences for misusing his weapon and scaring off livestock would be the catch-all charge of 'Conduct Prejudicial to Good Order and Discipline.' With the evidence now in his possession, linking the incident to a capital crime, mere military jurisdiction would no longer suffice. He would have to get a letter from the Mayor asking the Colonel of Ed's regiment, the Earl of Oxford, for permission to arrest and question the man.

There was still the wound to examine. Robshaw pumped out water into the can and prepared a solution of soap, while Luke took his surgical scissors and sliced away the shirt and waistcoat from around the point of entry. He then took up a silken cloth, soaked it in the soapy mixture, and began swabbing the affected area – gently so as to preserve the shape. It took several minutes to dissolve and clear away the dried blood, but they were rewarded with a clear sight of the skin break on Harbord's lean frame: a narrow isosceles triangle in profile, with an acute angle at the top and a broader fuzzy edge below. And it was big: no wonder he'd bled out quickly. ''Twas only sharp on one side,' Robshaw observed.

'But what knife these days has only one edge?'

'I seen such a thing before. Could be a Scotch dirk – they're like that. Wide blades an' all.'

'But you'd think it would be the other way round, surely – sharp side downward?'

'Maybe he just got it the wrong way up,' the deputy said – and, Luke had to admit, he could not improve on this explanation for the moment.

'Right, well, let's observe the formalities. Fetch the horse and cart and take the body to the charnel-house. I'll write a note for you to give to the coroner. Then I think we'll call it a day.'

'Yessir,' Robshaw replied, and was gone. With his tweezers, Luke placed the remaining fragments of burnt blue cloth in the envelope and sealed it, wrote the details of date, time and place and signed it, then locked it in his desk drawer along with the mysterious magpie note from Harbord's pocket. He had just finished jotting a short official notification of the MP's death when the men came with the cart and removed the body from the parlour. He would have to talk to Ed, at least to give him due warning – and at some point, he and Robshaw would need to go back to The Unicorn and Jacob's Well, to question Unsworth again and examine the dead man's room and belongings. For now, those jobs could wait. Alone in his office and savouring a precious interlude of quiet, Luke put away his treasured microscope, retrieved a bottle of canary and a cup from their hiding place, and sipped slowly as the shadows lengthened, pondering the day's events.

Chapter 17
A Fireside Tale

At the farm, the soap had been satisfactorily finished off and was now drying. As there was still plenty of daylight, Emily had next been set to cheesemaking; her mother reckoning to keep her busy to take her mind off her ordeal on the London road. The puny pailful or two of milk she'd gathered from the cattle that morning was at an early stage of manufacture, having been separated into curds that were then cut up into small cubes, and gently warmed in the sun, to firm and settle. Under Mistress Hopkins' watchful eye, she was now concentrating on the other end of the process, begun the previous autumn: bandaging the circular finished truckles top and bottom, and round the sides, with muslin, and smearing in a fine layer of lard to make the fabric stick to the cheese. These she would be in charge of taking to market in Oxford the next day, where they were destined to be sold and taken to kitchens and pantries to mature to the individual customer's taste before being consumed.

Emily looked out from the open side of the cheese-loft across the valley, the breeze catching in the spinneys and the hawthorn boughs shaking their blossoms by way of mute reply to the sallies of songbirds and the turning of seasons. Her thoughts flew unbidden to the day when she and Richard found themselves alone in the cottage – sundry minor farmyard emergencies having called both her parents to their duties at once – and 'one thing led to another', as it was later said. The youngest of three surviving children and the only one remaining in the family home, through early years she had always been their 'pet-lamb'.

Now, she had been obliged to grow up quickly as she contemplated her own portion of adult responsibilities.

Weeks of worry, followed by the awful hardening certainty occasioned by missed periods, had culminated in a tearful confession to her mother. That encounter had been gentler than she had feared, however, and – notwithstanding a few knowing grins from the labourers, which crimsoned her cheeks – Emily's 'condition', as it was known, had been accepted seamlessly into the warp and weft of farm and family life. Initially shocked, Jacob had rapidly come round to an optimistic cast of mind, being of the view that Richard was 'a steady feller', who evidently intended to do right by his daughter. Indeed, the first banns of marriage had lately been read at St Andrew's.

Now, just as the dripping of the whey seemed to take up Emily's inner lament over the fate of her two milch-cows, she suddenly espied a far-off but familiar figure striding purposefully up the path towards them. Yes! It was Richard. She felt her heart lift within her breast for the first time since last night's misadventure.

The young couple would be allowed time to walk in the sunshine, but not to be indoors unsupervised: a stipulation Richard seemed happy to accept, to Emily's relief. She recalled with a shudder the occasion, shortly after the revelation of her pregnancy, when her mother had seen fit to issue some indelicately phrased advice not to 'let him eat of the pie before he's paid the price' – a form of words she would go to some lengths to avoid having to listen to again.

'So how come you're here at this hour?' she asked, when they were together.

'Ain't you glad to see me then?'

''Course I am, silly! Only 'tis usually later.'

'They finished us a bit early. Short of stone.' Oxford since the Restoration had seen a building boom, which had placed considerable stress on supplies of limestone. Headington Quarry was all but worked out, at least of the best-quality material that was in demand by the colleges for such projects as their precious libraries.

'So you heard, then, what happened last night to them poor milchers?' she enquired, her features taking on a mournful expression.

'Aye, Jacob came by the site to tell us, about the shooter, an' all. What a rogue! Said you was in low spirits, like. I got away soon as I could, after that.'

Through bright orange bills, the gaggle of white farmyard geese hissed disapprovingly as the couple picked their way past. Presently, they reached a narrow, overgrown laneway which meandered down a slope towards a long-neglected out-building. Unobserved, they slipped inside. 'Richard...!' she said warningly as she felt the passion of his embrace, and her own answering inner thrill. The structure was earmarked for conversion to their own cottage after the wedding. 'We haven't long to wait now – then we'll come in here whenever the fancy takes us.' The man looked down into her face with a merry twinkle:

'We'll only come out when the fancy takes us, you mean.'

Disengaging from their clinch, Richard ran his fingers along the tiles that he was in the process of fitting to the roof, when the master mason could spare him.

'So Father came by your site this morning, with Master Pawling?' she asked.

'That he did.'

'They went for to see Luke Sandys at the Guildhall, and he said he'll get the shooter and put him on a charge.'

'Oh, aye?'

'Only Master Pawling said some odd things when he came back. As how he'd given something to Master Sandys, and the feller might hang for it.' She was wide eyed at the thought.

'Well, you know what they say – Mayor Pawling do like the sound of his own voice.'

'Fie, Richard Bourke! He's been that kind to us,' she said reprovingly. 'Given us our new cottage, for one. Now, see you do put up the rest of them tiles!'

That evening at the cottage, the women were gazing silently into the fire, each lost in her own thoughts, as Jacob enjoyed the last of his frumenty.

'Now, heed me, Liza, and you too, Emily,' the father said, pushing away his empty bowl. 'I heard a strange tale in town earlier. Aye, a strange tale indeed, and a sad one.' Liza regarded her husband with some scepticism – she had heard such tales from him many times before, and what struck Jacob Hopkins as strange often turned out to have a simple explanation.

'This one's about a ghost,' he announced, relishing the surprise with which this news was greeted. "Tis said 'twas the ghost of old Noll Crumble himself.' The women settled themselves into their chairs.

'There was these two old soldiers, see, what fought in the Holland wars, and they was both wounded. Jack ended up with a hump-back, and Tom lost his leg, and had to walk with a crutch.' Mother and daughter now gave their full attention – mutilated war veterans had been familiar figures in both their lifetimes, not only from the Anglo-Dutch wars but also the Civil War, decades earlier.

'Well, anyways, these two fellers, they was both out drinking one night in Oxford, and got to jawing, and they realised they'd miss the curfew. So Jack ups and says, "I better take a short cut home, across St Thomas's churchyard."' They shivered involuntarily. St Thomas the Martyr's was an ancient church in Osney, from King Stephen's time it was said – and the subject of many a tale concerning supernatural events and manifestations.

'But when Jack's halfway across,' Jacob continued, 'out from behind a gravestone pops a ghost – the ghost of Noll Crumble. And he says to Jack, "Here, what's that on your back?" And Jack says, "It's a hump." So the ghost says, "Well, I'll have that," and quick as a flash, takes the hump away and disappears, like.'

The mention of Noll Crumble – or Oliver Cromwell – was enough to impart at least a slender thread of plausibility. Soldiers from Cromwell's parliamentary army, captured by Royalist forces in the Civil War, had been locked up in St Thomas's – a portion of recent history that was rued locally because the imprisoned men, Puritans all, had promptly smashed the stained-glass windows, for their supposedly idolatrous imagery.

'So, the next night,' Jacob continued, 'the two of them meets up again, and Jack's standing straight now, for the first time in years, and he tells his mate all that have happened. And Tom says, "I shall have to try that tonight, I might get my leg back."' Liza leaned forward to poke the fire into life.

'So he sets off, and sure enough, the ghost pops out again. But old Noll, he says, "Here, what's that on your back?" and Tom says, "There ain't nothing on my back." So the ghost says, "Well then, here you are, have a hump!" And sure enough, poor Tom's still got no leg, only now he's got Jack's hump an' all! So – like I say, 'tis strange – and sad.'

Emily struggled to stifle a guffaw at her father's air of solemn satisfaction with the climax to this narrative, but her mother burst out:

'Why, you clodpate, Jacob Hopkins! Have you checked your own legs, to see if one's not longer than the other? 'Cause they've surely been pulling it for you, whoever told you that tall tale!'

'Why, 'twas some of Luke Sandys' men, at the Guildhall,' the husband replied, a misty sense beginning to form that he had, indeed, been the butt of their joke. The three of them looked at each other and laughed out loud.

'Ah, but 'twas rich, going in there with Farmer Pawling,' Jacob recalled. ''Twas as though he owned the place. We was left in there, when Master Sandys and Master Robshaw was called away, and Pawling, he was on his legs and off straight away into the back parlour, for to look at a corpse that was in there, on a table. 'Twas said 'twas from a murder.'

'Cussed if I'd have cared to look at a corpse,' his wife exclaimed. 'Was it covered in blood, like?'

'Oh, I never looked,' Jacob replied. 'I had no stomach for it, but Pawling, he couldn't wait.'

Chapter 18
An Arrest Warrant

Ed was in the hall when Luke returned to Magpie Lane. With Elizabeth absent on church-related duties, Luke came straight to the point.

'Robert Pawling came to see us this morning, at the Guild-hall.'

'Last year's mayor? What did he want?'

''Twas about your Guardsmen. You never mentioned one of them had fired his flintlock and stampeded some cattle.'

'Slipped my mind last night. Stupid thing to do, though. Trooper, name of George Gregory, one of Tom Lucy's company. How did Pawling know about it?'

'You wouldn't have heard what happened to the animals, then?' Ed shook his head. 'Well, the beasts were from Magdalen Farm, where Pawling's been the tenant for many years. I'm afraid two of them died.' His brother made suitably sympathetic noises. 'It seems they stumbled down a steep slope and into the ruins of an old chapel that's being demolished for the stone. One was impaled on a pickaxe the men had left there, and the other broke a leg and had to be destroyed.'

'Well, Gregory's on a charge – "Conduct Prejudicial" – that should cover it. The Colonel will make sure Pawling's compensated.'

'It's not quite that simple,' Luke pressed on. 'Did you see that trooper again after you reached Oxford?'

'No, I came here as soon as I could get away. They were all off for the night by then. I could find out where he's billeted.'

'That would be helpful. I'll need to talk to him myself. In fact we'll have to take him in.'

'What, for frightening a herd of cows? We'll deal with that within the regiment. 'Tis standard military discipline.'

Luke looked evenly at his brother.

'I've reason to believe that the same man who fired that pistol later stabbed William Harbord to death.'

It took a moment or two for this to register, whereupon Ed exhaled with an audible 'pfff'.

'I hope you're sure of your facts, Luke. The Colonel will hate it.'

Luke confirmed with Ed that Gregory's gun had backfired, and explained the connection with the singed blue cloth found on the body. The pair both examined Ed's own matching tunic through the magnifying glass, which Luke had brought home for the purpose. Sure enough, it was of the same fabric he'd seen at the Guildhall an hour or two earlier. A murder is a murder, the brothers agreed – and firmly in the bailiwick of the civil authorities to investigate and prosecute.

Positively ambushed at his breakfast table the next morning, above his mercer's shop on the High Street, Mayor Bowell acceded to Luke's request with bad grace: 'Very well, I'll sign your damn letter.'

His face pruned in anguish as the implications sank in. Two powerful interests – the Whig faction in Parliament, and the Royal Guards – were now to be set at odds, with the City seemingly in the role of troublemaker.

'You'll have to take it in to the Guildhall, and get Paynton to seal it.' Paynton, the town clerk, cultivated a dusty, disobliging manner to deter what he considered excessive demands on his time, with the paradoxical result that any request for his services tended to drag out into a lengthy, nitpicking argument over protocol. Having finally persuaded him to seal the mayor's missive to the Earl of Oxford, seeking permission to take one of his men into custody, with the City's official imprimatur, Luke betook himself to meet Ed at Merton College, where the regimental top brass were billeted.

'What the Devil d'you mean by it, sir?' Aubrey de Vere, 20th Earl of Oxford, was quivering with indignation. The City's request had not gone down well on top of the alcohol he'd consumed and its after-effects this morning. His luxuriant chestnut wig draped over the corner of his chair, the Colonel's head was instead covered with a damp towel. The effort of shouting sent a fresh paroxysm of pain through his temples. Snatching for his phial of Goddard's Drops, he knocked a quill pen from its inkwell and sent it skittering across the desk, spreading dark blotches in its wake.

'Slingsby!' he roared, then winced again.

The Sandys brothers had met the chastened figure of Captain Lucy on their way in. Failure to lodge the requisite paperwork pertaining to the charge against Trooper Gregory had earned him the rough side of the Colonel's wine-furred tongue, and the aide-de-camp, Captain Slingsby, was now in the anteroom, instructing the young officer on what it should say. At his master's summons, he scurried back in. Rubbing his eyes, the Colonel lowered his voice to a tone of generalised disgust with a deeply unsatisfactory world.

'Captain Sandys' brother here wants to arrest Gregory and take him into the custody of the City.'

'Out of the question, sir,' Slingsby snapped. 'Discipline is a regimental matter.'

'He is wanted for murder,' Ed volunteered, provoking a fresh eruption.

'You'll speak when you're bidden, sir!'

However, the Colonel soon tired of holding up his end of the argument, indicating his grudging assent to the arrest and mumbling an instruction to bring him coffee and small beer. He countersigned the mayor's letter, which Luke carefully folded and slipped into his inside pocket. In the anteroom, they held a hurried conclave with Slingsby before he embarked on his latest errand. The aide-de-camp pored over a sheet of paper, on which the addresses of the Guards' Oxford billets were listed.

'Yes, it says here – Gregory and Ladlow are staying at number two, Goat's Head Yard, wherever that may be.'

'Off St Michael's Street, over by the north gate,' Luke said. 'We should be able to pick him up there.'

'Well, Godspeed to you. If he's gone out, you'll have a job finding him – the men have a day's leave today, they'll be in mufti.'

'They would,' Luke remarked grimly. 'And, as it's market day, it'd be like looking for a needle in a haystack.'

'Better make haste,' Ed said.

At Goat's Head Yard, however, the Sandys brothers drew a blank. The door was answered by a tow-headed youth with a pink complexion, who was apparently either a simpleton or intimidated out of his wits by the appearance of a constable and a Guards officer together on the doorstep. Wordlessly, he disappeared back inside to be replaced by a middle-aged woman, a greyish mob-cap surmounting her distinctly disagreeable countenance.

'Worrizit?' she enquired, smoothing her apron. The cook-maid proved a voluble, though singularly uninformative interlocutor. 'I ain't been paid nothing yet,' she complained. 'Do you tell your colonel that, cavalryman!'

The new Disbandment Act, passed by Parliament two years earlier, meant soldiers could only be billeted on householders by consent, so it was a chance to earn a bit of extra cash – but the system was already notorious for long arrears. In answer to their questions: the men had been gone that morning by the time the household rose for the day; to exercise their horses, she supposed, which were stabled at Christ Church. No, she didn't know where they were going next; no, they hadn't discussed any plans, 'least not in front of me.' At Luke's prompting, she yelled for the boy: 'Cuthbert! Get back here!' But, when the same queries were put to him, Cuthbert merely blushed still redder, and shook his straw-coloured head.

'Well, let's go to my office,' Luke said. 'Could you draw a likeness of this Gregory, with pencil and paper? Then Robshaw and I can take that, and you can take one of the other constables, and we'll just have to look everywhere we can think of, till we find him.' In childhood, the outdoors-minded younger brother had just about sat still for long enough to absorb basic principles of draughtsmanship from their father, and, seated at the desk in the room at the back of the Guildhall, he quickly produced a serviceable sketch, showing the moustache and beard and capturing the suspect's characteristic expression of barely suppressed anger.

'Looks a choleric sort of character,' Luke observed.

'Not the most biddable,' Ed agreed. 'Mind you, he'll come quietly enough, I would think, at least if I reach him first. He knows he's on a charge, so he'll probably assume the Colonel wants to deal with it there and then.'

'But he doesn't know he's wanted for murder.'

'Quite so. I can imagine his face when he finds that out.'

Chapter 19
Market Day

Magdalen Farm was all a-flutter. There were chicken's necks to wring – a task Emily's mother performed with brisk efficiency – along with eggs to place in boxes lined with straw, and Emily's own special job of arranging the cheeses in a wicker basket, with a fresh linen cloth over them to keep off the sun's morning rays. All were destined to be sold to market traders for eagerly anticipated bonus rates, as Oxford strove to meet the surge in demand from its suddenly expanded population. Mistress Hopkins took the reins as her husband fixed the shafts of the old cart into the halter worn by the piebald nag, while Emily made herself comfortable behind as best she could.

The master mason was filling in time between deliveries of stone by instructing Richard in some of the finer techniques of his trade, but the apprentice might be released to look round the market for an hour or two.

'Maybe see you there, then,' she'd said casually, as they parted the previous afternoon. 'Aye – maybe,' her lover had grinned. So, today she put on her best bonnet – somewhat old and worn now, as it had been her mother's, but of excellent quality, with bobbin lace decoration – and a gown with the seams discreetly let out by a thumb's breadth either side. She settled herself carefully against the side of the cart to avoid creasing it.

Leaving the farm, they turned right at the fork in the lane towards Oxford. To the left lay the path to the London road, which Emily registered with a small involuntary shudder. The cart then rolled and jolted along the causeway across the Marston meads, as Peasmoor Brook chuntered on through its loquacious shallows alongside, and was nearly at the city wall when Farmer Pawling trotted up behind them on his grey gelding.

'Mind you get best prices for them goods, Mistress Hopkins!' he called out jovially, raising his hat as he overtook them. 'I'll see you in the market, by and by.'

On market days, Pawling would call in at his old mercer's shop on the High Street. The University authorities had 'discommoned' him as a supplier when he muscled in on their exclusive right to patrol the streets by night and enforce the curfew. Now, the business was recovering, having apparently passed to Pawling's apprentice, Thomas Coombes – though he was still, in fact, pocketing the proceeds. The women watched the tall, erect figure on the dappled horse as it dwindled into the distance.

'He looks quite the dand,' Emily remarked.

'As well he might,' Liza snorted. 'He'll be picking up his money from Master Coombes on the way into town.'

Haunches of mutton and pork were suspended in approximate order of size from the rails across the top of the stalls; there were coneys, splayed on the wooden benches, and geese, whose long, lifeless necks lolled over the sides, as the women picked their way along the shambles on Queen Street. Liza had strung the chickens together in braces, and together they carried them through the already teeming crowd with a ''scuse-me' here and a 'begging-your-pardon' there – until they reached Master Bulstrode's stall.

'Good day to you, ladies,' the ruddy-faced butcher called out. 'Pleasant day for it.'

Emily was glad of the fresh breeze that carried away the pungent odour of the blood and offal the men sluiced into the channel running down the centre of the roadway, when they'd prepared the meat for their customers.

She had tagged along many times on this errand over the years, but now she was observing the transactions of adult life with renewed interest. Bulstrode had customers waiting, and his apprentice boy was serving them all very slowly, as he strove to avoid making mistakes. The master moved to the side of the stall to deal with Mistress Hopkins in person, keeping a nervous eye on the purchases already under way.

'Thruppence a pair – best price,' he pronounced, with an air of finality.

'Now, Master Bulstrode, we've knowed each other a long time, and you know you won't see better birds than these in a month of Sundays.'

'One and six the lot then?' She went to reply, then paused, calculating.

'Why, 'tis the same amount, for twelve birds! Are you trying to catch me for a coney?'

There was a twinkle in her eye, for this was a ritual long established between them.

'Very well then, Mistress Hopkins, seeing as how 'tis you, and them birds do look plim, I must say… how about fourpence a pair?'

'Done.'

Delving under his blood-spattered apron, the butcher quickly counted out two shillings, which Liza slipped into a recess of her bag. 'Thank you kindly, Master B,' she said, smiling as they bade farewell.

Chapter 20
A Manhunt Begins

Luke took the sketch and headed off with Robshaw up Fish Street. Apart from the Colonel's aide-de-camp, Ed was the only member of the Horse Guards in Oxford that day to be wearing full uniform – calculated by the brothers as likely to induce compliance from Gregory in his arrest. By the time they set off, another constable, Tim Blount, had reported for duty at the Guildhall, so Luke paired his brother with the new arrival. Blount was serving his six-month before resuming trade as a blacksmith. They would head up Corn-market Street while Luke and Robshaw peeled off along the High, looking inside the inns, taverns and coffeehouses as they reached them. Having checked all such premises on their allotted route, the two City men walked back towards the market, looking left and right as they went; but the crowd was thickening, and the task felt hopeless.

'It'll just be dumb luck if we see him in this lot,' Luke said. 'I've got an idea: come on.' He struck out briskly towards the City church of St Martin's at Carfax, on the corner of Queen Street, with Robshaw scurrying to keep pace. Luke knocked loudly on the door, then again when there was no answer. 'I know you're in there, Wheaton – open up.'

'Patience is a virtue, master, patience is a virtue. Thus saith the Lord,' a voice wheezed from within, accompanied by a jangling of keys – and the door finally opened, albeit only a crack. 'Church is closed, Master Sandys. Can't be too careful, what with these London types around, and with it being market day an' all.'

'We need to get to the top of your tower,' Luke said, without ceremony. A practised frown settled on the verger's features.

'I shall have to ask the Rector, sir, about that. Come back later.'

'No, this can't wait. We're on the trail of a man wanted for murder.'

'Well, I don't know what his Reverence would say to that. I never heard of such a thing.'

'Very well, fetch the Reverend Duckworth. I've been meaning to have a word with him since I caught you selling the "healing water of St Frideswide" last year. Penny a bottle, wasn't it? I'm told "his Reverence" takes a dim view of simony.'

'Come to think of it, I might have the key to the tower on this here bunch,' Wheaton said, hurriedly pulling the door ajar.

Once inside, Luke was gratified to find his hunch was correct: the scaffolding was indeed still in place from the latest adjustment to St Martin's new bells, commissioned by Richard Duckworth, the rector, who was an expert campanologist. He'd ordered an extra bell, to create a set of six, the previous year, and their ringing combinations and sequences were generally accounted as being among the wonders of the age. Robshaw protested mildly as they started to climb, but found his head for heights from the midpoint as they reached the top of the wooden apparatus and stepped out on to a broad landing, through which the bell-ropes passed by means of small round holes, then resumed the ascent up some sturdy stone steps. At the top, some seventy-five feet up, they paused for breath and drank in the cruciform city view: to the east, the spires of All Saints and Saint Mary the Virgin, with its pink flush of almond blossom at street level; the Castle and Castle Mound to the west; Christ Church Cathedral to the south; and St Michael's church at the North Gate, along Cornmarket Street. 'If he sticks his nose out, we'll see him from here,' the deputy said, gazing downwards at the market area and its throng of comers and goers.

Chapter 21
A Game of Cup and Ball

At the cheesemonger's, the Magdalen Farm produce fetched, as Mistress Hopkins said, 'a pretty penny' – in fact, fully fifteen shillings. Emily flushed with pride to be introduced, even in jocular fashion, as 'our new head cheesemaker', and the women came away well satisfied with their morning's bargaining. Emily's senses filled with the more agreeable experiences of market day. The melodious flageolet player stood by the road-side and fixed passers-by with beseeching eyes for coin, competing with the cries of merchants' apprentices: 'What d'ye lack, sirs?'

There were fishmongers, with shoals of silver flanks glistening in the late-morning sun, while other stalls offered dried figs and quinces, cinnamon and black peppercorns. At one or two, there were even some of the new ingredients now beginning to find their way to England from the Orient: nutmeg and cloves, and earthenware jars of ground garam masala. One day soon, she would be purchasing market goods for her own household: a realisation that thrilled and alarmed her in equal measure. What would garam masala taste like, in a bowl of pottage? Or should it be tried first in porridge? Aye – that'd be the plan.

Looking around, Emily could suddenly no longer see her mother. No matter: she would simply head back to the stable yard behind The Mitre, where they had left the horse and cart, and wait there. Master Ingram, the ostler, an old friend of her father who had a daughter of about her own age, would let her sit in his comfortable chair. Just then, however, she glimpsed from behind the longed-for silhouette in the middle distance:

Richard. It must be him: at his side she identified his friend Paul, who was apprenticed to another mason engaged on a college building project nearby, and also therefore subject to the vagaries of stone supplies. They'd evidently been given time off together.

She was forming a call of greeting when the words suddenly died on her lips. For as the pair made their way down Fish Street, two older men who walked in front of them turned and gestured for them to follow, turning left into Blue Boar Street. And she recognised one of them, she was sure. Not in uniform this time, but that facial hair was unmistakable: it was none other than the Guardsman whose gunshot had stampeded her cattle. What had Farmer Pawling called him? A 'rogue and a rascal'!

Emily's head was spinning. Shouldn't she report this sighting to someone? Her father had said Luke Sandys would take up the matter, and Pawling implied the man was to be severely punished. And yet here he was in plain sight, with her Richard. As she looked around for a constable, however, she saw none – and the scurrying passers-by all seemed so preoccupied with their own affairs, there was no ready opening to approach any of them. Conflicting impulses led Emily to a rapid resolve: she would follow the four men herself, but at a safe distance. She must know what was afoot, but she would rather avoid another personal encounter with the soldier, even with Richard there. Hitching up the sides of her gown, she fairly trotted down Fish Street, attempting to catch up, heart in her mouth at the combination of curiosity and peril that drew her onwards.

As she neared The Bear Inn, she saw them, seated around a table in a quiet corner of the courtyard. Drinking would begin in earnest later, when market business was done, but for now the crowd back here was thin, and they had the space to themselves. Moving quickly to avoid being spotted, Emily dodged into the back end of an alleyway belonging to another inn, The Chequers – a long, narrow establishment which fronted on to the High Street – and positioned herself to peer unobtrusively round the corner. However, she need not have worried unduly: the men seemed intent on the activity in front of them.

With his bandaged right hand, the Guardsman set out three upturned wooden cups on the table, then held up a small ball to show Richard, who nodded as if in approval. This he placed under one of the cups, and proceeded to slide them around the table; taking the leftmost, switching it with the one in the centre, then moving the rightmost across to the other side, and repeating these actions several times. He then stopped, and motioned to Richard to take his pick. Emily watched with bated breath as her fiancé stared long and hard at the cups, and eventually tapped one of them with his index finger. The Guardsman lifted it to reveal the ball underneath, whereupon Paul clapped his friend on the back; the older man raised his shapeless grey hat and offered a handshake by way of congratulation, and the Guardsman took a coin from his purse, kissed it and handed it to Richard.

The apprentices started to rise from their chairs as if to leave, but Grey-hat gestured for them to sit back down. There was to be another game, apparently for higher stakes: Richard drew back out the coin he'd won, along with another from his pocket. Emily saw the silver glint as he set it down. It must be a whole shilling. The same sequence unfolded, only this time, as the shuffling of wooden cups was about to begin, Grey-hat was suddenly afflicted by a cacophonous and pitiable fit of coughing. The younger men looked round in concern, and, while they were momentarily distracted, Emily clearly saw the seated Guardsman lift one of the cups, quickly remove the ball and place it in his pocket.

Having ascertained that Grey-hat was recovering, the men

returned their attention to the table. She wanted to cry out, 'No, Richard! He's cheating!', but – having secreted herself to watch them – she felt she must stay hidden. So, she was forced to watch in miserable silence as her lover scrutinised the three upturned cups, knowing what he evidently did not suspect – that his chances of winning were precisely nil.

On the disappointing outcome to the second game, copious commiserations were offered to Richard, along with the chance to win his money back, but this time the two apprentices were determined to leave, and duly did so, disappearing up Bear Lane towards the High Street. The two older men rose as well, and Emily's heart skipped a beat on seeing them walk towards her hiding place. Before they reached her, however, they turned sharp right up another narrow alleyway, Wheatsheaf Yard, and – after waiting for what seemed like an agonisingly long interval, but was in fact the shortest time she dared allow, to make sure they would not return – she emerged, relieved at having escaped discovery but suffused with righteous indignation on Richard's behalf. She set off as fast as her by now rather shaky legs would carry her around the inn and up Bear Lane, intending to find him and reveal how he'd been duped.

Chapter 22
Paths Converging

On the top of Carfax tower, Robshaw at that moment clutched Luke's shoulder and exclaimed: 'Look there! That feller yonder, by the end of Wheatsheaf Yard, on the High. Is that our man?'

Luke shaded his eyes with cupped hands, and followed the direction in which his deputy was pointing. Two men stood at the edge of the great thoroughfare, one bare-headed and the other wearing a grey hat of indeterminate shape. They first looked up the street, then down – and, on a brief exchange of words, disappeared down Bear Lane. Even from a distance of a hundred yards or so, and their high elevation, the likeness of their sketch to the sullen set of the bare-headed man's face, with its dark moustache and beard, was noteworthy. Luke could even just about make out that his right hand was bandaged.

'It might be, Robshaw,' he said, excited. 'It might very well.'

They took the stone steps two at a time, heads inclined to avoid bumping them on the underside of the spiralling; half-clambered, half-slid down the scaffolding, then, having passed a bewildered Wheaton at high speed, jogged off in the direction of the High and the entrance to Bear Lane. As they wove in and out of the market crowd, Luke spotted Paul and Richard.

'Bourke! Come with us,' he panted.

'But I'm not on duty, Master Sandys,' the apprentice protested.

'No matter, it's an emergency. You're sworn in, so you can make an arrest. Come.' And, with that, the younger man had no option but to tag along behind the two senior constables.

There was a slight kink about a third of the way up Bear Lane, formed by the jutting-out walls of adjoining buildings. Just as Emily made her way around this obstacle on her right, she almost ran straight into two pedestrians coming the other way: one bare-headed man, and another wearing a distinctive grey hat. Her soft little 'Oh' on recognising them scarce did justice to the seething admixture of recognition, shock, fear and outrage she felt inside.

'Whoa!' Gregory exclaimed, as they disentangled themselves. His face changed as he stepped back to a distance enabling him to have a proper look at her. 'Why, if it isn't the young cowherd from the London road? I never forget a face. You've got me in trouble with my Colonel, missy. What d'you think, Ladlow? 'Tis a pretty chance indeed, to have borne this into my way.'

'Aye – pretty,' Grey-hat leered unpleasantly.

'Now, girls who get gentlemen in trouble with their Colonel don't know their place. And girls who don't know their place need to be taught a lesson,' Gregory continued.

In panic, Emily looked up and down the lane, but, the three of them aside, it was empty of people.

'There's no one to run to here, missy.'

''Tain't just your Colonel what you're in trouble with,' she said tremulously, finally finding her voice. 'Luke Sandys is after you an' all. He's a City constable.'

'D'you hear that Ladlow? A City constable, indeed!' the man taunted. 'Well, the City can't touch us. Discipline is for the reg-iment. And now I'm to have my wages docked for a 'Conduct Prejudicial', all because you came along with those beasts at the wrong time.' He half-turned his head towards his companion, swivelling his eyes to keep them fixed on Emily's face. 'How do I feel about that, Ladlow?'

'You ain't happy, George.'

'You've hit the nail on the head there, my friend. I ain't happy. Not happy at all.'

Emily could keep it in no longer.

'And you was cheating at that game with the cups and the ball. I saw you.' Straight away she would have bitten off her tongue, if in doing so she could take the words back. Gregory's face, up to now darkly sardonic, set into a tempestuous, threatening scowl.

'I'll decide what you did and didn't see, you brazen-faced hussy,' he growled. 'Spy on me, would you? You're coming with us.' With that, he seized Emily by one arm, roughly spun her round and clamped his own arm tightly around her waist, then began marching her back down Bear Lane whence she had come, his companion loping alongside. 'Don't even think of crying out. What'll happen if she cries out, Ladlow?'

'Why, she might have to make acquaintance with Solly here,' replied the other, drawing the first few inches of his sabre.

'You see, Ladlow's a sentimental creature,' Gregory grunted as he half-pushed, half-carried her along. 'He's given his sword a name. "Solly". Ain't that sweet? But I'm not sentimental. You don't think I'm sentimental, do you?'

'N-no, s-sir,' Emily replied, her breath coming in short bursts.

'"No, sir." No I am not – on that you may depend.'

Emily quickly lost track of the route they were following. They turned now left, now right, then left again – in fact weaving between the high, impermeable walls of Oxford colleges: Oriel, Corpus Christi and Merton.

'W-where are you taking me, sirs?' she cried.

'Somewhere away from prying eyes,' Gregory replied. Clasped in the Guardsman's iron embrace, Emily was miserably aware, as she looked around in vain for succour, that only banks of cold unfeeling stone, with indifferent narrow windows, rose away on either side of her.

Chapter 23
'You need putting in your place, my girl!'

Luke, Robshaw and Richard Bourke reached the south end of Bear Lane and looked either way, but the quarry had vanished.

'Right, let's split up – Robshaw, you go towards Fish Street. If you don't see Gregory, try to find Ed and Tim, and bring them to help. Dick, you come with me.' Unfurling the sketch as Robshaw hurried off, Luke added: 'This is the man we're looking for – the Guardsman who stampeded Emily's cattle.'

'Ah, so he's that one,' Richard replied, his eyes widening with surprise. 'She said you was after him.' He looked more closely at the picture. 'But... this feller – I just been with him.'

'Where?' Luke looked at him sharply.

'In the courtyard of the inn, yonder – we was, er, playing a game.'

'What kind of game?'

'Why, 'twas nothing, just a game of cup and ball.'

'Well, it might be his last. We're after him because we think he killed William Harbord.'

'That there politician?'

'The same. And he could be dangerous, so have a care.'

Luke unclasped the stave from his belt and, with the other hand, felt the hilt of his dagger. It should not come to that, surely – and he had no desire to cross blades with a trained soldier – but 'hope for the best, prepare for the worst' had ever been his motto. Whereupon the Chief Bailiff's Officer and the apprentice stonemason set off to find the suspected murderer.

The pair strode smartly off down Blue Boar Street; the road now narrowing, then widening as it swung right around the back of Christ Church and opposite Oriel College gate, next turning sharp left along the front wall of Corpus Christi. All the while, Luke and Richard were careful to look on either side, but of Gregory there was no sign. As the steeple of Merton College Chapel hove into view, Richard emitted a sound of surprise, mixed with alarm.

'What's the matter?' Luke demanded, impatiently.

By way of reply, the younger man pointed to an object on the ground, lying between the gateposts of the path alongside the chapel leading to Christ Church Meadow.

'Why – 'tis Emily's bonnet.' He bent down to pick it up.

'Emily's bonnet? Are you sure?'

'Sure as eggs is eggs, Master Sandys. 'Tis her favourite – belonged to her mother, like. I'd know it anywhere. Aye, here's the stitching she put in,' he said, examining it.

'But what's it doing here?'

'She was coming to market today. I hoped to meet her in town.'

The men looked at each other with sudden surmise as the implications of this discovery sank in.

'So, Emily's bonnet is lying on the ground, close to the last known sighting of the Guardsman whose gunshot stampeded her cattle,' Luke said slowly. 'I don't mean to alarm you, Richard, but I can't believe that's a coincidence.'

Moments earlier, Gregory had propelled his captive down the self-same route until, as they made to turn right down the path to the meadow, Emily seized what might be her last chance to try to escape. She durst not let herself be taken away from the road, she'd started to think as she was whisked along, for there, surely, lay the only chance of encountering a passer-by who might help her, or raise the alarm. In trying to squirm free, however, she reckoned without the full extent of the Guardsman's strength and skill at arms. A second later, the grip had merely tightened still further and a short, cold blade, which appeared in his other hand as if from nowhere, was at her throat.

'Don't you wriggle, missy. I'm not finished with you yet,' he seethed, through gritted teeth.

Unnoticed by the men, who were now moving considerably faster along the path, the momentary struggle, while unavailing, had dislodged her bonnet, which fell to the ground and was soon left behind them. The spring flowers in the Merton Chapel garden nodded their heads in a sudden zephyr as they passed, but, to Emily's stricken gaze, they looked merely as if they were affirming her worst premonitions, that the colourful blooms were the last of their like she would ever see on earth.

At the end of the path, the meadow opened out in front of them, with the walled garden of Corpus Christi College on their right. At the near end of that wall was a large recess filled with an evergreen laurel bush, and it was into the confined space behind the dense foliage that Gregory and Ladlow now pushed her.

'You need putting in your place, my girl.' The moustachioed Guardsman unhooked the sheath and scabbard – containing sword and knife respectively – from his belt, slid the strip of thick brown leather out of the loops on his breeches, doubled it over and grasped it in one hairy fist.

'Lucky for you I'm suddenly feeling generous. It'll just be the belt for today.'

Emily shook and sobbed as he thrust his bewhiskered face close to hers – so close, she could smell the whisky and tobacco on his breath.

'But if you ever breathe a word to anyone about that little

game with the cups and the ball, well,' – and he nodded towards the dagger, now propped against the base of the wall – 'it'll be something else. D'you catch my drift?'

'Yessir,' she whimpered.

'Very well then – bend over and take your punishment.' He planted her hands against the wall, so her rump was sticking out, and raised the heavy belt to strike her.

At that moment, a substantial figure came crashing round the other side of the bush and hurtled into Gregory, knocking him sideways and on to the floor. It was Richard, armed only with the small hammer that was the first mason's tool he'd managed to buy for himself. His senses were so attuned to his lover and the mother of his unborn child that he'd picked up the sound of her sobbing, and reacted to the situation before anyone else.

That advantage was now at an end, however. Following close behind, Luke thanked his lucky stars they'd decided to take the path rather than continue along Merton Street after finding the bonnet; but he gasped at the speed and agility with which Gregory absorbed the blow, rolled over and sprang to his feet – seemingly in one fluid movement – then grabbed and unsheathed his sabre. His companion followed suit.

By now, Richard had reached Emily and pulled her away on to the path. She collapsed into his arms, face hidden in his chest and shoulders heaving with massive sobs. Luke swiftly stepped between the couple and the two Guardsmen, holding out his wooden stave in one hand, dagger in the other, knees slightly bent in readiness to spring or parry. Gregory twirled his sword, then suddenly shifted his weight forward and feinted to thrust. Luke leapt backwards, turning slightly as he landed to avoid being blindsided by the second swordsman, who was moving to outflank him.

Seeing his attention was divided, Gregory did now strike, a right-to-left slash that Luke just about managed to deflect by crossing the stave and dagger in front of him as he whirled round again to face the attacker. A crunching sound told him the steel had made at least a glancing contact with the wood. Christ, that was close! Surely he could not keep this up – he was outnumbered and equipped with inferior weapons, and his breath was becoming shorter as they circled each other on the path. Gregory grinned with relish, and began to move in for the kill.

'Gregory! That's enough!' Ed's most impressive officer's voice rang out across Christ Church Meadow as he sprinted towards them, Robshaw and young Tim Blount trailing in his wake. True to their military training, the heads of the two Guardsmen snapped round at the distinctive note of command, Gregory's face creasing into a bitter scowl. Ed slowed to a brisk walking pace as he drew near.

'Trooper! Sheathe your weapon! That's an order,' he barked. 'You too, Ladlow.'

'Captain Sandys! We were attacked, sir, we're entitled to defend ourselves,' Gregory protested.

'If I have to draw steel, it'll go ill for you with the Colonel,' Ed said, moving his hand towards the hilt at his waist.

The two troopers slowly and reluctantly put their swords away, whereupon Luke felt a huge knot begin to unwind in his stomach.

'That bully rook came at me with a hammer,' Gregory kept up his protest, jerking his thumb towards Richard.

'Aye, 'tis true, Captain, then this here feller drew his dagger on us, and that stave,' Ladlow added.

'This "feller", Ladlow, is my brother, Luke. He's a City constable, and – Gregory – you'd do well to listen to what he has to say.'

'I should think so an' all,' Robshaw exclaimed, still panting as he caught up.

117

'The distress of that girl tells against you, man, for one thing,' Luke said, nodding towards where Emily cowered in Richard's arms. 'That's abduction – even kidnapping.' He sheathed his dagger and drew out the folded document from his inside pocket. 'And I've a letter here, signed by both the Mayor and your Colonel, authorising your arrest on suspicion of murder.'

'Murder?' Gregory repeated incredulously, as Emily gasped, and burst out in tears all over again. 'Who am I supposed to have murdered?'

'I'm arresting you for the murder of the MP, William Harbord.'

'MP? Harbord? I don't know any MPs. Never did – I avoid such men like the pox,' he said, quickly scanning the letter and handing it back. 'Why the Devil should I murder one of them?'

'You'll be able to have your say later, Gregory,' Ed cut in. 'The Colonel will see you're treated fairly. But for now you must go with these men.'

Robshaw made as if to apply the iron shackles he carried, to restrain the Guardsman at the wrists, but Ed motioned for him to stop.

'I'll vouch for him, Robshaw. He won't disobey orders.'

Richard volunteered to take Emily to The Mitre to be reunited with her mother.

'I shall want to talk to her,' Luke warned, 'but that can wait till tomorrow.' The Sandys brothers set off to escort the prisoner to the Castle gaol, where he would be booked in and locked up in a holding cell. Robshaw went with Richard and Emily, then to the lodgings at Goat's Head Yard, to retrieve Gregory's blue Guards tunic, and Tim Blount resumed his position on patrol in the market. Shaken and dog tired as he was, Luke could not help feeling a profound sense of satisfaction as they walked along Queen Street towards the Castle. They had got their man.

Chapter 24
Vindication for Pawling

Luke returned to the Guildhall with Ed to find visitors already waiting. First, there was Captain Sutherland of the Foot Guards to deal with. At the brothers' approach he straightened and fastened the top button of his red tunic, seeming to accentuate the clash of colours with his ginger facial hair.

'Ah, there you are Sandys – and, ah, Sandys,' he blustered. 'I'll come straight to the point. We need support from the City this afternoon. King's going to the Sheldonian Theatre. We're moving the whole Court. Could do with some local knowledge.'

Luke puffed out his cheeks. Did the man not realise how busy he was?

'Very well, Captain, I'll see if I can find someone to send.'

But Sutherland would not be fobbed off.

'I'll call for you later, then. That's all!' And, with that, the officer turned on his heel, and was gone.

The next visitor was content to wait in the shadows, but had evidently been looking forward to this moment. It was Robert Pawling.

'So, you picked up that rogue then, Luke?' he began, a gratified expression on his face.

'If you're referring to Trooper Gregory, sir, nothing is proven against him, not yet,' Ed said.

'You must be Captain Sandys?'

'Indeed, Master Pawling, this is my brother, Edwin.'

'At your service, sir.'

'And at yours, Captain,' the farmer said, with a nod. 'And at yours.'

Luke wondered how he knew about the arrest already: probably from The Mitre.

'I'd be grateful if you could keep that to yourself, for the moment,' he said. Ed's response reminded Luke that the regiment would need to see clear evidence of Gregory's guilt, if he was to be prosecuted for the murder. Having details of the case bruited abroad by the likes of Pawling could only risk polluting it.

Robshaw, however, chose that precise moment to blunder in, carrying Gregory's tunic. Sure enough, its right cuff was a mess of singed blue shreds, which he held aloft in triumph.

'So, 'twas the coat as gave him away in the end then, Luke?' Pawling enquired.

'Aye, them bits we found on Harbord came off this here cuff, sir, and no mistake,' the deputy blurted out.

'Yes, that is the evidence in chief against Gregory, though again I must ask you not to spread that information, Master Pawling.'

'I'll speak to my Colonel about getting compensation for your livestock, sir,' Ed said, sensing a propitious moment to change the subject.

'Thank you kindly, Captain,' the farmer replied, twinkling. 'Five should cover it.'

'Pounds?'

'Guineas.'

'Very well – five guineas it is.'

'That'd be handsome – handsome indeed. Well, good day to you, sirs!'

'He seems full of himself,' Robshaw remarked, after Pawling closed the office door behind him.

''Twas ever thus,' Luke replied – though, he had to admit,

there was something unusually self-satisfied about Pawling's manner, even for him.

Master Ingram, the ostler at The Mitre, rustled up straw and some old blankets to make the back of the cart more comfortable, and Emily nestled into her fiancé on the way home. As the old horse plodded on through the warm part of the afternoon, and the vehicle gently rolled and jiggled, long before they arrived at Magdalen Farm she was sound asleep in Richard's arms.

'She's had a terrible shock, poor lamb,' the mother said, as Jacob Hopkins presented a concerned face around the cottage door.

'Another one?'

'Aye, only now that rogue what did it's been locked up, and not before time. Why, he grabbed our Emily and held a knife to her throat. Said as how he'd beat her with his belt!'

'Richard saved me,' Emily piped up weakly. Awakened when the motion of the cart came to a halt and helped indoors, she'd been plied with a weak rum-and-water and tucked up with a blanket.

The father shook and scratched his head in alternate outrage and wonderment as the story was retold – a story long on recollections of derring-do from Richard but notably shorter on events in the courtyard of the Bear Inn – and, from Emily, disconnected segments of her ordeal that were now acquiring a firmer shape in her memory. Some details of these she shared with her parents, while withholding others out of a disinclination either to alarm them or to dwell too deeply on her darkest moments. At regular intervals the couple were interrupted by narrative prompts from Liza, along with the occasional 'he never!' or 'well, I should say!'

'By Heaven, Richard, t'would seem she'll have a good husband, and a brave one,' Jacob exclaimed at last, clasping hold of the details that stood out most vividly from the tale, multi-handed as it was. 'And he murdered a feller, an' all, this here Guardsman?'

'So it seems,' Richard replied. 'Master Robshaw told us about it on the way to The Mitre. Said there was bits of his coat sleeve, what was burned when he shot Emily's cattle, found on the body, like.'

Emily, who had been oblivious through that particular journey, lifted her head from the pillow. 'Is that how Master Sandys knew he was the killer?'

'Aye, so 'twas said.'

At this, there came a familiar rap on the cottage door, which could only be from the handle of Farmer Pawling's horse-whip.

'How's the patient?' he beamed kindly at Emily, who was now sitting up. Mistress Pawling had sent a suet pudding from the farmhouse kitchen, which Liza received gratefully. 'I was sorry to hear about what happened, Emily,' he said, then, addressing the assembled company: 'I said that shooter was a rogue and a rascal, and that he wouldn't have long on this earth to do more mischief. Well now he'll most likely hang, and good riddance.' The sentiment was greeted with noises of approbation from Richard and Jacob. 'I should add, Hopkins, that Luke Sandys' brother Edwin, who's a Horse Guards captain as you know, has agreed to get five guineas from his regiment in compensation for them two milchers.' The arrangement was immediately endorsed by all concerned as eminently satisfactory.

Arm in arm, Emily set off with Richard for a restorative turn around the farmyard before dusk. She was the first to break their companionable silence.

'Thank you for rescuing me.'

'You've already said that.' The couple looked at each other, and laughed.

'Richard…'

'Hmm?'

'You ain't never going to bet money on that game again, are you?'

'Not if you don't want me to, sweet.' He was being his agreeable best. But her contented smile soon gave way to a frown.

'What did you think of what Farmer Pawling said?'

'About the five guineas? Not a bad price, for a pair of milchers.'

'No – I mean about Gregory. He'll like as not hang now, for murder.'

'I should think so, an' all. The scoundrel!'

She squeezed his arm in acknowledgement, but continued with her train of thought.

'But none of us knew about that till today. Farmer Pawling, he seemed to be saying that yesterday, when he came back with Father from seeing Master Sandys.'

'This again? Why trouble ourselves with it now?'

'There's something there what don't seem quite right.'

Richard stopped for a moment, looked at her, and sighed – surmising, from her expression, that she would not simply let the matter drop.

'Why, the rascal had already fired his flintlock by then, and killed poor Daisy and Cassie.'

'Aye, but a Royal Guardsman'd never hang for that, surely? So how did he know, like?'

'Well, he do know a lot, don't he, about the world, and that? Probably more than you and me,' he replied gently.

''Tis strange, though. I saw him that morning, dead early,

riding off towards the London road, he was. Then a bit later he came back to pick up Pa, and they went into town together.'

Richard made a flummoxed shape with his lips, and breathed in and out through his nostrils, shaking his head.

'Well, we've to go and see Master Sandys ourselves at the Guildhall on the morrow – he wants you to tell him what happened with Gregory and Ladlow,' he reminded her presently. 'You can tell him about this, an' all.'

Chapter 25
An Appointment with the Bishop

One of the grooms in the stables at Christ Church was a boy-hood friend of Ed's, and, for what was, after all, his day off (as he reminded his brother), the pair had promised themselves a hack out to the top of Boars Hill to enjoy the views across the county. So, Luke called at the college with Robshaw, and they climbed the stone steps to keep an appointment with the Dean, who was also the Bishop of Oxford, John Fell.

In the reign of King Charles I, his father had been Dean before him, and, during the Puritan ascendancy of the Interregnum, the younger Fell taught Classics to undergraduates while keeping the Anglican flame alive from a modest house on Merton Street. Now a leading figure of both academic and ecclesiastical Oxford, he was credited with restoring order and dignity to college life by enforcing distinctions designed to keep undergraduates in their proper place – their classrooms – and by burnishing and safeguarding its scholarly reputation. Pawling had wanted the Freedom bestowed by the City on Titus Oates, accuser-in-chief of the Popish Plot, to be matched with an Honorary Doctorate of Divinity from the University, but Fell blocked the scheme, thus incurring the then-Mayor's undying enmity.

'Ah, Sandys. Come in, come in,' the Bishop exclaimed with a beatific smile as the pair reached the open door of his chambers. '*Felix qui potuit rerum cognoscere causas*, eh, my boy?' An eminent Latinist, Fell was amused and fascinated by Luke's trajectory from, as he put it, 'classical scholar to constable'. When

they met, he invariably repeated this quotation from Virgil –
meaning, 'happy is he who can ascertain the causes of things' –
to test the memory of his former student with an aphorism he
considered particularly fitting.

'Quite so, your Grace, quite so,' Luke replied.

'So, what can we do for you today?' the Bishop asked.

'I need your permission to interview the college porters, sir.
We believe they may have seen something that might help
in our inquiry. We're investigating the murder of the MP,
William Harbord, on Monday night.'

'Ah yes, we heard about that. A bad business. May God rest
his soul,' the cleric replied. 'Well, you may certainly ask them if
they saw anything.'

'Thank you kindly, sir. That will be most helpful.'

'Think nothing of it, dear boy. Whilst I have you here, let me
show you something.'

Fell unfurled a large sheet of paper in front of him. Beckoned
to join the Bishop on the other side of his desk, Luke stood
alongside him and looked down at an elegant drawing he
immediately recognised as the work of Christopher Wren.

'Know what that is?' Fell asked.

''Tis a tower, sir – in the Gothic style, unless I'm much mistaken.'

'Gothic, that's right, Sandys, Gothic, indeed. We've got Kit
Wren to lift his head out of his work on St Paul's Cathedral to
design us a tower to complete the college wall on the Fish Street
side. It'll go over the gates to Great Quad, you know. 'Tis to
be a bell tower: we'll move Great Tom there from the chapel.'
He gripped the younger man's arm, the intensity of his vision
burning in his eyes. ''Twill be the crowning glory of my work
here, Luke – the crowning glory!'

As College Dean, Fell had presided over an extensive building programme at Christ Church, making improvements to the

Great and Peckwater Quadrangles, and laying down the Broad Walk, with its twin lines of elm trees, across the meadow. He and Wren had become firm friends through Fell's energetic promotion of the Sheldonian Theatre, one of the building projects that had confirmed the architect's reputation as the foremost of the age.

'A fitting legacy for you, sir,' Luke said.

'A monument to Providence, and the limitless bounty of our Lord,' the Bishop immediately corrected him. 'But it's good of you to say so, dear boy. There's just one problem.'

'And what's that?'

'Stone! We can't get enough. Back when the College was built, Cardinal Wolsey got the stone from Headington Quarry, of course, but that's mostly worked out now. Wren's engaged a master mason, you know – a very capable man, Christopher Kempster, of Burford. Of course he's got his own quarry over there, but the stone is too dark a shade – doesn't match. Also, it's a very long way, which adds greatly to the cost.'

'Is there none to be had in Oxford?'

Fell's countenance took on what Luke would call, if it were not in an eminent man of the cloth, a crafty expression.

'Ah, well, there are ways, of course. *Magnum vectigal est parsimonia*, hmm?'

This was from one of Cicero's Paradoxes, which Luke remembered well.

'Economy is a great revenue?'

'That's right, Luke, economy is a great revenue, indeed. And that's where I need your help,' the Bishop went on, grasping Luke's elbow in conspiratorial fashion; '*ad susceptum perficiendum*: to finish what we started.'

Sandys momentarily caught Robshaw's eye, which was fixed in a meaningful stare; but immediately looked away. Having witnessed many such scenes in the past, the deputy let out an all-but-inaudible sigh. His master was susceptible to flattery, at least of the intellectual variety, and he knew full well what was coming next. They would be asked to undertake some errand for the Bishop in exchange for his assent in this portion of their investigation: a request to which Sandys would readily accede, with reckoning of the cost – in time and perhaps even risk – made only afterwards, when it was too late to back out. To cap it all, it was invariably Robshaw's participation in such escapades that he would blithely pledge, as well as his own – without ever thinking to consult him on the matter.

Sure enough, Fell now elaborated on the situation impeding his supply of limestone. He planned to save money by sourcing the material from the still-substantial ruins of Osney Abbey, whose lands were seized at the dissolution of the monasteries under King Henry VIII to establish Christ Church in the first place. So, what was stopping him?

'Vagabonds, Luke. Sad to say, the ruins have become a redoubt for vagabonds and masterless men. I'm afraid Kempster downright refuses to send his labourers there to fetch the stone: says it's too dangerous.'

'Begging your pardon, your Grace,' Robshaw cut in, 'the University proctors can't go along and look after them, then?'

'Hm-hm!' Fell chuckled. 'You'd think so, wouldn't you? But no, the statutes won't allow it. The proctors are strictly confined to University premises by day, and then, after nine o'clock, the city within its established walls. No further.'

'Well, that is the limit of our own jurisdiction, sir, if it comes to that,' Luke pointed out.

'These boundaries, Luke, that divide us. These walls – whence came these walls?' the Bishop asked rhetorically. 'Mere lines on a map, drawn by a man. God knows no earthly boundaries, my boy. *Incepto ne desistam* – may I not shrink from my purpose.'

Now came the moment for which Robshaw had been bracing himself.

'So, how can we help, your Grace?' Luke asked. Thus it was that Sandys and Robshaw ended up agreeing to escort a crew of Christopher Kempster's men, the following day, to the Osney Abbey ruins, where they would begin the job of taking away stone for the new building.

'That's how he rose to be both Bishop and Dean,' the deputy observed, as they made their way back downstairs. 'He knows how to get men to do what he wants.'

Two porters were on duty at the lodge: short-sighted old Greening, who spent the interview squinting at the two constables disturbing his peace and quiet and revealing, in the process, an unprepossessing set of half-rotten teeth; and his junior colleague, by the name of Hignett. In deference to their order of seniority, Sandys and Robshaw questioned the older fellow first, but, finding his answers confined to indeterminate monosyllables, they soon gave up to concentrate on the younger. And indeed, Hignett, they quickly established, was the very man who had performed the duty of walking round from the lodge with a bunch of keys as Great Tom sounded the nine o'clock curfew on Monday night, and locking the heavy oak doors that secured the Great Quadrangle on the Fish Street side of the college. The spot was more or less opposite The Unicorn and Jacob's Well, and he distinctly recalled surveying the street in the clear moonlight, and noting with satisfaction that it was empty:

'There was nothing outside that there door when I locked up the House, sirs, I'd swear to it.'

As they walked the short distance back to the Guildhall, the pair discussed the implications of Hignett's evidence for the possible time frame of the murder.

'So, how long passed, then, would you say, between the nightwatchmen calling at your place to tell you about the body, and the time when you knocked on my door?' Luke asked.

Robshaw gurned pensively.

'Could only have been ten minutes, at the most.'

'I wish I could remember what time that was. Actually, come to think of it, Ed said he was admiring the pendulum clock in the hallway at that point – he'd never seen one before. When he's back I'll ask him if he can recall where the hands were pointing.'

Chapter 26
A Trip to the Theatre

At the office, Captain Sutherland was already waiting. Luke was to go with him to a meeting where plans for the Royal party's progress to the drama were to be finalised, then straight away implemented. The Foot Guards' commanding officer, Colonel Russell, greeted Luke with evident relief.

'Ah, Sandys, this is Lord Finch, the Lord High Steward and Lord Chancellor, who's in overall charge of His Majesty's security. This other gentleman is…'

'…with me,' Finch said testily. Cold grey eyes quickly appraised him from a lean, weathered face, and Luke surmised the tall, strong-looking figure, who stood slightly apart from the other two men, to be one of Finch's intelligence officers.

'Sandys will advise us on the local situation,' Russell continued, looking at Luke expectantly.

Lying on the desk was the college's copy of Scholae Publicae Universitatis Oxon, open at the double-page print of the map of Oxford made by David Loggan a few years earlier, and Luke traced with his finger the route he'd decided to recommend for the King to reach the Sheldonian.

'Well sirs, the Royal carriage should probably leave Christ Church through the side gate on to Blue Boar Street, here. That way, we'll avoid the junction of The High with Cornmarket and Queen Streets, here. The market'll be winding down by now, but that's the busiest area.'

'And it's where the Whig mob tends to gather,' the supposed intelligencer said.

'If there's a mob, sir, we can disperse it. But yes, there are men who seem to spend a lot of their time loitering in and out of the taverns around there.' Luke did not care for the implication that control over the streets of Oxford was in question, but he was still inclined to avoid the possibility of any trouble. 'Then we can bring His Majesty across The High by Oriel Street, here, and into St Mary's Passage, down the side of the church.'

'And then, when they get out of their carriages, we can take them into the courtyard of the Bodleian and come through the Divinity School door,' Russell finished for him. 'Excellent suggestion, Sandys. Lord Chancellor?'

'Yes, well, I see no objections.' He turned to his intelligence officer.

'Seems sensible to me, sir.'

'One thing,' Luke said, as Russell closed the valuable book. 'Why is the play not being performed in the College Hall? Dramas were put on there in the past, were they not? For the King's father when he was here?' The other men exchanged glances.

'Theatrical fashion,' Finch pronounced disdainfully. 'The players have decided their set won't fit in there.'

'I see. What's the play, by the way?'

'By some chap called Charles Saunders,' the Lord Chancellor replied. 'Tamerlane the Great, apparently. No idea what it's about, but the King seems to be looking forward to it.'

The passage for the Royal party, and the dozen or more carriages required for the whole Court to follow, was lined by heavily armed Foot Guards, hurriedly deployed on Russell's orders once the route had been finalised. Luke had instructed Robshaw to make sure the City constables were all on patrol in the High, and to come and find him straight away if trouble flared at any point. As for Luke himself – he was going to the theatre. Plays and players had thrived in the reign of Charles

I, but were banned outright under Oliver Cromwell. At the Restoration, two rival theatrical companies – the King's and the Duke's – were awarded Royal Patents, and now vied for audiences in London, but performances in the provinces were almost unheard of. He would be there on duty, to be sure, and in his official capacity – but that would not stop him enjoying the show.

Looking upwards from his seat in the Sheldonian, Luke had an oblique view of the lurid ceiling fresco, depicting the revelation of truth in arts and sciences, with a cherubic figure at its centre perched somewhat implausibly on a smoky-orange cloud. As ever when he entered this, the most striking of all the city's recently added buildings, however, he was more impressed with the ceiling itself. It was a mark of Wren's genius to have solved, at a stroke, a problem with which countless generations of architects had struggled in vain: how to construct and support a roof whose single span exceeded the longest timbers available, without recourse to pillars or pediments. John Wallis, Oxford's own Savilian Professor of Geometry, first proposed the geometrical flat grid design, as theoretically the strongest structure – but it took a man of Wren's ingenuity and audacity to be the first to put theory into practice.

From his position in the top tier of the steeply banking auditorium, Luke's attention shifted to the figure in the centre of it all: His Majesty, lavishly bewigged and clothed in gorgeous silks and velvets, with a ruff like a white-foamed waterfall cascading from his neck. Even after more than twenty years on the throne, the so-called 'merry monarch' made no concessions to public disapproval of his love life, flanked as he was by his two favourite mistresses of the moment, red-haired Nell Gwynn – herself a former actress – and Louise de Kérouaille, Duchess of Portsmouth, in a blue satin cloak.

The action on stage unfolded, in blank verse, a bloodthirsty tale of wars and rivalries. Outside, cloud had been thickening all afternoon, and the dramatic effect was in no way diminished by the faintly audible thunder from the darkening sky. In the story, Tamerlane – played by Thomas Betterton, one of the foremost actors of the London stage – began by boasting of his conquests:

'Far greater's our renown in glorious arms,' he declaimed in suitably resonant tones, 'who know to conquer too, enlarge our sway, and teach the haughty Ottoman to bow.'

Luke had difficulty following the plot as it became more involved, with a developing quarrel between Tamerlane and his son. He must have missed the reason why, but suddenly one of the numerous courtiers on stage dramatically snatched up a sword and made as if to attack the potentate – only to be restrained and disarmed. Just as he was redoubling his concentration, he happened to glance down to see an all-too-familiar figure entering the theatre by one of the doors on the far side: Robshaw. What did he want?

Chapter 27
Trouble on the Streets

Sure enough, the deputy wanted Luke's attention, and – judging by the expression on his face and the urgency with which he beckoned his master to descend from his perch 'in the gods' – something was amiss.

'We got a riot on our hands here,' Robshaw reported in agitation as the pair huddled at the bottom of the stairwell. 'There's mobs has been forming all day, with students at one end, and them London folk up the other. Now they're squaring up, like, and it's us caught in the middle.'

Attracted by the kerfuffle, Captain Sutherland joined them.

'Sandys – all well?'

'Not entirely, Captain. Apparently there's a disturbance brewing on the High Street between rival mobs.'

'Bit of cold steel would soon put them in their place,' Sutherland growled, jutting his chin.

'Hold back, Captain, please,' Luke said. The Guards had more than enough weaponry at their disposal to quell any civil unrest – but at what cost? It would be the City authorities who would have to cope with any continuing ramifications if the incident ended in bloodshed.

'Get your men to deploy on all the routes from the High to the Sheldonian: Catte Street, Turl Street, and the Broad. Then the King will be protected. We'll deal with the trouble at source.'

'That man to whom all Asia bowed has learned to kneel,' another of the characters intoned as the men quit the theatre, 'to Tamerlane's more mighty power. Avert, ye gods, all nations

cry, from us the hand of the all-conquering god-like Tamerlane.'

The sound was unmistakable: a weighty pebble landing and
skidding on the paved surface of the High, marking an escalation in what had been, until shortly after Luke and Robshaw
arrived, a largely verbal confrontation. From one side came the
Whiggish mob, dotted with blue ribbons in the hatbands of
London men, but with clearly audible undertones of Oxford
voices in their battle-cry of 'No Popery, No Slavery!' Several
held placards aloft bearing the name, 'William Harbord MP',
where the initials for 'Member of Parliament' had been used
to spell out 'Murdered by Papists', in a suitably lurid shade. It
was answered in the other direction by the Tory taunt 'The
Devil hang up all Roundheads!' – and, more ominously, from
the undergraduates, 'Make ready! Stand back! Knock 'em down!
Knock 'em down!'

Reinforced by a dozen University proctors now seconded
to daytime duties – following Luke's request to the Provost,
as he'd promised Mayor Bowell – the constables were holding
a narrow band of the High Street separating the two groups.
Luke crossed first one way, then the other, straining to locate
the stone-thrower. Suddenly, he spotted a group of four young
men – almost certainly students – emerging from the end of
Queen's Lane. They were carrying a coat by its corners, which,
as they set it down on the edge of the High, revealed its load as
a pile of cobble-stones.

'Robshaw!' Luke shouted immediately, pointing in their
direction. 'Take a snatch squad and get those men! And for
God's sake don't let them throw those cobbles!'

Tamerlane's lines flashed into his mind, in Betterton's distinctive ringing delivery: 'Gazing on the golden prey, you thought

it looked too great to be so cheaply bought, then seizing it with danger, and the famous lot of war, made it your merit's due, and valour's right.' Robshaw and three burly colleagues closed quickly on the students, quelling the young men's appetite for the fray with sharp blows from their wooden staves to the knees and shoulders. Two of the constables gathered up what they could of the cobbles – levered out with a strong knife, no doubt, from the surface of Queen's Lane – but it was too late to avoid the escalation entirely, for some had already been picked up by other students. A volley of stones across the line was met with an answering surge that the constables and proctors were powerless to prevent.

Suddenly the rival mobs were mingling in chaos under the now slate-grey sky. As if in response to the distant rumbles in the heavens, the noise at street level ratcheted up, and in the fading light Sandys could see weapons being wielded above the heads of the crowd: sticks and clubs, but also the occasional flash of a sharp blade. Forced to the side of the High Street, Luke formed his men into squads of three or four, directing them to pick out what seemed like leaders amid the press, and move in to seize, arrest and shackle them.

'There, man, there – that tall fellow with the pitchfork!' he yelled at Tim Blount and his team.

He was so preoccupied with watching the riot that he didn't notice a cobble tracing an arc in his direction until it was almost too late. At the last moment he turned aside, ensuring that the blow was a glancing one, but he felt a white-hot shaft of pain, and – dabbing the side of his head – noticed the scarlet stain on his fingers as he pulled them away. Luke sat down sharply on the pavement, took out his handkerchief and pressed it to his right temple, and forced himself to take a series of deep breaths.

Chapter 28
Binding of Wounds

John Radcliffe held up his jar of salve to the candlelight from the end of the bar at The Mitre and scraped his spathomele round its inner edges to lift off what little remained of the mixture: a reduction of plantain leaves in sheep's tallow, beeswax and oil of turpentine. For the last hour-and-a-half, since the rioters had been dispersed by the brief, intense and long-threatened shower the clouds had finally unloaded on the city just before dusk, he had been applying a dressing here and a splint there to the limbs and heads of the walking wounded.

Now, his medicinal supplies were exhausted, and – having smeared the last of the ointment over a nasty gash on a young man's shin – he packed away his instruments and turned his attention to the caraway cake and mug of ale that Cate Napper had placed on the counter for him.

'Most palatable,' the physician opined, as he finished a mouthful of the crumbly confection. 'Your own work?' he asked, as he caught Cate's expression of satisfaction out of the corner of his eye.

'Yes indeed, Doctor. 'Twas a good batch.'

Luke Sandys wholeheartedly agreed: on the plate in front of him were the last few crumbs of his own portion, which he was surreptitiously scooping up between forefinger and thumb. Waste not, want not.

At the first pattering sound on the pavement beside him, Sandys had turned his eyes heavenwards and thanked God for the timely arrival of the rain. It fell, literally, on the just and the unjust, as Matthew's Gospel said. The constables' efforts to identify, isolate and arrest the ringleaders on either side of the disturbance were abruptly curtailed in the rush for shelter, but that seemed a small price to pay for the restoration of the King's peace on the streets of Oxford. Just yards away, His Majesty sat enraptured by the fictional conflict unfolding on stage at the Sheldonian, blissfully unaware of the real-life blows, missiles and insults being exchanged between rival factions of his subjects outside.

'Still, no one's died, eh?' Radcliffe enquired.

'Not that I know of,' Luke replied. He himself had escaped the danger of any more serious injury thanks to Robshaw, whose strong arm had lifted him up and helped him to where he knew his master would receive both practical help and sympathy.

'Strange,' Radcliffe said as he supped his ale. ''Tis the second evening this week that I've been called away to deal with a medical emergency.' An old friend of the Nappers, he had been summoned by Cate from his Lincoln College rooms, just across Turl Street, at the first arrivals from the riot. She'd spent the evening bringing fresh supplies of muslin cloth for bandages, even once slipping out to knock up Gibson, the apothecary, for a small quantity of opium, for a patient whose ulna had sustained an especially painful fracture.

'Well, many people in Oxford know you as a good doctor and a good man,' she said. 'Take it as a compliment.'

'Kind of you. It certainly shows the trouble we've brought on ourselves by having Parliament come here.'

'So what was the first incident?' Luke asked. 'Not another political free-for-all?'

'Not exactly. This involved a soldier, a Royal Guardsman

judging by his uniform. He'd have come in with the King on Monday.'

'You'll have to put in for a regular appointment as physician to the regiment,' Cate said teasingly.

'Ah, well, I'm pretty sure this was all highly *ir*regular,' the doctor replied. 'Fellow had discharged his pistol and had a back-fire, by the look of it. I had to patch up his wrist and hand as best I could.'

Despite his sore head, Luke sat bolt upright.

'Where was this, Doctor, and when, if you please?' His companions looked at him in surprise at the sudden tone of urgency.

'I was with friends in The Spotted Cow, on Hell's Passage.'

'No, I mean, where were you called out to?'

'Oh, I see! Well, the surroundings were not the most salubrious, I must say: the upstairs room of a house in a rather grimy alleyway off St Michael's Street.'

'And when?'

'Monday evening, as I said.'

'No, I mean, what time Monday evening?'

'Well, to be honest, I was rather frogmarched over there by the man's comrade, who said I was to attend to his colonel. I knew that was a lie. Anyway, as we were setting off I remember hearing Great Tom sound the student curfew, so that must've been nine o'clock.'

Luke's head was ringing: with the imagined sound of the Christ Church bell; with the after-effects of the blow he'd received; but above all with the shattering impact of the physician's tale on his assumptions about the murder. If Gregory had been undergoing treatment shortly after nine o'clock, then – given the firm recollection by Hignett, the college porter, that Fish Street had been clear when the bell tolled – how could he have killed Harbord? What about later?

'How long were you with the man, Doctor?'

'Well... there were many small burns to be cleansed and salved. One likes to do a thorough job, of course. And it was slow going because they only had the one rushlight. Not like the decent candles the Nappers keep here. So, I might have been there about twenty minutes, all in.'

Luke still had Ed's sketch of Gregory folded up in his inside pocket, he realised. He drew it out and showed it to the doctor.

'Was this the man you attended?' Radcliffe held the drawing close to the candle flame.

'Why, yes! That captures him rather well: the Cavalier whiskers, and the disagreeable expression. Yes, that's a decent likeness.'

'That's a sketch of the man we're holding in the Castle for the murder of the MP, William Harbord.' Radcliffe and Cate made suitable noises of astonishment. 'And now I'm rather afraid we're going to have to let him go, because your story, on the face of it, provides him with a rock-solid alibi.'

Chapter 29
'The Protestant Whore'

Luke stalked off down the High towards Magpie Lane in a state of inner turmoil even more unsettling than usual when leaving Cate's company. The evidence he'd seen for himself, which pointed so clearly to Gregory as the killer: how could it be wrong? As Robshaw said when he brought in the trooper's dark blue military tunic, there was no doubt the fibres they'd found in the wound had come from there. The colour, and the singeing from the gunpowder, were a precise match.

One slight possibility remained, that Gregory had left Goat's Head Yard after being bandaged up, and headed straight for The Unicorn and Jacob's Well, where he'd then slain the MP. Would he have had enough time to do that before the proctors found the body, and reported it to Robshaw? It seemed highly doubtful: but, Luke now recalled, he'd intended to ask Ed what time was showing on the pendulum clock in the hallway when his deputy had knocked on the door that night. That would allow him to calculate the likely time bracket for the murder, and determine whether Gregory could possibly have done it.

His brother was in at home, together with Elizabeth, who took one look at Luke's bandaged head and turned sheet-white. 'By God, husband, what's happened to you?' she wailed.

'It looks worse than it is – got caught by a flying pebble in the riot,' he replied. She was used to his habit of playing down the dangers that occasionally came his way in the line of duty, but, after being allowed to inspect the wound and dressing for herself, she was somewhat mollified.

'But why didn't you come home? I'd have tended to you myself, as a wife should.'

He was touched.

'I know you would have done, my dear, but Dr Radcliffe was at The Mitre.'

'You and that Mitre, you want to spend more time there than you do here,' she exclaimed – striking a nerve more sharply than she could possibly realise, he told himself – but her overriding emotion was clearly one of relief. When Luke had changed into dry things, she poured out cups of sack and the three of them began to settle back down.

Before Luke arrived, Elizabeth was nearing the climax of an anecdote she'd heard in the market, which she evidently found highly amusing. Now she insisted on starting all over again. A luxurious carriage had, apparently, been making its way down the High Street, past the junction with Cornmarket and Queen Streets, when a rumour rippled through the semi-permanent mob hanging around that area that the vehicle contained none other than Louise de Kérouaille, the Duchess of Portsmouth and the King's French mistress. In common parlance, the Duchess was known, as Elizabeth reminded the brothers, as 'the Catholic whore'.

'Anyhow,' she went on, 'they followed the carriage, till they were all standing round it, and the driver says "make way, make way", only they wouldn't! "Not for the Catholic Whore," says they. Then what d'you think happened?' The brothers looked blank. 'Cussed if the curtains didn't open, and out pops a head of red hair. 'Twas only Nell Gwynn! And she says to the crowd, she says, "Calm yourselves, good people... I am the *Protestant* whore!"' Elizabeth threw back her head and laughed long and loud.

'And what happened then?' Ed enquired at last.

'Why, the people gave a great "hurrah," and let the carriage go past,' Elizabeth said, dabbing her eyes. 'Just imagine – "I am the Protestant whore!"'

'Where did you say this took place?' Luke asked.

'Just by the end of Turl Street, 'twas said.' At this, he felt a throb of ice through his veins. An image of Cate, in her kitchen at the back of The Mitre, sprang unbidden to his mind's eye. How many yards was that from the hate and fury of the mob, during the incident his wife was pleased to recount as an amusing anecdote? Ten, at the most.

With an effort, Luke changed the subject, and turned to Ed.

'When Robshaw came to knock us up the other night, after we'd had supper, you said you happened to glance at the new clock, in the hall. Can you remember what time it said?'

'Yes, surely: five-and-twenty before ten. Why?'

Luke pulled a face.

'Wind changes, you'll stick like that, Luke Sandys,' his wife remarked. 'Pray tell – what's on your mind?'

'Why, 'tis the case, my dear – the one against Trooper Gregory, from Ed's regiment, for the murder of that MP the other night.'

'What of it?' his brother asked.

'Well, if that was the time when Robshaw called, then I'm pretty sure it's just collapsed,' he said wearily.

Ed pricked up his ears.

'Really? How come?'

Luke briefly outlined Radcliffe's story. If he'd been walking towards the house on Goat's Head Yard at nine o'clock, starting from Holywell Street, he would have arrived at perhaps five past the hour. The body was not there when the porter locked up at Christ Church, bang on nine, so Gregory would not have had time to get back from there before Radcliffe turned up. The physician reckoned to have been with the men for about twenty minutes. Robshaw's estimate of the time that elapsed between the knock on his own door from the proctors and his arrival on Magpie Lane was ten minutes; so, if that was at five-and-twenty to ten, the body must have been discovered at around five-and-twenty past. There was simply no way for Gregory to have been at the tavern on Fish Street at the time the murder must have been committed.

Chapter 30
Solace in the Workshop

Luke rose early from a disturbed sleep. Taking care not to wake Elizabeth, he put on the same dry clothes he'd chosen the previous evening after returning home damp from the riot, and peered in the looking-glass at the bandage on his head. Dr Radcliffe had done a characteristically neat job: it would hold for another day. He licked his fingers and smoothed down a stray lock of thick, dark hair, which had been displaced by the dressing. Were there a few more flecks of grey? Perhaps. Angling the mirror downwards, Luke took a moment to step back and scrutinise his outline, checking off the still-flat stomach, and – if he said so himself – rather fine calves, well displayed below the knee-straps of his new breeches.

In the kitchen, he found Joan, the ancient cook-maid, plucking disconsolately at a capon that would form the basis of a boiled dinner for the household.

'Why's everybody getting up at sparrow-fart?' she demanded. 'I've already had to fetch breakfast for Master Ed.' The regiment was to escort the King to the races at Burford for the day, which necessitated starting at first light.

'Well, you know, Joan, early to bed…' As an attempt to leaven her mood, it was misguided.

'And dead, you mean?' she snapped back.

'Dead?'

'Aye – 'twas what my Ma used to say. The English don't know how to sleep in, of a morning – they're always wanting to be up and about, and it kills 'em. "Early to bed and early to rise, makes a man healthy, wealthy and wise" – that's what you think. Only turn it around – early to rise and early to bed, in the end makes 'em all dead.'

Luke pondered this homespun wisdom as he kindled the meagre fire she had set in the kitchen grate. The daughter of a slave girl who'd absconded from a Portuguese boat in London and fallen into the strong arms of an Irish labourer, Joan possessed both a choice vocabulary and her own distinctive outlook on life, which Luke had learned to treasure through upbringing and experience.

'Well, if you'll let me have some bread and a cup of milk, Joan, I'll get some of those dried figs from the jar and leave you to it.' Thus provisioned, he walked through to the back of the house, into the capacious workshop his father had installed when it was built, decades earlier.

When his chance of a college Fellowship was stymied by Elizabeth's pregnancy with Jane and their hasty marriage, Luke was bound instead to old Samuel Sandys as an apprentice furniture-maker. As it turned out, Providence had blessed him with nimble fingers and a steady hand to go with the virtues of patience and concentration he'd cultivated over years of scholarship. Before long, the father began steering him towards the finer work for which his own ageing faculties were now less suited.

By the time his apprenticeship formally ended and he became a Freeman of Oxford in the Guild of Joiners, Luke was already bringing in and fulfilling valuable commissions to carve picture frames as worthies of the University and its constituent colleges sat for ever more extravagant portraits, and wanted suitably ornate edgings to match. Later, the family fortunes had received a boost through his appointment to the Bodleian, which then promptly decided to ask all the colleges to contribute pictures of their respective founders to hang in the newer Selden End of Duke Humfrey's Library.

Now, with constabulary duties taking up so much of his time, Luke accepted a mere trickle of work in comparison. His own eyesight, declining with the onset of middle age and aided by a pair of spectacles, was equal to the really detailed carving only on clear mornings, when light flooded in through the workshop's large east-facing window. But he looked forward to these interludes of peace and quiet and, today, with so much to trouble his mind, a couple of hours concentrating only on the texture of the material and the precise movements of his tools represented an especially welcome form of solace.

Picking up one long edge, he peered along the bolection, the plain wood separating the two decorative strips, for what seemed like the hundredth time, ensuring its edges were straight, before turning his attention to the scrolling foliage that formed the main adornment, gingerly shaving here and there with his slender file and smallest chisel to bring the fine detail of the pattern into perfect symmetry.

Propped at his side and protected by a cloth was the canvas itself, a somewhat flattering likeness of Sir Thomas Millington, an old friend from the Wadham scientific meetings of Luke's student days, who was now both Oxford's Sedleian Professor of Natural Philosophy and a Fellow of the Royal College of Physicians. The desire of his medical colleagues to honour him by displaying his portrait in their London headquarters was not matched by the Royal College's finances, which were in poor health; so Millington had discreetly commissioned the work himself.

In truth, the frame was just about finished, and would need only to be fixed into place and gilded with gold leaf before he could take it across the High to the Professor's rooms at All Souls College. As Luke carved and scraped, his mind could not help but return to the murder. The process of an investigation rather resembled a frame, he'd often reflected: ever-tightening to exclude irrelevant material piece by piece, and homing in on just the key components of evidence and testimony required to make a case for the magistrates. Now, however, that process had gone into reverse, and Gregory, who'd been firmly in the centre of the frame, was suddenly just one more detail in a diffuse and baffling picture.

All too soon, it was time to disengage from the gratifyingly responsive oak, and apply himself once more to the murder of William Harbord, which felt, by contrast, impervious to his efforts. As yet, he had no stomach for an encounter with Mayor Bowell and his vapourings, so he waylaid Robshaw on the deputy's habitual approach to the Guildhall and diverted him across the road to the New Inn, there ordering hot chocolate for them both.

'Rare treat, this time o' the morn,' the deputy said gratefully, spooning in sugar as the steam beaded his whiskers.

'You'll need something sweet to wash down the news I've got,' Luke replied, grim-faced. ''Tis bitter, indeed.' He imparted the gist of Radcliffe's encounter with Gregory and his own calculations of the timing, effectively ruling out their prime suspect.

'But if Gregory was away on Goat's Head Yard, how come bits of his coat sleeve ended up in Harbord's blood from that stab wound?' Robshaw demanded.

'How indeed? But that's a secondary question now. The main question is the same one we started with: if Gregory didn't kill him, who did?'

Chapter 31
Pulling Threads Together

The master mason and his wife had heard tell of both Emily's abduction and Richard's heroism by the time the apprentice called on them on his way home from Magdalen Farm, and his request to delay his arrival at the Jesus College site until noon the next day had been sympathetically received. So, that morning, he went straight to the cottage adjoining the barton and climbed into the back of the cart with Emily, the couple making themselves comfortable on the straw and blankets, while Jacob haltered the old piebald horse and slowly drove back down the path across the marshes.

The young couple found increasingly raucous amusement in playing pinches, and an improvised version of loggits with bits of stick and small pebbles they found in the bottom of the cart – until at last an exasperated Jacob broke his silence:

'You're in better spirits today, missy, and no mistake.' As they neared the Guildhall, however, Emily fell silent. Scenes from her ordeal of the previous day were horribly vivid as they drove up the High Street and past the end of Bear Lane. Still, she knew her duty, and – with Richard and her father alongside – she was ready to give Master Sandys a full account of yesterday's events. And to think, all along, the man who'd carried her off had actually murdered someone!

Luke and Robshaw were gazing glumly at the samples of singed blue cloth retrieved from Harbord's body when Jacob, Emily and Richard arrived.

'You know we've been holding Gregory on suspicion of murder,' Luke began carefully, after listening to Emily's recollections. 'Did he say anything, at any point, about that? Anything about William Harbord, or MPs in general?'

'No, sir – nothing,' she replied, as Richard and Jacob exchanged puzzled looks.

'Are you charging him today then, Master Sandys?' the apprentice asked.

Now it was the turn of the two constables to glance meaningfully at each other. With a sigh, Luke concluded that it would be wrong not to take them into his confidence.

'I'm afraid it looks as though we're going to have to let him go.' Emily let out an involuntary noise that was half-gasp, half-sob.

'Calm yourself, my dear,' the father said tenderly, placing his hand on hers.

'But Master Robshaw said you'd found them bits of cloth from his sleeve on the body, like,' Richard persisted. Now Robshaw avoided meeting Luke's irritated glare.

'Well, Master Robshaw clearly spoke out of turn, but yes, we did find them on the body. However, we've since heard from a reliable witness that Gregory was somewhere else at the time of the murder, so he couldn't have done it.'

'Mystery is, how them bits of cloth could've got where they got,' Robshaw broke in.

Somewhere deep in Emily's consciousness a set of connections now finally fused with a distinctness that made her physically flush with realisation, swiftly followed by an equally powerful conviction that she must have got something wrong. From Gregory's volcanic response the day before, she well recognised the potential perils of her instinct to speak out in the face of injustice. However, she felt compelled to press on, even if it got her into trouble.

'Master Sandys, did Farmer Pawling give you something when he came in with Father the other day?'

'Give me something? Why yes, he gave us some information, I suppose. That's when he told us about the shooting, and your cattle.'

'Had a hard week haven't you, love?' Richard said sympathetically.

Emily still looked doubtful.

'Father, tell Master Sandys and Master Robshaw what you told me and Ma the other night.' Jacob gave a slight start at finding himself directly addressed, having assumed his role would be confined to conveying them back and forth.

'The other night?'

'Aye,' his daughter reminded him, 'when we was sitting by the fire.' The man looked suspiciously at the row of expectant faces. Was she trying to make a fool of him?

'What – about Noll Crumble and the hump?'

'No! The other thing – when they was called away.'

Comprehension slowly dawned on Jacob's countenance.

'Ah, you mean when Farmer Pawling went in to look at the cadaver, yonder?'

'That's it, aye.'

''Tain't still there, is it?' he asked Luke, alarmed.

'No, we had it taken to the charnel-house.'

Luke was slowly catching up with Emily, although he, too, could not quite credit the way the conversation was heading.

'Tell me exactly what Pawling said.' Emily had shared her misgivings with Richard, of course – and, before that, with Jack, the farmyard donkey. Now it came to the moment when she must raise them officially, however, they suddenly felt puny and implausible.

'Why, he said as how he'd given you something – something as'd mean the shooter wouldn't have long on the earth to do any more mischief. Seemed like he was saying he'd hang for it!'

There – she'd said it. As she noticed Sandys' intense, grave expression, she experienced a vertiginous wave of nausea, and a conviction that she was about to be scolded for nurturing ideas above her station. But no: she was evidently being taken seriously, which if anything was still more unnerving.

'But we had nothing to link Gregory to the murder at that stage. I remember telling Pawling: the matter of scaring cattle would be for the regiment to deal with. And they were never going to hang him for that.'

Robshaw, too, had now cottoned on, and blurted out what the others were thinking.

'You're not telling us Pawling put them bits of cloth on the body?'

'But how could he have got hold of them?' Luke said, turning his head slightly towards his deputy by way of acknowledgement, while keeping his gaze firmly on Emily.

The young cowherd cast her mind back to when she'd been summoned to the farmhouse to tell her story to the former mayor in person.

'I told him about the feller taking off his coat and stamping out the fire on the ground.'

'Perhaps he went and picked up them shreds off of the road?' Robshaw speculated.

There was one more detail that had been troubling Emily, so she thought she might as well add it to her story.

'And I saw him ride off out the farm Tuesday morning, at first light, then he came back a bit later to pick up Father, and they set off again to see you and Master Robshaw.'

For a brief interval, nobody spoke. Then, sitting back in his chair, Luke thought aloud, summing up their joint surmise.

'So, Pawling is angered by the death of his cattle, that's understandable. He learns from Emily that Gregory had a back-fire, then threw his coat down and stamped out the sparks, so he thinks to look for evidence to try and get us to take up the matter. He rides off to the London road, where the incident took place – that's close enough, from Magdalen Farm.'

'Aye, 'twould only be a short trot,' Richard said.

'He looks on the ground, finds a few shreds of singed blue cloth lying there and picks them up, planning to give them to us later that morning so we can prove which Guardsman fired the pistol.'

'We told him about the murder, and the corpse lying back there,' Robshaw reminded him.

'So we did, when he came in. Then we had to go and see the Mayor. So now he has an opportunity to get the shooter into more trouble – trouble that couldn't be dealt with internally. It would lead to Gregory's arrest and trial, and probable execution.'

'Where was you when he went into the parlour?' Robshaw asked Jacob.

'I stayed sat down – dead bodies don't agree with me.' The man paled at the mere thought.

'We were gone for ten minutes or so, getting Bowell to calm down,' Luke recalled. 'He'd have had plenty of time alone with Harbord's corpse to plant the evidence – if he'd had it with him.'

''Tis the only way them bits of cloth could've got there, if Gregory never put them there himself,' Robshaw said, shaking his head.

'Old Night-Mayor' just about summed him up, Luke thought bitterly. Would they ever be able to prove that Pawling had deliberately interfered with a murder investigation, in an attempt to get revenge on a man who'd wronged him? Almost certainly not: but the thought seemed inseparable from the pronounced air of self-satisfaction both he and Robshaw had noticed in the farmer when news of Gregory's arrest for murder became known. Why, now he remembered, the man had even urged him to 'take a good close look at that dead body' before leaving the Guildhall that day: an injunction that now felt like gloating over his successful interference with the evidence. Would he have knowingly sabotaged their inquiries, in the crucial first forty-eight hours after the crime, in pursuit of his own personal vendetta? He was often rash as to the consequences of his actions, in Luke's experience, but he had never known Pawling do anything calculatingly wicked. Still, it was difficult not to be angry.

Chapter 32
Rats of Oxford Castle

Conditions in Oxford Castle were not improved by rainfall. These days, the moat was largely silted up, but renewed moisture seemed to stir its secrets of times past. Occupants of the houses built in recent years all round the bailey wall had to contend with a near-constant smell of damp. The great crack in the medieval keep spoke volumes for the building's inability to keep out water, and they found Gregory in a bedraggled, if not exactly chastened state.

'Come to pin something else on me, have you?' he scowled at the jingling of keys as Sandys and Robshaw approached his cell door with one of the warders.

'I should say, Gregory, that your conduct of yesterday was disgraceful,' Luke began. 'In the first place, a Royal Guardsman should know better than to go coney-catching at a market.'

'I had to make back the money somehow, since my pay's to be docked!'

'As to that, you should prepare yourself to go without whisky and tobacco for a long time. I shall give a full written report to the Earl, and it will make clear just what a scoundrel you've been, to treat a young woman in that rough and ungentlemanly way.' From over Luke's shoulder, Robshaw fixed the trooper with a glare, but the latter's scowl merely deepened.

In truth, the warders were desperate to get rid of Gregory. The prisoner had complained incessantly: about the food; about the water that formed runnels across the cell floor; and about the noise of rioters as they were brought in. The few cells at the City's disposal – here and in the Bocardo, the tower at the

157

north gate – were full of men the constables had arrested in the disturbance, who'd been escorted to gaol with help from Captain Sutherland's Foot Guards and were now facing charges of 'riotous and barratory behaviours likely to lead to a breach of the King's peace.'

Ed had stipulated that the trooper must have a cell to himself, and Luke had paid for the privilege, at least for one night – which exacerbated the overcrowding everywhere else. Gregory's defiant attitude must be catching: the Castle's notorious rats, far from scuttling off at the sound of footsteps, today stood their ground, staring insouciantly back at the human interlopers in their dark domain. It was with a heavy heart that Luke imparted the news that both Gregory and his attendants wanted to hear: he was to be released with immediate effect.

'It'll be for the Colonel to deal with you now. I'm sure he'll take appropriate measures.'

'But I'm free to go?'

'Yes, you're free to go.'

True to form, Bowell fretted long and loud when brought the news that Gregory was now off the list of suspects (not an extensive list, Luke thought to himself – though he did not exactly share this intelligence with the mayor).

'I suppose 'twould be out of the question, then, sir, to get a warrant to arrest him on a charge of kidnapping instead?'

'Yes, Sandys,' Bowell snapped: 'You suppose right.' Luke's humour was not improved by Calvert simpering and snarking in the corner of the mayoral chamber as he delivered the ill tidings.

And Emily? She was, if anything, relieved that her tormentor was not now going to be put to death. Luke had explained, as best he knew, how Gregory's transgressions would be dealt with under military discipline, but she was inclined to dismiss that as a domain entirely beyond her experience. As Richard went off to his building site at Jesus College, the couple thanked God she had emerged unharmed from her week of traumas. She had, as her mother put it, been 'scared half to death' – but, they reflected, it could have been far worse.

Chapter 33
Another Close Shave

Luke curled his toes inside his boots as the deadly steel blade hovered inches from his throat. All of Jackman's customers would surely experience the same frisson of fear at this moment, as the barber-surgeon doubtless realised – but he showed no sign of it. Did he practise that blank look, lest a minuscule tic inadvertently vouchsafe to the man sitting prone in his chair a shared knowledge of potential doom in one rogue swish of the razor? To betray even the slightest glimmer of awareness would be to risk fatally undermining his trade.

Feeling grimy after his encounter with Gregory in Oxford Castle gaol, Luke headed to Jackman's establishment through the maze of streets around St Ebbe's Church to have his stubble scraped off. During his apprenticeship, Luke would often tag along with his father on visits to the colleges to see clients, paying particular attention to the portraits displayed in libraries and common rooms. In many, dating from earlier in the century, the sitters were bearded, but that was before hair became politicised: Puritans were nicknamed 'roundheads' for their close crop and bare chin, whereas Cavaliers would grow out their own locks or wear a long wig, and cultivate a distinctive T-shaped ensemble of moustache and beard. But it was a long time since any portrait he had been called upon to frame showed any arrangement more hirsute than a modest covering on the upper lip: the style favoured, in fact, by the King himself.

As a craftsman, Luke appreciated the deftness and confidence of Jackman's movements, honing his jawline just as he himself had chiselled and refined the patterns of the wooden frame hours earlier. We are all made of malleable material, he mused; the face we present to the world, shaped and whittled by experience. What about the soul we present to God? There, he was on more treacherous ground. Old Samuel Sandys had gone to his grave as he had pushed bull-headedly through life, in the unshakeable conviction that he was predestined to sit at the hand of the Almighty. The dark side of his outlook was that fellow beings – with whom he mingled daily – would inevitably include many who were doomed to eternal damnation, no matter what pains they took to live virtuously.

Luke had disavowed his father's nonconformist religious beliefs chiefly for reasons of convenience; but on this question, the difference of opinion was genuine. Evidence accumulated from close acquaintance with felons and felonies had convinced him that most of us, confronted with sharp enough exigencies of anger, fear, frustration or temptation, are capable of either good or evil. Take Pawling, for example: they had unthinkingly trusted him when leaving him with just Harbord's dead body and Jacob Hopkins for company, just as Luke had willingly put his jugular within easy reach of Jackman's razor. For the ex-mayor to have succumbed to an urge and opportunity to exact revenge would not make him irredeemably bad. And what of his own temptations? Unbidden, the image of Cate Napper came to mind, and Luke felt his stomach positively churn as the blood supply in his midriff started to pump downwards. He licked his suddenly dry lips and, with a conscious effort, turned his mind to reviewing the investigation so far – such as it was.

Turning this way and that along narrow alleys on the way back to the Guildhall, Luke was halfway through replaying the moment of first hearing about Gregory's alibi when he passed Jethro Cox's yard. The two men who were deep in conversation with the wheelwright, by the open door of his workshop, looked familiar, he thought – before placing them, a heart-beat later, as members of the Green Ribbon club. One, clad all in black, was a thin, dyspeptic-looking character, the man whom Norton had introduced as the pamphleteer. What was his name? Settle – Elkanah Settle. The other was his compan-ion, or perhaps bodyguard: the blackamoor, in a three-quar-ter-length plum-coloured coat, standing with hands propped casually in the pockets of his breeches and a sleek capotaine hat slightly askew atop his large head. They still had to go back and talk to them again at The Unicorn and Jacob's Well – along with a private interrogation of Unsworth, the landlord. Better do it soon: if they were in need of a cartwheel, perhaps they were planning on going somewhere.

Chapter 34
The Abbey Ruins

The deputy grabbed the saddle by its pommel and cantle and heaved it up on to the back of his thickset Welsh cob, while Luke tightened the girth around his own mount, a fine chestnut mare, as she flared her nostrils. She would need the martingale today too, being apparently in one of her flighty moods. Dowling, the foreman in charge of Kempster's two labourers, had been vague in response to questions about their previous visit to the shell of Osney Abbey. Luke inferred that they had not actually run the gauntlet of the 'vagabonds' they'd reported to their master at Burford as an obstacle to their work. Instead, on finding that the ruins were not deserted as they had expected, 'they turned yeller', as Robshaw put it contemptuously after the men had quit the office to prepare their cart for the onward journey.

Whoever was taking shelter in the remains, would they really pose such a threat? The constables mounted their horses with a determined, if somewhat sceptical attitude: ready for trouble if it came, but not expecting it. The route out of the city took them west along Sleyng Lane, named for the slaughterhouses which, in former times, accounted for the main business done there. Now, the old City Wall on their right-hand side formed one edge of Pembroke College, established during the reign of Charles I when the University was expanding at a gallop.

For Robshaw, in particular, the journey was a familiar one, taking them past his place of work: a large brewhouse, whose malty aromas were a pleasant companion on the mild midday air. Oxford had grown and changed rapidly in their lifetimes, with students, attracted from far and wide by its burgeoning scholarly reputation, bringing prosperity to the city, along with new ideas, tastes and perspectives. And scholarship did seem to work up a terrific thirst, as the deputy was wont to point out.

Luke looked at the crack in the keep as they skirted the south side of the Castle. The stark fissure seemed to symbolise a break from the insularity of the past. Where once the building was dedicated to keeping folk out, now its residual function was to keep them in, when they had shown they could not behave themselves. He shortened the mare's rein as she slipped on a cobble and tossed her head. How fitting, he reflected, for Wren's soaring neo-Gothic vision to be realised at Christ Church College by using materials from a medieval monastery. For centuries, the old stones had enclosed a nest of mummery and superstition. Now they would turn outwards to the modern world.

The cartwheels creaked placidly as the drayhorse ambled across the twin bridges over the prongs of Castle Mill Stream and past a higgledy-piggledy row of cottages. With a left then a sharp right turn, they came out on to the path across the meadow, and the pale gap-toothed remnants of Osney Abbey jutted into view. The earliest of the snake's heads were just in bloom, turning their gorgeously purpled gaze demurely downwards as the horses plodded by – too close for comfort, it seemed, for a flock of magpies, who issued a sudden scolding 'chack-chack-chack' and took off towards the ruins in apparent disapproval.

'Damn magpies again,' Robshaw remarked tersely. Grunting rueful agreement, Luke did a double-take and looked sharply at the pugnacious set of his deputy's profile. The man seemed to be slightly, but distinctly sweating: odd, given the pleasant freshness of the spring sunshine. Anyway, they were now arriving at the building.

A wisp of cooking-smoke from somewhere behind the ravaged façade confirmed that human habitation was indeed under way. As they dismounted, a face poked out from round the side of a wall – then just as quickly vanished. Moments later, a tall, upright figure in a black ankle-length cassock pulled back the evergreen ivy and emerged to squint at them through a pair of eyeglasses balanced on the bridge of his nose. Below the brim of his hat – also black – a shock of silver-grey hair was clearly visible.

'Silver! Silver Birch! I'd know you anywhere, you old dog!' Luke was delighted to find one of his student contemporaries. 'What in God's name brings you here?!'

'Luke Sandys, as I live and breathe! Well met, sir, well met,' the other replied warmly, removing his spectacles and slipping them beneath his cassock as Luke dismounted and the pair shook hands.

Peter Birch – nicknamed 'Silver' by fellow undergraduates in honour of his luxuriant but prematurely grey locks – had stayed on at Christ Church to study for a Master of Arts degree and, eventually, graduate as a Doctor of Divinity.

''Tis God's work that brings me here, Luke, in faith.'

'What, among rogues and vagabonds?'

'Aye, men call them vagabonds, my friend – but that doesn't mean we should think of them as rogues. How did they become vagabonds, Luke, eh? Answer me that!'

Luke shrugged, a doubting half-smile on his face, and Birch abruptly took his arm.

'Come, let me show you what we're doing for them,' the cleric said, as Sandys signalled to Robshaw and Kempster's crew to wait. He led the way around the undergrowth to the back of the facing wall, to where one end of the roof was intact. This canopy, along with a nearby cloister that was still standing, was obviously keeping the worst of the elements from making life too uncomfortable for perhaps as many as twenty people. A row of wary expressions greeted Luke, with eyes fixed on him as an intruder who – if he was not clearly in favour with their patron – would doubtless be treated as hostile. He began to realise what had deterred the Burford men from proceeding to take away the stone as planned.

At one end of the cloister, a screen fabricated from oddments of threadbare muslin and calico, crudely sewn together to ward off flies, hung from a rail that was secured in place with wooden props. Birch pulled the curtain back to show food supplies inside including a basket of loaves.

'You bring them bread?' Luke asked.

'Indeed, the Osney parish is blessed with a bread charity. A bequest of twenty guineas from Thomas Faulkner, a merchant who passed over in the reign of King James – God rest his soul. The income pays for bread to be distributed among the parish poor.'

'But that's only for settled parishioners, surely?'

Birch's face contorted in disapproval.

''Tis iniquitous, that system! There are so many parishes round here that fail in their duty,' he said. Poor relief was supposed to be administered according to the so-called Settlement Act, adopted by the Cavalier Parliament shortly after the Restoration. Under it, every man should have a settlement certificate: a badge of belonging which ensured that, if certain conditions were fulfilled, his needs of food and shelter – and those of his family, if any – were to be met by the authorities of his home parish. But many such authorities were apt to find or contrive a pretext to withhold the requisite documents, to limit their liabilities: and, if a man could not prove residency or employment, he was effectively cast out from this social safety net.

'You know the most common denominator among these poor wretches?'

Luke raised his eyebrows.

'Orphans, Luke: or abandoned by their parents in childhood. Their lives never get back on course. So, I bring the surplus bread down here, once we've seen to the settled families. Else they'd be forced to resort to begging – or worse.'

'I thought most vicars spent any spare income on repairs to the roof?'

'Why, 'tis true,' the other replied with a sigh, 'one can always find work to be done on the fabric of our churches. But that would be to go against the benefactor's wishes.'

'Well, you're a clergyman of rare principle, Silver, I'll give you that,' Luke admitted. 'But you know, they can't stay here for much longer. Bishop Fell sent us to watch over these men while they take away the stone.'

'I know, he wants it for his great tower. We've thought of that. Step this way.' They picked a path through weeds and brambles towards the more overgrown and tumbledown end of the old abbey, and Birch outlined his scheme for Kempster's labourers to begin by removing the material from there. He had a point: structurally, this part of the building was useless, but among the vegetation Luke could see that many of the stone blocks were still intact. Prise them loose with sufficient care and they could go straight into Wren's ambitious new edifice: it would just take a bit more patience than starting with the stuff that was more easily accessible.

Chapter 35
A Mysterious Apparition

Sandys returned to where Dowling and his men were waiting with Robshaw, and briefly gave instructions. He was momentarily struck again by his deputy's slightly odd, flushed appearance – but, having no wish to be distracted from the interesting discourse of his old friend, he dismissed the thought.

'So, these nets were being discarded by a local fisherman,' Birch was saying. 'A kind parishioner found some sewing materials and these vagabonds, as you call them, mended them. They take a few roach and chub from the river. Then, on Fridays, we put on a fish supper, with guests – a few friends and even relatives turn up, sometimes.'

'And they sleep here? Must get cold in winter.'

'Yes. I suppose they… huddle together for warmth.'

Looking at the neat piles of blankets and straw stacked against the cloister's back wall, Luke wondered at a clergyman speaking as if approvingly of such a practice. The homeless were mostly men, it was true, but there were some women – and it was hard to imagine any parish actually refusing to help a married couple. Birch read his thoughts.

'They're welcome to the message of the Gospels at any time, Luke – they need only turn up at St Thomas's with an open heart. Sin is sin, whether committed by rich or poor. We're all fallen creatures.'

Dowling had taken down a large bag from the cart, from which he and his men removed leather aprons and gloves, heavy chisels, hammers and a pickaxe – and at last set to work. Seeing Robshaw position himself with half an eye on the vagabonds,

Luke seized the chance offered by a rare conjunction of time and circumstance, and set off with Birch to reminisce and talk politics on a leisurely stroll around the meadow.

'So, 'twas a tense time at Christ Church at the end of the Protectorate?' he enquired. Luke had left after taking his BA, just months before the death of Oliver Cromwell plunged the young English Commonwealth into a crisis from which it never recovered.

'That would be a great understatement, my friend. Many were the Fellows wondering every day whether it was time yet to come out openly for King and country.'

'What about Fell?'

'Ah, well that was when he really rose to greatness, in that time of upheaval. Never hid his allegiances, as you'll remember. Didn't make a great show of ramming them down men's throats, as some did – just never hid them.'

'Always had that look of supreme inner confidence, didn't he, that things would pan out?'

Birch nodded, swiping aside some undergrowth with his staff. 'Of course, it helped that he was such a brilliant scholar, they couldn't very well get rid of him. Wouldn't do to hound out the leading Latinist in England just because he believed the King would come back one day.'

'And now he's in his pomp.'

Luke remembered the gleam in the Bishop's eyes as he talked about the culmination of his rebuilding programme.

'Practically runs the University, they say.'

'He probably does. And he always saw past people's politics, anyway. Take you, Luke: he liked you because you were interested in Virgil and Cicero.'

'Despite my "Calvinist background" you mean?'

'Indeed. But you're Anglican now, I presume?'

'Aren't we all? I take Communion at St Martin's, the City church.'

'Ah! With old Dick-Duck.'

'Dick-Duck?'

'Yes – Richard Duckworth. The Vicar of Bell End.' Luke laughed out loud.

'For a Reverend gentleman, Silver, I must say you're not very reverent, are you?' Birch chuckled.

'Call it old age. Or perhaps… perhaps getting to know people here has given me a certain amount of perspective. One loses patience with ecclesiastical niceties,' he went on, suddenly serious again as they approached the ruins. 'They all have a tragic tale to tell.'

'What about this chap?' Luke asked. A still well-built gentleman, now frosted with old age, was standing some way off, watching some of the men as they carried out repairs to a beehive.

'Ah – yes, interesting. Come, I'll introduce you. Good day, Martin! Martin Fletcher, this is Luke Sandys. Friend of mine from university – now Chief Officer of the Oxford Bailiffs.' The man swiftly appraised Luke, a frown knitting his brow over piercing blue eyes, before offering his hand.

'Well met sir. You'll be busy then, looking into the murder of that Harbord?' His features twisted into a momentary expression of contempt at the name. Must not have shared the late MP's politics, Luke thought.

'Why, yes, so we are.'

'Not looking for clues here, though?' Birch cut in. The others laughed.

'No, indeed! So, are you one of the… "residents"?'

'Nay! 'Tis my grandson.' Fletcher made a vague gesture in the general direction of the knot of men at the beehive.

'And he enjoys it here?'

'Prefers it to living with me.' They exchanged pleasantries and moved on.

'How does he come to be here, then?' Luke asked Birch. He had not wanted to interrogate Fletcher directly on first acquaintance.

'Well, many years ago, his daughter got into trouble. Scoundrel made himself scarce, before the child was born.' Luke made a suitable noise, combining sympathy with disapproval. 'Then later, she died. Drowned, I think, now I come to remember.'

'Terrible way to go.'

'Indeed. Anyway, so the lad was left an orphan, to all intents and purposes. Now he's here.' They had looped round to their starting point at the other side of the ruins, where they had left Kempster's crew.

The labourers were hard at work, painstakingly levering out the cuboid chunks of limestone intact and loading them on to the cart, while the Abbey's itinerant population seemingly pursued their own diverse purposes. The horses cropped patiently in the afternoon sunshine. But where was Robshaw? With Birch still by his side, Luke came across his fellow constable sitting on a low wall in a patch of shade and gibbering – yes, there was no other word for it – positively gibbering.

'Oh M-master S-sandys, sir,' he began, shaking violently. 'I s-seen a ghost!'

'A ghost? What're you babbling on about, man?'

'Oh, s-sir, I hope as how 'tis just the m-marsh fever! Making me s-see things, as well as all this here sh-shaking and sweating!' Robshaw had contracted malaria – 'marsh fever', as he put it – some years earlier, and Luke now realised the symptoms he'd noticed earlier prefigured one of his occasional attacks; however, he'd never known the condition to produce delusions, at least not in the stolid figure of his deputy.

'Snap out of it, Robshaw! Look at me!' he barked, as he

noticed the afflicted constable's eyes rolling. 'There's no such thing as ghosts. You're having a bad bout, that's all. We need to get you home.'

''B-but 'twas real, Master Sandys!' he wailed. 'As real as you s-standing there! 'Twas the ghost of W-william Harbord!' Luke glanced at Birch, who was obviously at a loss as to how to respond.

'Are you trying to make a fool of me, Robshaw, by God?' he growled, genuinely annoyed now. How dare he trivialise their investigation, in front of one of Luke's old friends? 'We'd better go. Dowling, that'll do for today. You'll need to leave room in the cart anyway, this one's in no condition to ride a horse, you'll have to carry him.'

Celia Robshaw opened the door of their little house on New Inn Hall Street and matter-of-factly helped her stricken husband inside. 'I'll take care of him from here, Master Sandys, thank you.'

Once the working party reached Christ Church, word was sent to Bishop Fell, who descended from his eyrie to oversee the proceedings in person as the first batch of stone was unloaded and stacked in a large lockable shed, set aside for the purpose at the side of the College stable block.

'Splendid, splendid,' he purred, as Luke returned from handing in their horses to the ostler at the Guildhall. 'No *creato ex nihilo*, eh, Sandys? It's *creato ex materia* from now on, my boy.'

'Yes, there should be plenty of material to create with now, your Grace,' Luke replied with a smile. 'Kempster's men can go back any time – they know they're to take the stone from the tumbledown parts of the ruin first. They won't get any trouble from the vagabonds in that case.'

'Splendid, splendid,' the Bishop repeated.

Chapter 36
Some New Information

When Luke finally returned to his own office and slumped down behind his desk, he was startled by a sudden movement at the edge of his field of vision. He jerked his head round to find his glance met steadily by a pair of cold, calculating grey eyes. As their owner rose from a chair in the corner and approached to offer his hand, Luke recognised him as the man he'd guessed was an intelligence officer working for Lord Finch, when he'd been advising Colonel Russell and the Lord Chancellor the previous afternoon.

'Luke Sandys? We met yesterday,' the man said softly.

Relief that his chamber had not, after all, been invaded in his absence by a complete stranger mingled in Luke's breast with a creeping dread. How had the man got in? And how had he managed to sit there so silently that Luke had been unaware of his presence? The catlike grace of the visitor's movements, and something about the set of his weatherbeaten face, suggested an efficient ruthlessness that was no doubt common currency in his trade.

'Good day to you, sir,' he replied, striving to master his misgivings. 'And you are?'

'In the Lord Chancellor's service, as you know. You can call me Tom.' Seemingly in no mood for small talk, he came straight to the point. 'Do you want some information about the late William Harbord?'

'Why yes, I suppose so...'

'You should.' The spy reached inside the front of his coat, and Luke could not altogether dispel the notion that he was about to draw a weapon: a stiletto, perhaps, or even a pistol. In fact he merely produced two documents, and proceeded to unfold them on Luke's desk.

'These are copies of two notes from the French Ambassador, Paul Barillon. Each confirms a payment to Harbord of five hundred guineas, both made over the last eighteen months.'

Luke whistled through his teeth.

'Where are the originals?'

'I can't tell you that,' 'Tom' said with a half-smile. 'But our man went to his grave believing they were safely locked in a bureau in his study at the ancestral pile in Norfolk.' This seemed to make no sense. Harbord had been the unofficial leader of a group dedicated to the crackdown on Papists and the exclusion of James, Duke of York from the line of succession; and was well known from his speeches in Parliament as a critic of France, one of the leading Roman Catholic powers in Europe.

'So what were they paying him for?'

The intelligence officer stretched his long form as he leant backwards in the seat at the other side of Luke's desk, put his midnight-blue felt hat on the floor and clasped his hands together behind his head.

'Politics is a world in which nothing is quite as it seems,' he began expansively. Harbord had been instrumental in the impeachment of Lord Danby, formerly head of the government, 'Tom' reminded him. As Luke remembered from reading the murdered MP's file at the parliamentary clerks' temporary office in the Bodleian, Danby had been exposed in the House of Commons as having secretly sued for peace with France while asking Parliament to approve 'supply' – that is, leave to spend money raised in taxes – for a standing army, ostensibly to go to war with the same country. For this service, it seemed, the late Member for Thetford had received the first of his generous remittances from Barillon.

'Why should the French pay him for that, I don't understand?'

The spy leant forward in sudden intensity.

'*Cui bono?* What's the situation after the impeachment, and who stands to gain by it?' Luke shook his head. 'Danby went to the Tower – bad luck for him. So who now is going to propose raising taxes to set up a standing army? That cover's blown. England is defended, but by part-time local garrisons. Hodge with his rusty halberd is hardly going to make trouble for France in her quarrels with the Dutch and Spanish.'

The second of the two notes was much more recent, indicating a payment for introducing a bill during the so-called Second Exclusion Parliament, which had been dissolved just two months earlier in January, prohibiting the government from raising loans on the London money market.

'If there's no supply, what happens?' The Lord Chancellor's man was taking it upon himself to give his host a short course in the ways and means of political chicanery. 'Does government just cease altogether?' Luke supposed not. 'So, where will the money come from, to allow ministers to pay people to carry out the King's policies and his wishes? Thanks to Harbord's bill, they can't borrow it in London, which leaves only one real option – the one across the Channel.'

This was, Luke realised, what the fellow was driving at. The King of France, Louis XIV, had just stunned Europe with an ostentatious show of his vast wealth, accumulated through absolute rule: the magnificent palace at Versailles, just outside Paris, living quarters for which had recently been completed. The opulence of both grounds and interiors was already the stuff of legend.

'This Parliament is supposed to forget about the Exclusion. Now we've left London, everyone is supposed to realise they were really good friends all along, and start agreeing with each other,' Tom continued sardonically. 'I'd give it a fortnight of sitting, at the most.'

'That's going to disappoint a lot of people here,' Luke replied. 'Oxford has been looking forward to rich pickings.'

'Can't be helped. The point is, the "Honourable Members" won't agree supply without Exclusion, and that'll get blocked in the Lords, where Old Rowley has a rock-solid majority. If he can't get cash from Parliament or the money-lenders, he can only turn to Louis. They're cousins, after all, did you know?' Luke nodded. 'And that will put England pretty much in Barillon's pocket.'

Leaning his elbows on the arms of his chair, the Chief Bailiff's Officer tented his fingers.

'So let me see if I get this straight. Harbord's public image is as a hammer of the French, so to speak...'

'A Gallophobe, yes. Which is exactly what made him so valuable. No one would suspect him...'

'...of secretly serving French interests,' Luke finished off the sentence.

'Very good! Now you're starting to understand politics!' the spy said with a cold smile.

'But what of his friends in the Green Ribbon Club? They didn't know about these payments, surely?'

His guest's demeanour grew grave, and he continued only after a slight pause, during which he seemed to be debating with himself.

'I'll take you into my confidence, Sandys. I've been told you're reliable.' Luke inclined his head. 'Frankly, there's no need for me to be involved in discussions about the King's security in Oxford. Colonel Russell has all that under control, he's a competent officer. No, that's just a cover story: I came when I heard about the murder, because it made me think we must've had a leak somewhere.'

A new shape and pattern to Harbord's killing, and its political context, was beginning to form in Luke's mind.

'We did wonder whether someone on the other side of politics might have had him killed…'

'But?' the spy prompted.

'But what if someone found out about these payments? Someone on his own side?'

'He'd be seen as a traitor.'

'And a target.'

Luke took his turn to brief his companion about their investigation. Tom already knew about Gregory's arrest and subsequent release, though the source of the trooper's alibi was evidently news, along with their suspicion that the shreds of cloth that seemed to incriminate him had instead been planted on the body by Pawling. On one thing the two men ended up agreeing: it was now imperative to track down the mysterious caller who'd evidently disturbed Harbord's composure at The Unicorn and Jacob's Well, as the Green Ribbon Club met there on what turned out to be the MP's last day on earth. As they rose, Luke made to pick up the copies of Barillon's notes, but the spy was too quick for him. Pocketing them, he did at least promise to share any new leads that came his way.

'So, how do I contact you?'

'You don't,' the other said with a grin. 'I contact you.' For a while after Tom took his leave, Luke sat alone in the gathering gloom, then, on a sudden resolve, pushed back his chair, grabbed his hat and coat, locked the office door behind him and set off on the short walk to New Inn Hall Street.

'Hello Patch! All well, old lad?' Luke fondled the spaniel's ears as it gave a toothy grin, panted slightly and wagged its tail in greeting. The Sandys had never had dogs when he was growing up, but for some reason the creatures often approached him with friendly intent. 'So what are we going to do with the big fellow, then, your master?' he asked Patch, with a nod towards the corner of the room, where Robshaw sat by the fire. 'He was in a bad way earlier.'

'Should be outside, that one,' his deputy said – but made no move to expel the dog into the cold. Instead, Patch settled back down beside him, resting his chin on his paws, as Celia Robshaw took a large pot from the grate and poured hot water into a wooden pail. She shoved it with her foot over to her husband's chair, whereupon he lifted a pair of thick hairy calves as she manoeuvred it into place, and settled his blackened, shovel-like feet in the bath.

'Aah – relief, at last. Thank you kindly, wife.'

It was a sentiment that Luke silently seconded, since the herbal waft from the bucket took the pungent edge off his deputy's own set of aromas. His pipe, for one, which he was relighting with a twig from the fire, amid copious deep puffing and snorting. 'There's mint in there, with ginger, and soldier's woundwort,' Celia said, nodding at the foot-bath as she caught Luke's enquiring eye. 'Or you might know it as yarrow. All good for a fever.' She went back to her embroidery, under a candlelight on the far side of the room, as Robshaw invited Luke to sit, and transferred ale from an earthenware jug into two pewter cups. Now he was closer, the pair of coneys, hanging from a nail in the soot-covered wall, added their own distinctive bouquet. He felt Robshaw look up from pouring to catch his line of vision.

'Of course, they'll have come off common land?' Luke said, nodding at the rabbits.

'Aye, there's plenty round the edges of Port Meadow. Mind, you've not come here to ask me and Patch about poaching.'

'No, indeed. How are you, first of all?'

'Nothing a good pipe can't put right.' He took a long draw of tobacco.

Luke summarised his briefing from 'Tom', and the pair shook their heads, lost for a moment in silent thought as the embers in the grate shimmered grey-and-orange. Robshaw leant forward and threw on another log.

'I don't see how we're going to find the killer, if it was all to do with these political intrigues in London,' Luke grumbled presently. 'With an Oxford man down, of course we'd know where to start looking.'

'We'll get him sir, or my name ain't Jack Robshaw.'

Luke was glad of his revived good cheer. It seemed like a propitious moment to take him back to the events at the Abbey.

'So – your hallucinations, earlier.'

'Halley – what?'

'Seeing things that aren't there.'

At this, the deputy's chin jutted and he shifted in his seat. 'Why, it was there – a man, with the face of William Harbord, plain as you're in front of me now.'

From the corner of his eye, Luke glimpsed Celia shake her head, and pull a stitch through her sampler with added vigour. The dog sat up and yawned.

'How can that be, Robshaw, really? We know Harbord's dead.'

'There's some things as can't be explained, Master Luke Sandys – not even with your science and book learning.' He jabbed the air with his pipe-stem for emphasis. Patch raised an ear, tilted his head slightly to one side, and let out a little half-whine, half-growl of agreement.

'Maybe it was someone who looked like Harbord?'

'Aye, maybe. Could have been his brother I suppose.'

'Older or younger?' Robshaw took another puff on his pipe as he thought back.

'Younger, for sure.' Now Luke remembered, Harbord's parliamentary file contained something about a brother, but he'd been lost at sea. Another dead end. He sighed, and his deputy seized the opportunity of changing the subject.

'Least we got Kempster's men going with that there stone.'

'That we did. Fell was pleased.'

'So he ought to be, with the trouble we took.' They supped their ale.

'What did you make of that "colony" at the Abbey?'

'Load of cullions,' Robshaw replied contemptuously. 'In their own little word, ain't they?'

'Mind, they'd heard about Harbord.' At the other's raised eyebrows, Luke went on: 'I was surprised, too. After all, his seat's in Norfolk.'

'About as far away as you can get.'

'Indeed.' And, with that, the pair drained their cups, and bade each other goodnight.

Chapter 37
Cate on her Round

Catherine Alexandra Napper
The Mitre Inn
High Street
Oxford
England
The World

Cate looked down at the childish script on the inside cover of her little prayer book with a nameless feeling of unease. To carry it with her and be able to feel it in her fingers was one of her chief comforts through these dark days. A reminder of happier times, when she had learned her letters at Father Huddleston's knee. 'Bright as a button', he'd always called her. And what lustre those days wore now, in retrospect: before her family's hopes for religious freedom in England, under its newly restored monarchy, were dashed by political fervour.

Seeing the book nestling on the bottom of one of her two bread baskets as she pulled back its wickerwork lid, Cate instinctively felt in the pocket she had sewn into her skirt to keep the leather-bound litany out of sight. No: the tiny volume was an item in the wrong place, which was disquieting enough, given its all-too-clear Romish origins and its capacity, therefore, to give her away to ill-wishers as a 'Papist'. That such an unexplained accident had occurred amid the unrest now roiling on the streets – as Oxford nervously awaited the opening of Parliament – imbued it with a still more disturbing aspect. She slipped it back into its hidey-hole with a frown.

The influx of strangers to the city had cranked up the tensions engendered in the past couple of years by the so-called Popish Plot. No doubt the murder of the MP had also played its part, as Luke Sandys had prophesied. Not that her family's religious allegiances had stopped those injured in the sectarian riot earlier in the week – outsiders and locals alike – from turning automatically to The Mitre to find care and comfort, she reflected ruefully.

Notwithstanding its role as a community hub, the inn still needed to pay its way, and Cate's parents were far from alone in seeing the coming of Parliament as an opportunity for profit. But her mother's face had assumed its most careworn aspect when Cate suggested taking her wares to sell in other nearby establishments.

'But she'll be out on her own! A young widow – most folk don't even know about that: they'll see her as a maid, without a chaperone!'

But Jim Napper had glimpsed Cate's mutinous expression.

'Fie, Mary, we're among friends here. And she'll just be going from one tavern to the next – they all know her, they'll look out for her.'

'I'll only be gone for an hour at a time, Ma – two at the most,' the daughter protested. So, it was settled. Cate had a job that gave her a bit of precious independence. Where the parents were in agreement was over the quality of her output: both bread and cakes were the object of regular favourable comment among their clientele.

She sat down and leafed through the prayer book, whose text set out the Rosary in full: first the Apostles' Creed, then the Our Father. 'Give us this day our daily bread.' Well, that was her task now. The Lord was acting through her to meet the needs of her fellow beings, which enabled her to feel useful, at least, as she earned her keep. She particularly enjoyed setting out on clear mornings, when she would play a game of walking in the long shadow cast in the rising sun by the steeple of the All Saints Church, where the Nappers went to be checked off in the parish register every Sunday in minimum observation of the law. Once her footsteps took her beyond its shade, her heart would give a little leap for joy, as if temporarily freed from the oppressive influence of Anglican orthodoxy and the depredations it had visited on her own people.

Jim had now whittled a small notch on the side of the wooden oven door, into which Cate could insert a metal hook to loosen it when the contracting air within sealed the board tightly in its cavity. Removing a batch of caraway cakes to cool, she felt her mood lighten as she recalled the day Luke had come into the kitchen to help her open and rekindle the oven. He had met her gaze for slightly too long, causing her to look down in modesty; then, when he passed her the flame, their eyes had met again, bringing a smile unbidden to her face.

Small past mysteries suddenly made sense. She remembered his consideration, during visits to Hanage House to brief them on the court case. She realised at the time that he must come into contact with far too many grieving relatives for all to be given the same care and attention they themselves were receiving. She assumed it was out of respect for the Weston family. But there were clues, when Cate looked back, that she herself was the chief object of his ministrations. In her grief, she had dismissed them, but, in retrospect, it was clear that his feelings were rapidly deepening. Why, at one point, he had leant in towards her, to speak confidentially about aspects of the investigation, and she noticed he was trembling. When they shook hands on his departure, Luke's grip would linger, as if longingly, on hers.

But what were his intentions? Indeed, what could they be, as a married man twice her age? Divorce – even for Protestants – was, she knew, difficult and expensive, and thus extremely rare. She would not altogether put it past Luke Sandys to get one. Even if he did manage a legal separation from his wife, however, neither her family nor her Church could accept him as a husband. Gazing absently at the kitchen window, Cate took up two freshly starched linen cloths and used them to line the baskets. She might contemplate defying Father Morris. Whether she was truly willing to shock, even scandalise her mother and father – that was an altogether different question. One she regularly asked herself, without ever coming up with a convincing answer.

As she loaded up the last of the cakes for afternoon delivery, Cate decided to look on the bright side. Surely the political and public mood could not remain indefinitely at fever pitch, and it would be safe some day for Catholics to pursue their religion openly? This was the central thread of the rosier future she imagined for herself. Perhaps then she would be free to marry Luke Sandys; or even another suitor, of her own faith. No one could replace Marcus, who had been her first love – but surely his death would not altogether extinguish her chances of happiness?

Cate fingered her crucifix through the simple linen of her kerchief, under which it was safely concealed. Next to it she had tied a single black ribbon through her string of rosary beads, which were threaded on to the same cord. They had married in secret, as a public ceremony in a Roman Catholic place of worship was considered too dangerous amid the overwrought political atmosphere brought about by the Popish Plot. Instead, the wedding mass had been quietly administered in the old chapel at Hanage House, with immediate family and their retainers the only guests. So, she must now mourn in secret. With a sigh, the young widow Weston passed the straps of the twin baskets over her shoulders, laced on her bonnet, slipped out of the side door and set off on her round.

Chapter 38
Back to The Unicorn and Jacob's Well

It was half an hour or so later when Luke and Robshaw once again pushed open the door of The Unicorn and Jacob's Well. Their arrival caused the already low level of conversation to hush further. A smattering of locals were evidently trying out the new option for a quick jar, along with a much-reduced number of Green Ribbon men compared with their first visit – though Luke noticed they included Settle and his black friend, the slightly convex crown of his hat visible on the seat beside them. The pair followed the constables with a glare of unconcealed hostility from their position at the back of the room.

'You're not too busy, Unsworth, you can spare us a few minutes.' It was not put as a question. 'In the back.' Luke jerked his head towards the rooms at the rear of the premises, and for the avoidance of debate Robshaw grabbed the landlord's arm, although he put up scant protest. Through a door from the bar they entered a back parlour with a stone floor, which had another door to the yard outside, and corralled Unsworth into a corner.

'I want you to tell me exactly what you overheard when the man Harbord said was "not a member" of the Green Ribbon club came to call on him on Monday.'

'Aye, I heard you'd had to let that feller go,' the innkeeper said, features settling into his trademark sly grin as he rubbed his sore arm.

'There's more where that came from, if you don't cough,' Robshaw growled.

'I'm sure that won't be necessary, Robshaw,' Luke said. 'Master Unsworth values his new liquor licence, so he's obviously just collecting his thoughts before telling us everything he knows.'

Unsworth switched to another of his favourite facial expressions: one of injured innocence.

'Why, I was coming to see you, Master Sandys, at the Guildhall, I swear!' he protested. 'Only you've been that busy, what with arresting the wrong man.' Robshaw fingered the heavy wooden stave at his side.

'Less of your lip,' he said. Luke lifted a hand, keeping his eyes fixed on the landlord, who gulped and glanced at the door to the bar, which they had closed behind them.

'There's things I could tell you about them there Green Ribbons as'd make your hair curl,' Unsworth said, lowering his voice. 'I listens from behind the bar when they holds their meetings. Their plots and plans – why, some of them sounds like treason.'

Luke glanced at Robshaw. Perhaps he would have to let his deputy loose on this annoying specimen after all.

'Very well,' he said with a deep breath, resolved to give the innkeeper one more chance. 'You can tell us about the Green Ribbon Club and their meetings in due course. But let's begin with Monday. You said a man came to see Harbord and they had a quarrel, at the door?'

'Well, I heard raised voices, so I assumed.'

'You assumed. What was it you heard said? Think, man, it could be important.'

'Why, he said as how Harbord should meet someone, now he was back in Oxford, like.'

'Meet whom?'

Unsworth shook his head.

'That I never heard, sir.'

'Was that what made Harbord angry?'

'Well... there was one particular word this feller used, what seemed to get him proper batey.'

At that moment there came an almighty crash-and-thud from behind the closed door, followed by the unmistakable '*zhush*-ing' of broken glass being strewn in shards across the floorboards and a shout of 'Hoy!' The constables jumped, their heads snapping round towards the source of the noise. Unsworth subsided, as if in stages, against the wall, his breath immediately beginning to come in shorter and more audible gasps.

'Stay here!' Luke barked at the innkeeper, who could scarcely have moved if he'd wanted to, frozen in panic as he evidently was. The pair unhooked their staves from their belts, and Robshaw flung open the door to the bar.

Luke braced himself: he had intervened in tavern brawls many times, and knew that trouble could erupt without warning when drink was being taken, almost as a change in the wind. As they re-entered the bar, it took a moment to register that, in this case, the antagonists had already quit. The only remaining customers were two locals: an older man, bleeding from the forehead where a sliver of glass had evidently flown too quickly for his age-dulled reflexes to permit evasive action, and a younger one – his son? – who was now supporting him.

Luke walked quickly over to the pair, feeling in his coat pocket for the spare dressing Dr Radcliffe had given him when treating his own head injury after the riot. That was a mere graze, after all: and this fellow's wound was fresh.

'Here – take this,' he said.

'Why, thank you, sir,' the older man exclaimed, as the younger quickly unfolded the bandage and began to wind it around his head.

'You were lucky – an inch lower and 'twould've been your

eye,' Luke said. 'So – was it a fight? Where are the combatants? Gone, obviously?'

'Why, all them fellers what was in here went straight out, sir,' the younger man confirmed. Robshaw had already surmised as much, and was now on the doorstep, looking up and down Fish Street.

'Only 'twasn't no fight,' the drinker was continuing as Luke moved to join his deputy. 'Just a great big smash through the window.'

They peered first south, towards Bacon's Tower and the bridge at the entrance to the city, then north towards the junction with Cornmarket, Queen Street and the High. Among the still-copious foot traffic of late afternoon, however, there was no way to pick out anyone who might have attacked The Unicorn and Jacob's Well, nor any sign of the Green Ribbon men who'd apparently quit the premises en masse at the first sign of trouble. They went back in.

'So where is it, then – presumably it was a big rock or something, that was thrown in?' Luke asked the father-and-son team.

'Why nay sir, 'twas that there,' the younger replied, gesturing towards a mess of overturned stools behind the broken window. Luke still could not see the missile – strange, as it must have been substantial, given the size of the hole it made.

'I can't see it.'

'That, sir – that chair there,' his informant replied.

'What... you mean, one of the pub's own bar-stools?'

'Aye, sir, that's what I've been trying to tell you. Them two as was sitting yonder, the thin man and the big blackamoor,' – he inclined his head towards the back of the bar, where Settle and his companion had been – 'they got up soon as you took off into the back, and went out the door, in a fearful hurry, like. The black one, he picked up that stool on the way, then next thing we knew, 'twas flying back in here through that there window.' Luke shook his head and frowned.

'But why would them Green Ribbons attack their own tavern?' Robshaw wondered.

A great throb of dread rose in Luke's gorge.

'Why indeed, Robshaw? Come on!' He led them quickly back towards the rear parlour and thrust open the door. The sight that greeted them confirmed his worst forebodings: Unsworth, his stricken form folded into the angle of wall and floor, a flow of deep crimson emanating in time with his laboured breaths from a gaping wound in his lower chest. The door to the outside yard swung on its hinges, and in two quick steps Robshaw reached its threshold and looked out.

'No one,' he said, as Luke snatched a grimy linen covering from the corner table and crumpled it over the innkeeper's punctured midriff, applying pressure in an attempt – futile, he already knew – to stem the bleeding.

'Unsworth! The word! There was a word the man used to Harbord, that made him angry. You were about to tell us – what was it?' Luke was beside himself – how could they have been so stupid? Throwing the stool through the window had been a classic diversionary tactic to draw their attention from the matter in hand, and they had fallen for it. Unsworth moved his lips inaudibly, and Luke lowered his ear to the dying man's face.

'Be... be-betray,' he gasped out. 'You betrayed us.'

'You betrayed us?' You're sure that's what he said?' The slight affirmatory nod of his head was the last act on earth by the landlord of The Unicorn and Jacob's Well. Unsworth's chin slumped on to his chest, his eyes glazed over, and he was gone.

'Morraine seize us!' Luke looked up at his deputy, aghast.

'We've been played for a coney, and no mistake.' Robshaw spat disgustedly on the floor. Luke's mind was racing, the pieces of the mystery now starting to fit together. Could Monday's caller have been from the Whig side of politics, and known about Harbord's treachery with the French? Hence, perhaps, his accusation that the MP had 'betrayed us'. Maybe Harbord's fellow fanatics in the Green Ribbon Club caught wind of it too, and maybe some of them killed him for it. Luke would be amazed if Settle and his friend were not involved. With Gregory's arrest, the investigation was, from their point of view, barking safely up the wrong tree. But news of the trooper's release, and the constables' arrival at the inn later the same day, had changed the picture. The pair must have decided Unsworth needed to be silenced before he could tell Luke something that would incriminate them. They had to act fast: they had left in a 'fearful hurry', the young man said.

Realising the constables would react immediately to an apparent outbreak of unrest, they had managed to cause a commotion in the bar, and sure enough Luke and Robshaw had come running. Then they had simply dodged round the side of the building and entered the back parlour through the door from the yard, stabbing the innkeeper before he could say anything. Luke's gall over being so easily fooled was mitigated by two things, at least: he had managed to get Unsworth to 'cough' – Robshaw's word – before he breathed his last. And now at least they knew who they were looking for: in connection with not one murder, but two.

'Go over to the Guildhall and fetch a few men,' he told Robshaw. 'And make sure you get the names of those two drinkers in the bar – we may need to speak to them again.'

'Yessir. And you?'

'I'm staying with the body,' Luke replied. 'After what happened with Pawling and Harbord, I'm taking no chances. I'm not having any more evidence tampered with.'

Chapter 39
Cate at the Mermaid

Cate had called on all her usual customers on Cornmarket Street. Not The Golden Cross or The Star, for they were sizeable coaching inns like The Mitre, and had their own ample kitchens. No: it was in the smaller taverns where she prospered, and found, moreover, a friendly welcome. So, heading north up the east side, Mistress Tuplin at The Bell greeted her with a cheery 'Afternoon to you, my pretty. What've you brought for us today?' And the return journey down the west side of the old thoroughfare would be incomplete without her regular confidential discourse with Miss Lizzie Carter, who helped her parents to run The Blue Lion – and who somehow found time to keep abreast of the latest London fashions; even, on occasion, adding them to her own wardrobe.

'I got something really lovely the other day,' Lizzie was saying, as she delved into a trunk in the little room next to the scullery where the two of them just about had room to sit. She pulled out a swatch of silk in a rich salmon pink.

'Ah, 'tis beautiful, Lizzie, truly,' Cate said admiringly. 'What will you make of it?'

'Why, 'tis just the right length to make a scarf. 'Twill be just the thing on a cold morning.'

'There'll be some left over.'

'Aye – have you seen those gloves, Mistress Bowell has a pair, with curled ribbon decorations at the wrist, like a ruff?' Cate nodded encouragingly, feeling the material in her fingers.

'I've a pair of suede gloves, of a shade that should tone perfectly.'

'And the off-cuts from a scarf will give you enough for that too. How clever.' At that point, however, the conclave was curtailed by Lizzie's exasperated mother.

'Back to work, miss! We've customers been waiting five minutes or more.' Cate and her friend exchanged sympathetic looks. Even Mistress Carter was mollified, however, by the newly baked caraway cakes, and promptly purchased three to offer for sale that evening as well as one for 'Master C', who would, as she put it, 'never forgive me if there weren't some for him an' all.'

Now Cate must enter the portals of her least favourite establishment: The Mermaid on the corner of Queen Street, one of the city's oldest, on whose floors and windowsills, she fancied, the dust of ages had accumulated with little if any interference by the human custodians whom the ancient premises had witnessed coming and going through the centuries. Still, there was business to be done, so – unconsciously giving her crucifix a little squeeze through her kerchief, and brushing the prayer book in her skirt pocket with the fingertips of her other hand – she nerved herself to go inside.

To add to the off-putting qualities of ambient odour and dim lighting, the extra crowds in Oxford now included a group of London men (she assumed) who'd apparently taken up semi-permanent residence here, and who turned as one to devour her with their eyes as she crossed the floor. Growing up, Cate had come to regard her features as slightly too sharp, and the residual set of her countenance too earnest, to be considered conventionally pretty. The extent of male attention she received always came as a slight surprise, therefore, and sometimes a nuisance. So she composed her special 'cross expression', consisting of a frown, pursed lips and an angry glint in her eyes, and flashed it across the room. While the gesture usually succeeded in causing local men to look away, these strangers appeared oblivious, however, and merely stared insolently back at her.

Then, the landlord, Master Moreton, presented an alarming aspect, his rubicund visage framed by a shock of matching reddish-brown hair and his beard seeming to separate out its constituent colours, so alternate clutches of whiskers were black, fair and ginger, like a tortoiseshell cat.

'Now then, missy,' he boomed, emerging suddenly from the shadows behind the bar. Cate quickly gathered herself after an involuntary start.

'Good afternoon, sir. I've a few caraway cakes left, if you've a need of them. Freshly baked.'

'Mighty fine they smell an' all,' the innkeeper replied, snuffing deeply. Cate wondered how he could discern their aroma among its plentiful competitors for olfactory attention, but she pressed on regardless to close the bargain.

'A penny each then, sir. They're a good six ounces, every one.'

'Six ounces? Why, 'tis the weight of a ha'penny loaf, not a penny!'

She sighed inwardly.

'That is for bread, sir, this is cake. With sugar.'

Moreton delved into the basket Cate had set down on the counter and pulled out one of her cakes, weighing it critically on his upturned palm and regarding it through narrowed eyes. She wondered if his hands were clean, but did not care to look too closely to check.

'Very well then missy – we better have four of them,' he said at last, disentangling eight copper ha'pennies among a mass of paper scraps dredged from his coat pocket. Her purse would be heavy, but her baskets were now much lighter – just a few cakes left for the inns and taverns down Fish Street. On previous rounds, she'd reached The Unicorn and Jacob's Well, opposite Christ Church, but – such was the demand that day – her wares would surely be exhausted before she got that far along.

Chapter 40
The Lost Wallet

Unsworth's body had been taken under guard, placed on the trestle table and safely locked inside the parlour behind Luke's office at the Guildhall. The constables had secured the side door of the inn, and one stood at the front entrance, stave at the ready against any attempt to enter, as the Chief Officer and his deputy briefed four others among the overturned furniture in the bar area.

'We now believe Harbord was killed by members of his own political group who…' He was chary of revealing any more details than they needed to know of his briefing by the Lord Chancellor's intelligencer – '…who may have thought he'd double-crossed them in some way.'

'That's what Unsworth said, aye,' Robshaw nodded in affirmation.

'That's right, we got him to tell us just before he died what in particular angered Harbord when a man came to call on him on Monday. "You betrayed us" were the words, apparently: that fits with other information we've received, that he may have been playing both ends of politics against the middle.'

'So, who we looking for then?' Tim Blount asked.

'Well, we clearly need to find that man, but two others now as well – the men we believe killed Unsworth.'

'One's a weedy-looking feller what thinks he's Lord Muck,' Robshaw pronounced contemptuously. What this description lacked in detail, Luke felt, it made up for in its evocative quality.

'That's Elkanah Settle. Slight build, clean-shaven, prominent nose and noticeable overbite. He writes their pamphlets –

quick-witted, and dangerous in a cunning sort of way, but I doubt it was him who actually stuck the blade in.'

'That'd be the blackamoor. Big blighter, reckons himself quite the dand,' the deputy added. Luke nodded.

'Younger man of African descent. Well built, plum-coloured coat and pale breeches, with a distinctive hat, a capotaine, sides of the crown bulge out slightly. No beard or moustache, but thick black sideburns.'

'Green ribbons?' Blount asked.

'Good thought, Tim, but they've probably taken them off by now.'

As the men fanned out in search of Unsworth's killers, Luke and Robshaw turned their attention to the inn itself. They climbed the winding staircase to the bedrooms: the landlord's own, predictably slovenly, and cluttered with the debris of rudimentary bachelor's personal hygiene and dressing arrangements; and another, by contrast, conspicuously bare, with its bed neatly made and floor clean swept.

'Must've been where Harbord was lodging,' Luke said. 'Well, if there was anything here to shed light on his death, we missed it. Mind you, his letters from Barillon were supposed to be at his home in Norfolk.'

Back downstairs, as Luke righted the chair that had crashed through the window, together with others upended by its impact, the deputy let out an indeterminate grunt of surprise from the back of the bar.

'What's that there? Under where them two was sitting?' Luke followed the direction of his finger and picked out a slender dark shape in the shadows beneath the bench from where Settle and his henchman had glared at them earlier, as they'd frog-marched Unsworth for interrogation. Robshaw knelt on a stool at the end of the table and bent down to retrieve the mystery object. They turned to each other with excitement as he placed it on the table top: a slim document wallet in black leather of fine quality. If, as seemed likely, this belonged to Settle, it was a find indeed. Luke gave a low whistle.

'Must've dropped it when they got up to run outside,' Robshaw murmured, turning it over in his hands. 'That feller said they was in a hurry, like.'

With The Unicorn and Jacob's Well secured, the pair sat at the desk in the office at the back of the Guildhall and looked down at their discovery. Dusk had now fallen outside, so Robshaw lit candles as Luke gingerly opened the silver clasp and pulled the wallet open. Inside, sure enough, the innermost compartment of the portfolio's left lobe contained four engraved visiting cards: one, somewhat dog-eared, from Sir Thomas Armstrong, an MP and former army officer; and three in pristine condition announcing Elkanah Settle Esq., Playwright, Poet & Pamphleteer.

'Well, that confirms it – this is Settle's all right,' Luke said. 'Must have got up so quickly to leave, the minute our backs were turned, this dropped out of his pocket and he never realised.'

They turned their attention to the wad of papers in the main body of the folder. The top two sheets were full of close-wrought doodles, as if the writer's pen had to keep busy with something to allow him to concentrate – while listening, perhaps? Luke felt a sudden thrill that experience had taught him was a sure sign of proximity to some kind of connection in a case, or even a breakthrough. Turning eagerly to the next page, it was clear immediately that the wallet's contents could be of considerable importance. At its head was the inscription: 'Meeting of Green Ribbon Club, 18th inst. – Minutes.'

'The eighteenth – that was Tuesday! This is a record of what they've been up to in there.'

'Unsworth reckoned it might be treason,' Robshaw reminded him. Better still was the information Settle had recorded thereunder: a list of those present, whose names included Armstrong, as well as Edward Norton, who'd apparently taken over from Harbord as the Club's chief spokesman, and several others with the letters, 'M.P.' appended. James Cecil, the Earl of Salisbury, was also mentioned. Luke could imagine his new friend 'Tom' might take a close interest in this list – though its relevance to their own investigation was not immediately clear.

Disappointingly, however, the following pages shed no further light, covered, as they were, in a series of lines and curves with a superficial resemblance to letters of the alphabet, but no more than that.

'You'd know what that says then, sir – 'tis surely Latin or some such?' Robshaw asked.

'No, I'm afraid not. Looks more like Greek, but it's not that either. I don't recognise these letters at all.' Luke quickly riffled through the rest of the sheets, confirming that the folder merely contained more of the same. Every now and then he could make out, in the left-hand margin, a pair of letters that were surely initials: 'T.A.', presumably for Thomas Armstrong, featured occasionally, as did 'E.N.'

'That'll be Edward Norton,' Luke murmured.

Only on one page towards the back were there some different markings, which he and Robshaw now turned to study. On one line was an ink drawing that might have depicted – Luke thought – a raindrop exploding on contact with the ground. After staring hard at it holding his breath for a full half-minute, Robshaw finally pronounced with certainty:

'Nah. 'Tis a crown.'

'Of course – you're quite right, Robshaw, it's a crown. Obvious once it's pointed out.'

'So what do them letters mean then?' Immediately below the shape they had now identified as a crown, the initials O.R. appeared, and what looked like a downward arrow – or it could be one of the squiggles that filled most of the other pages. Next to that again was another set of initials, J.S., and an upward-pointing arrow.

'My God!' Luke clapped his hand to his forehead, quite forgetting about his graze, whose throbbing in response was lost in his excitement. 'That's what Unsworth was on about! "O.R." is "Old Rowley".'

'The King's nickname?'

'Indeed. And "J.S." must be James Scott, the Duke of Monmouth! They're plotting to down King Charles – that's the arrow – and replace him on the throne with Monmouth – the upward arrow!' The other images on the page faded into the background as Luke realised they had stumbled on a plot against the monarchy.

'That there Tom'd be interested in this, wouldn't he?'

'He would, Robshaw. He certainly would.'

'We should give this to him then.'

Luke's mind was racing.

'Not so fast, my friend. This is hot stuff, what's in this wallet. Settle would know that of course, and he'll have missed it by now. At some point he'll try to get it back from The Unicorn and Jacob's Well.'

'We should double the guard on that there door,' Robshaw said.

Luke pinched his lower lip between forefinger and thumb.

'We-ell… Yes, let's do that – for now. Then later we should put this back, and withdraw the guard – and I'll have to ask the Provost not to send any more of his proctors.'

'I don't follow you, Master Sandys.'

'Thing is, how can we prove it's his? It's got his visiting cards in it, but anyone could have put them in there. We'll have to catch him red-handed.'

'Ah,' Robshaw said.

'So – we keep the inn under guard, for as long as we could realistically still be looking for evidence in the murder inquiry. That way we avoid arousing Settle's suspicions. Then we put the wallet back where we found it, and wait somewhere out of sight to keep watch on the building. He'll surely try to retrieve it – and when he's got it, we'll move in and arrest the knave, for both murder and treason!' he finished triumphantly.

'Ah,' the deputy replied, 'now I follow!'

Chapter 41
Missing

As the pair savoured the triumph now in prospect, there came a thunderous knock at the office door. Robshaw opened it to reveal the substantial figure of Jim Napper, licensee of The Mitre Inn.

'Luke – thank God,' he exclaimed in a tone of urgent anxiety. 'It's Cate – she's disappeared!'

Luke sat bolt upright. 'What d'you mean, disappeared?'

'She's never come back off her round.'

'Calm down, Jim. What round?'

They ushered the man inside and got him to sit.

'She's been going out, some mornings but mostly afternoons, on a round for to sell her bread and cakes at the other taverns. She's usually back an hour or more before now – round about when it gets dark.'

'Could she be with someone? A friend?'

Jim shook his head.

'Mary's been to ask Lizzie Carter, at the Blue Lion, but she said Cate left there ages ago.'

'What inns does she go to?' Robshaw asked.

'Why, she calls up and down Cornmarket, then she goes down Fish Street. Far as that new one, The Unicorn.'

Luke leaned forward, now beginning to share Napper's alarm.

'She's been selling cakes at The Unicorn and Jacob's Well?'

'Aye – reckons as how 'tis one of her best customers.'

The constables went with Jim Napper first to the Falcon Inn, the next up Fish Street from The Unicorn and Jacob's Well, which should have been Cate's penultimate call. Neither there nor at the next establishment up the hill – The New Inn – had she been seen that afternoon; however, The Falcon's pot-man, and Taylor, The New Inn's landlord, both agreed to help with the search.

As the taverners struck out to pick up more volunteers along the way, Luke and Robshaw called at The Mermaid, where the landlord Moreton's disobliging gruffness melted to the extent of reporting that yes, he had indeed seen Cate: she'd arrived there about half an hour before dusk. No, she hadn't seemed agitated, or in any way different from her normal appearance or demeanour.

'Bought four of her cakes, and sent her on her way,' the innkeeper concluded his report of the encounter.

The pair paused on the pavement outside and took stock, as Luke struggled to contain his inner turmoil. Every instinct screamed at him to tear down the walls of Oxford brick by brick. Good job Robshaw was calmer: the only way to find her, surely, was by methodically thinking through the possibilities till a process of elimination pointed them in the right direction.

'So, something must've happened to her between here and the next one, then,' the deputy said.

They slowly retraced their steps, looking either side as they went; but there was nothing out of the ordinary, and nowhere else, apparently, where Cate could have gone. Running down the side of the New Inn was a narrow yard, leading perhaps seventy or eighty feet back from the road, but it seemed to serve merely as a temporary dumping ground for rubbish from the taverns and traders roundabout, and – if the smell were not off-putting enough – the cobbles stopped short of the ivy-clad wall at the far end, leaving a patch of earth and a dank thicket in which holly and hawthorn competed for the meagre light with nettles and bramble.

Calls at The Bear and The Wheatsheaf, where neither staff nor any of the thinning ranks of customers recalled having seen a young woman of Cate's description, seemed to rule out any chance that she had taken an unscheduled detour down Blue Boar Street. As the Nappers had closed The Mitre for the evening, Luke told a pale-faced Mary that he and Robshaw would be round the corner at The Golden Cross, where they could get a late supper. He spoke to Cate's mother in tones calculated to reassure himself as much as her.

'We'll find her, Mary. 'Tis only a matter of time, I'm sure. You'll send word, if anything turns up?'

'Aye, Luke, of course. Master Ingram's gone up the other way toward The Broad, to ask in the taverns round there. We're all praying for her.'

Chapter 42
A Chance Meeting

It was a rare occasion when the drooping moustache and doleful expression belonging to the landlord at The Golden Cross, Henry Hadfield, seemed entirely appropriate to the circumstances. The constables shook their heads in answer to his enquiry and raised eyebrows as to news of the search, and gladly accepted his offer of hospitality.

''Tis the least we can do,' he intoned.

Their meal had not yet arrived, and they had just placed their tankards back down simultaneously after each taking a sup of ale, when a familiar deep voice rang out from the other end of the counter:

'Evening, sirs!' It was Robert Pawling. 'You let that trooper go then, Luke?' he asked.

The brass neck of the man! Luke turned and glared at the ex-mayor. It was not an evening when he felt like being trifled with.

'Yes. The evidence we were relying on to hold him turned out to have been planted,' he replied.

'By you,' Robshaw interjected.

'You put those fibres on Harbord's body, to try to incriminate Gregory in the murder.'

Pawling grinned infuriatingly.

'Now, maybe I did, and maybe I didn't,' he began. 'But a man who can draw his flintlock on a herd of cattle and a young girl is capable of anything. How d'you know he didn't kill Harbord?'

'For the very good reason that he was somewhere else when the murder was committed.'

'Ah, well, you always was one for the details, Luke.' He sniffed, and took a sup of ale. 'And what about my compensation then, for those milchers? Shall I take it up with your brother?'

Luke sighed inwardly: nothing, it seemed, could so much as dent the former mayor's iron-clad self-confidence.

'If you're in town early enough, you'll catch him tomorrow. The Blues have a drill in the morning; you can have a word with him while they're saddling up. Probably Colonel de Vere as well.'

'They'll be mustering at the New House, then, as usual?'

Pawling's turn of phrase seemed to snag something, deep in Luke's subconscious, that now began swiftly surfacing.

'What did you say?' he asked with sudden urgency, spilling some of the ale as he put down his mug. Pawling misinterpreted it as a flash of temper.

'Now Luke, I can tell you're upset...'

'No, I mean what did you say? Those words you used, just then?'

'The New House?'

'That's it. What did you mean?'

'Why, 'tis the name the students use for Christ Church, ain't it? You should know, if anyone.'

'We always just called it "The House" – no "New".'

'Ah well, 'twas most likely before your time, then. It was called the New House, 'cause it took the place of the Old House.'

Luke and Robshaw exchanged glances. The Old House! The appointed meeting-place in the letter they'd found in Harbord's inside pocket – maybe it was not a reference to the Houses of Parliament after all.

'And what was the Old House?'

'The old abbey, at Osney. 'Twas dissolved, see, when the

cathedral and college got built.' Into the pause that followed, Robshaw released an audible breath.

From their responses, Pawling evidently knew he was on to something, and – to give him credit – seemed keen to help. Probably the result of a guilty conscience, Luke thought darkly: even he must possess one, somewhere beneath the self-righteous carapace he presented to the world at large.

'You've seen that somewhere recently, then?' he said. 'Part of the investigation?' For all his bluster, he was a perceptive old so-and-so.

'It was on a note we found in Harbord's jacket. Referred to a meeting at the Old House. "Friday at dusk", wasn't it, Robshaw?'

'Aye, that it was.'

'Well, where is it then, this note?' the ex-mayor demanded. 'Let me take a look, maybe I can help to make sense of it?' Luke calculated for a moment. Annoying as he was, Pawling possessed sharp wits. Despite himself, he concluded there was nothing to lose.

'Very well. Robshaw, fetch the note from my desk drawer.'

'But my soup's here!' the deputy protested – and indeed their meal was just arriving.

'Keep it warm for him will you, Henry?'

'Whatever you say, Master Sandys,' the innkeeper replied. So, a grumbling Robshaw stalked off in the direction of the Guildhall to retrieve the letter.

Chapter 43
Behind the Bay Tree

The dying rays of the setting sun were picking out purple and orange patterns in the mackerel sky when Cate emerged on to Fish Street from her successful negotiation with Master Moreton at The Mermaid Tavern. From the direction of Bacon's Tower and the Cathedral, two familiar figures hove into view: a pair she recognised from her visits to The Unicorn and Jacob's Well. The thin, saturnine character invariably caused her a slight shudder, and she had consciously avoided catching his eye when calling to sell bread or cakes; but the other, well built and well dressed as he was, had immediately caught her attention as one of the first black men she had ever seen. Even seated at the table of an inn, he seemed to possess a certain vitality, and comfort in his own dark skin, which had simultaneously fascinated and disconcerted her. Now, his movement carried a lithe hint of menace, as if he were somehow lighter on his feet than someone of his bulk ought to be.

As they saw her, they turned to each other for a brief exchange of words and quickened their step, which she thought odd, for they had seemed to pay her little enough attention as she plied her wares. At that point, however, raised voices distracted her from across the road. She frowned. Three or four men were engaged in a 'brabble'. Such an encounter had led to Marcus's death. When would they ever learn? But the build-up to Parliament had brought new tensions to the streets, apparently convincing many that they could not afford to go abroad in the city unarmed. Curiously, the quarrel seemed to involve others wearing green ribbons in their hatbands, which she could just make out in the shadows, thereby identifying them with the same group as the two she had just seen.

Suddenly she felt a powerful hand grab her wrist and twist it roughly up behind her back, rocking her slightly backwards on her heels. She half-gasped, half-screamed, but the breath seemed to have been drained out of her lungs by the shock, so that the noise came out as a barely audible squeak. A hard, pointed object jabbed into the space between her shoulder blades and a deep voice spoke close to her right ear: 'Nice and quiet now, miss, and you won't get hurt.' With implacable strength, her captor half-pushed, half-carried her a short distance down Fish Street and, in a trice, turned right into a narrow yard abutting the New Inn.

'Hurry up, Francis, for God's sake,' a different voice piped up reedily from behind her. 'Someone'll see us.' Sure enough, at this, the pace quickened again, and Cate felt her feet intermittently lift off the ground entirely – all without apparent effort on the part of the man in whose iron grip she wriggled unavailingly.

'Please, sir, no!' she gasped, as they hurtled towards the shadowy end of the laneway. Through the dusk she could see bushes and undergrowth in front of what looked like an ivy-covered wall – what did they mean to do with her?

At the last moment, however, the owner of the second voice – whom she now recognised as the thin man from the Green Ribbon Club – dodged in front of them, drew a short rapier from his waistband and used it to hold back a tangled thicket of holly, bramble and hawthorn, revealing a door in the wall that was previously hidden from view. Quickly glancing behind to make sure they had not been followed, he felt in the pocket of his breeches and produced a key, turning this in the lock and impatiently ushering them through.

The space behind the door, about eight feet in depth and the

Oxford standard fifteen-foot width, had been left largely forgotten about in the course of several interlocking ownership disputes as the city expanded over the previous century. A resident of Queen Street had taken legal action to claim it as part of his property; but this was opposed by several other nearby freeholders, whose claims were also at odds with each other. Eventually, the original plaintiff wrote off the squabble as a waste of time and money, and simply built a back wall closer to the house, reasoning that, if he could not have the space, nobody would. On his near side – the far side from where the men now entered with Cate – he planted a bay. Left untended, the bush grew in time into a tree of substantial proportions, whose evergreen foliage permanently blocked the offending patch of land from his rear view.

There had been a door into it from New Inn Yard since the wall on that side was built in medieval times (when the alley was called Kepeharm Lane), but that, too was generally forgotten. However, someone had remembered it; that someone surreptitiously got the old lock cut out and a new one installed, and made a few discreet snips in the stems of the evergreen ivy to enable it to be opened; the obscure enclave was cleared of the choking vegetation that had filled it over long years of disuse – and now it was a very handy secret refuge from prying eyes.

Hidden by the high walls and the bay tree from being overlooked on any side, the space was now partially sheltered by a rudimentary pitched wooden roof, with a bench and chairs sitting on planks laid across the earth below. Cate was shoved roughly into one of the chairs and, as the big man caught his breath, the other squatted down so that his eyes were level with hers, an expression of sly menace on his face.

'Now then, miss,' he began. 'Catherine Alexandra Napper, of The Mitre. And the Roman Catholic Church.' He spat these last words. 'Named for Saint Catherine of Alexandria, the martyr.'

She nodded miserably. 'Thought you could keep it secret, with that little Papist prayer book, eh?' Cate trembled, the air reaching her lungs only in short, shallow breaths.

'Want to know how we knew? 'Twas sticking out of your pocket when you reached up to put those cakes on Unsworth's high shelf, and we grabbed it, quick as ninepence. So from then on, you were unmasked, see? There'll be a rosary and crucifix under that kerchief as well, unless I miss my guess?' She nodded again, as the thin man rose to his full height.

'Then there was Father Morris, of course.' Cate gasped. 'Oh, yes! Simeon Ignatius Morris – he's been on our watch list for years. Thought he could slip away by night without anyone noticing. But a priest's hat makes a pretty silhouette in the moonlight. Not hard to guess what he's been doing in the vaults under your inn.' They had grown too accustomed to the easy tolerance of their friends and neighbours in Oxford, she saw now. To these newcomers, their situation clearly looked very different.

'Someone's got to watch out for our liberties,' Settle went on. 'The authorities in Oxford obviously turn a blind eye to illegal rites and superstitious sacraments. So we've been looking out for you, on that corner. What a piece of luck that you were passing that way today, just as we had cause to be walking up!' What luck indeed, Cate thought bitterly.

'Well, you'll be staying here for a day or two.' He turned the key in the lock and returned it to his pocket. 'With us.'

'And you'd best keep quiet,' Francis added, his hand straying suggestively to the hilt of his sword. 'You get my meaning?' Once again, Cate nodded mutely.

Chapter 44
Deciphering a Letter

There was seldom any room for doubt when Robshaw arrived somewhere. Bursting through the door of The Golden Cross, he slightly caught his stave, dangling from his belt as it was, on one side of the doorframe, then overcompensated and nearly barged into a customer on the other. The second man performed a veritable feat of juggling to avoid dropping the two tankards he was carrying back from the bar. Agitated apologies followed, to the amusement of the watching Luke and Pawling. Still, allowances must be made: the deputy had, after all, been kept too long from his vittles, and – after his master shot a meaningful glance at Hadfield – a steaming bowl was duly set down in front of him as he shambled on to a bar stool at the counter.

'Well?' Luke demanded.

'Well what?' Robshaw regarded him suspiciously, spoon poised on its way from the surface of the warm fluid to his lips.

'The letter, man!'

'Oh aye. Here 'tis.' He pulled it from his inside coat pocket and Luke opened it out in front of Pawling.

'Ah – magpies,' the ex-mayor said straight away.

'Yes – we thought they might be a coat of arms, in that pattern.'

'You did,' Robshaw corrected him, through a mouthful of soup-dunked bread.

'Well – it could be another connection with the abbey,' Pawling continued.

'How so?'

'D'you not know the story? The abbey was built by old Robert D'Oyly, see, right back in the time of King Henry – the first one. Well, this Robert married a woman, name of Edith, but before that, she'd been Henry's mistress.'

'I see.'

'Anyway, they're crossing Osney meadow one day, and she sees a flock of magpies. Well, you know they're reckoned to make a scolding sound: so when she hears it, she fancies they're scolding her, as a sign from God, for living a sinful life. So she says to her husband, do you build an abbey here, Robert, to atone for the sin.'

Luke listened intently to Pawling's tale. It did resonate with far-off recollections of hearing similar accounts in childhood, but he had not dredged up such material from his memory banks in a long time.

'It points to someone with local knowledge,' he mused. 'We initially thought – sorry Robshaw, I thought – the "House" must refer to the House of Commons, at Westminster.'

''Course, you'd know the old rhyme, Luke – "one for sorrow", an' all that?'

'Aye – "one for sorrow, two for joy; three for a girl and four for a boy". And there's four of them in the picture. But what could a boy have to do with Harbord's murder?' At this, the men shook their heads.

'Well, I must take my leave,' Pawling said, as he finished his drink and stood up. 'There was one more thing.'

'Oh yes?'

'Struck me straight away when I took a look at that body. Where was his dagger?'

'Dagger? He didn't have one.'

'Aye, that's right: he didn't have one. Wonder why not. He was a quarrelsome sort of customer, by all accounts, this Harbord?'

'You could say that.'

'Why, if I'd have been him, I wouldn't have cared to go about in Oxford this week without a weapon for self-defence, if it came to that. And yet he never had one. His belt was undone – 'twas almost as though someone'd taken his dagger off him.' Pawling evidently enjoyed the impact of his words. 'Well, goodnight, sirs.'

Robshaw put down his spoon in the bowl with a clatter.

'Right good that, Henry. Hit the spot, and no mistake.' As the innkeeper cleared away the things, he turned to Luke. 'What d'you make of that, then?'

'Interesting, about the weapon. I thought he'd just undone his belt to ease the pressure as he bled out – but I suppose it's possible that someone removed his dagger and scabbard.'

'And why would someone do that?'

'No idea. What about the magpies?'

'Well, I'd heard that about the abbey, that's what they told us when we was kids.'

'Me too. And "four for a boy"?'

'That an' all. But I can't see how that comes into it, neither.'

The pair bade Hadfield goodnight, and returned to The Unicorn and Jacob's Well to find Tim Blount, whom they had left on guard, in discussion with two of the University proctors, then just coming on duty for the night watch. Luke left Robshaw to sort that one out, and called in again at The Mitre on his way home. The stricken faces of Cate's parents told their own story: one by one, the search parties had returned with nothing but mumbled apologies and blank reports. That their daughter now looked certain to be missing for the night put a different complexion on her disappearance. He offered the few inadequate words of comfort that came to mind, and left them to what would no doubt be a sleepless vigil.

When he reached Magpie Lane, Luke found Elizabeth and Joan skeining wool by the light from the fire in the hall.

'Still up, wife? 'Tis late, indeed.'

Deftly winding the yarn around the back of a small dining chair the children had used when they began sitting up at the table, she looked him full in the face. 'Can you wonder, Luke Sandys? There's a man been stabbed, and the stabber is still abroad, somewhere. My husband's trying to find him. So what's this man like to do, when you catch up with him?'

'We can't sleep, master, as long as you're out of the house, 'tis the truth,' Joan added.

'Why, come now, there's no reason to worry. We're all looking for him, remember, not just me.' Luke took a taper from the fire and lit a sconce of candles. In turning, he caught the warm shade of the wool in the light.

'Is that from my good red cloak? I wore that this winter!'

'Begging your pardon, husband, but you did not. 'Tis high time the yarn was put to good use.'

The servant stood to pour two cups of canary and then – as Luke nodded in answer to her enquiring glance – a third for herself. He gave them an abridged account of the investigation, concluding with the magpies: 'four for a boy.'

'I do hope all goes well with our boy,' Elizabeth said wistfully, as she wound the last of the thread.

'Sam? He'll be fine. He's found a good place.'

'I know. But I can't help worrying about him.'

Almost despite himself, Luke felt the old impulse to ease his wife's anxieties – even those he knew to be groundless. 'Roger's not far away. I could write and ask him to look in now and again.'

Elizabeth brightened. The couple knew their son-in-law – who held a senior post at the Admiralty – was a substantial figure in his own right. She put her hand on his arm and looked at him again, this time with a gratified warmth. 'Thank you, Luke.'

He finished his drink; Elizabeth lifted off the skein of wool for Joan to put away, and they all turned in for the night.

Chapter 45
'What do you plan to do with me?'

Cate rubbed her arm and felt the circulation slowly returning to normal, along with her breathing. Calculation now vied for her attention with the initial shock, outrage and terror of her abduction. She must be on the lookout for any chance to raise the alarm – or even escape. And, for that, she must try to keep a clear head, and remain the mistress of her feelings. Before twilight deepened into full darkness, she snatched a sidelong glance at her captors. Each had his blade drawn and resting on his knee: a military-looking sabre, in the case of the larger man, and the shorter sword from Settle's thin scabbard.

Presently, Francis broke the silence.

'I'll go and get us some provisions.'

The other handed him the key.

'Don't be long.'

When, presently, the black man returned, he handed her a halfpenny loaf of bread and a ceramic bottle of small beer.

'Might as well eat and drink something,' he said, before he and his companion got stuck into their meal.

'Thank you, sir,' she replied softly. No point antagonising them – she would need the men to drop their guard at some point; so, she reckoned, she had best make herself appear as pliant and innocuous as possible.

Francis drew a tinderbox from his pocket and she heard the clicking of stone on steel before presently the tinder caught and he lit a candle. In the sudden glow, Cate took the opportunity for a quick, unobtrusive look at her surroundings. The oddest sight, which caused her an involuntary shudder, was of a full-sized cartwheel – newly made, by the look of it – leaning against the far end of the shed. It was an object seared deep into her consciousness: as Settle correctly guessed, she was one of many Roman Catholic girls named after Catherine of Alexandria, who was killed by being tied to a cartwheel with blades attached to it. On the window ledge of her room in the cockloft of The Mitre she had a small framed picture of the saint, who was always shown with a wheel to commemorate her martyrdom.

'Did you get that all down, then, what Norton was saying at the end of the meeting earlier?' Francis asked.

'Let me check,' the other replied, feeling in his coat pocket as he took a sup from his bottle of small beer. 'Wait... it's not here!'

'What's not?'

'My wallet, where I file my notes.'

'Well, where is it then?'

'I had it back at the inn... curse it! I must have dropped it there. Probably when we got up to leave.'

''God's sake, Settle. 'Twas careless, indeed – given what's written in there. You've never set down my name in those notes?'

'Why would I – you never speak in any meetings,' the other replied hotly.

'Sshhh!' Francis hurriedly put the candle on the floor and held up his hand for quiet. A moment passed while both men satisfied themselves no one was listening. 'Keep your voice down,' he hissed. 'It's definitely not in here somewhere?' The pair spent some moments checking all over the confined area they shared with their captive.

'You'll have to go back for it,' Francis said, as he held the lantern aloft.

'You mean you'll have to,' Settle retorted. 'That's what we're paying you for.' The other scowled, but merely said:

'I'll slip down there and take a look when we've finished eating.'

Round and round in Cate's mind went the questions she did not yet dare to ask aloud. 'Why are you holding me? What do you plan to do with me?' At least her immediate fear, on being pushed through the door into a confined space – that they would force themselves on her – had receded for the moment. To be closeted with two strange men was an injury to her virtue in itself; but surely no one would hold it against her, as she was not here by choice? They obviously intended to keep her alive, at least for the time being – else, why would they take the trouble to feed her? On the other hand, they had not concealed their faces, or even their names; which, she realised, would put her in a position to identify and give evidence against them – if she survived. But this train of thought merely gave rise to still-worse forebodings that she resolved to suppress for the moment as useless to her quest.

The nine o'clock bell for the student curfew, ringing out from just down the road at Christ Church, roused Cate from an intermittent doze, to the dismal realisation that her poor parents would by now be frantic with worry as they contemplated a night without knowing her whereabouts. She crossed herself and – clasping the crucifix through her kerchief – began to mouth the words of her litany, for comfort and support.

'Glory be to the Father, and to the Son, and to the Holy Spirit,' she recited silently. 'As it was in the beginning, is now, and ever shall be.'

A few minutes later, Francis rose to go out again, leaving her no nearer clarity, either on the mysteries of her captivity or on any plan to escape it. As the door closed behind him, she looked furtively at Settle, who was apparently staring at the wall oppo-

site. He lacked the unassailable physical strength of his min-
der, that much was clear from his narrow shoulders and pigeon
chest. She clenched her fists in a rush of anger. That this... this
pipsqueak dared to draw his blade on her, and address her in that
impertinent manner! To think what her father, or Luke Sandys,
would do to him if they were here. Why, Master Ingram, the
ostler, could snap him in two like a twig. With the advantage
of surprise, could she even overpower him herself? But these
musings were cut short by a scratching of the key in the lock,
heralding the other man's abrupt return.

'No good,' he reported. 'Door's still guarded.'

'What – by that constable? You might just have to knock him
over the head.'

'Two proctors there now an' all. Looks like they're settled in
for the night.'

Chapter 46
Morning at Magpie Lane

Luke finally snapped decisively into consciousness at first light after a disjointed sleep. Long periods of wakefulness had alternated with confused visions of boys, daggers, Africans, magpies bedecked in green ribbons, and Cate's receding form – always just out of reach – as the Osney Abbey ruins loomed on the horizon. A nightmare: or 'night-mayor', to use Robshaw's name for Robert Pawling. To think, the wretched man was still haunting his dreams, six months after leaving office.

A faint noise from downstairs told him Ed was up and about, so he went to join his brother in the kitchen, together with Joan, who was, it seemed, in a better mood this morning.

'Ah, but 'tis good to see you two boys both here again,' she told them, beaming. 'Remember when you used to come in from playing outside, and I'd give you tatie cakes off o' the roasting plate, with butter?'

'Aye, indeed, Joan. My mouth's watering, just thinking about it,' Ed replied. 'What've you got for us this morning?'

'Why, I set aside Master Luke's portion of mutton, when he never came in last night, so I've sliced that up for you both, and warmed it up nice in its juice, just how you like it.'

'Can't wait.'

'And I've kept you something else, an' all.'

Joan steadied her ageing wrist to lift a bowl from the pantry on to the table, and removed the upturned plate that was laid on top of it, to reveal coffee – not fresh, but welcome nonetheless. 'Brought round from Jacob's last night before they closed up. Stir some of that honey into it, and it'll put the skin on your back like velvet, so it will.'

'Thank you Joan. I needed this,' Luke said, tucking in to the meat along with a hunk of soft bread.

'You seem troubled, master,' the old woman said, narrowing her eyes. 'You've been working too hard again.'

'Why, we have much to investigate, and too few leads.'

'Ah well, you never know where a door will open. That's what my old Ma used to say: you never know where a door will open.' She nodded sagely, then left the men to munch their breakfast in peace.

'So, you'll have Gregory back with you for training today.' Luke pushed aside his empty plate, breaking off to call to the cook-maid, who was busying herself in the pantry: 'Do you need to wash these dishes, Joan?'

'Ach, I'll do it later. Can't be arsed right now,' she called back, and the brothers caught each other's eye with a grin. 'Anyway, Gregory: we had to let him go,' Luke continued.

'Yes, I was wondering about that. How come the evidence against him didn't hold up, then: the bits of cloth from his coat?'

'Well, last night, Pawling more or less admitted to me that he'd planted them on Harbord's body.'

'No! Because Gregory stampeded his cattle?'

Luke nodded.

'And he wanted to get him into trouble, not just in the regiment.'

'So what did he have to say for himself, when you confronted him?'

'Oh, the man's unembarrassable. Just changed the subject. In fact you might get a visit from him this morning. He'll have stayed in town last night above his shop, and he's still after compensation for his livestock.'

'Cheek of him!'

'Yes, he's completely brazen. This is what we had to contend with all the time, when he was mayor. Although he did actually suggest one or two other leads that might be useful. Robshaw and I ran into him, drinking at The Golden Cross.'

'Not The Mitre?'

'No – you remember Catherine Napper, the innkeeper's daughter?'

'Yes, of course.'

Ed studied his brother closely. He'd heard Luke mention her, and was too astute an observer not to notice the faraway look that came into his eye as he did so.

'Well, they closed The Mitre last night because she went missing.'

'I'm sorry to hear that. You know her well, don't you?'

Luke took a deep breath.

'I investigated the killing of her husband, about eighteen months back. He was stabbed in a brawl. So yes, I... I got to know Cate then.'

'This is more than just a matter of duty, then?' Ed persisted.

Luke cleared his throat to cover his discomfiture. Was it that obvious?

'Let's just say I'm very keen to get her back.'

'Well, I'm sure you know what you're doing,' his brother replied.

'They had search parties out, but if she's still not turned up this morning, we'll have to raise a proper hue and cry.' Men from all over the city would turn out, dividing up the streets between them and setting out to knock on every door, with the constables in charge of leading and coordinating the search.

'Well, that'll bring her back safe and sound, surely?'

Luke nodded, but swallowed and looked away before once again catching his brother's eye.

'There's something else. She's Catholic.'

Ed sat back in his seat and nodded.

'Ah. I can see why you'd be worried in that case. Might be tied up with this Harbord business?'

'I suppose we can only hope not, but it seems possible, yes.'

'In that case, Luke, you'd better hurry up and catch the killer. Plenty of men are blaming it on "Papists", as you'll know.'

'I'm not having people picked on, Ed. Not just because they happen to praise God in a different way. 'Tis wrong.'

As he waved his brother off into the morning chill – the hands on the pendulum clock in the hall pointing up the hour at a quarter after seven – Luke resolved to calm himself with a session in his workshop. In fact, he had tiptoed in there last night after the women had gone to bed and he found that sleep did not come directly; whereupon he had lit a candle and glued the frame into place around Millington's portrait. Now all that remained was to add the gold leaf and seal it with a layer of varnish. With daylight flooding in through the great east-facing window, he worked quickly, enjoying the sureness of touch and steadiness of hand that still returned readily at his command.

As Luke brushed the adhesive, or 'gilding size', onto the wood and pressed the delicate gold layer into the nooks and crannies of the gadrooned surface, a set of connections began to stand out from the crowded landscape of the past week's events: connections that sent a chill through his very marrow. Cate had been due at home towards dusk, which meant she would have been making her way down Fish Street at about the time Settle and his accomplice were fleeing The Unicorn and Jacob's Well, after Unsworth's murder. A coincidence? How often had he admonished Robshaw, in the course of an investigation, that there was no such thing; that the relations of cause and effect were merely waiting to be established? Ed had named out loud the suspicion that had been gnawing away at him all night:

that Cate's disappearance and Harbord's murder were somehow linked. Could the two Green Ribbon men be the connection?

When they'd met over coffee, he'd withheld details, he now realised, of the club and its anti-Catholic extremism, instead couching his warning in general terms. Had he even specified the inn where they met, and where Harbord's body had been found? In sparing her the full distasteful truth – that a band of zealots were in Oxford, stirring sectarian fears and plotting, as he now knew, to depose the King in favour of a pretender willing to crack down even harder on dissent – had he inadvertently deprived Cate of information that could have kept her safe?

Settle might well have enquired after the eye-catching young woman who brought the baskets of bread and cakes, and been told she was from The Mitre – and, while the Nappers made sure to observe the legal requirement to show themselves at an established church on a Sunday, their private adherence to the old faith was well known locally, if generally unremarked. The sacraments still administered and received below ground level were a different matter, of course. Could Settle have got wind of them somehow? And could he and the well-dressed blackamoor have intercepted Cate yesterday evening? If so, was she, in fact, with them at this very moment, as their captive?

It scarcely bore thinking about – and yet, having been thought, it could not now be un-thought. In fact, given the so far unexplained nature of her disappearance, it might even be the strongest lead. Luke held Millington's portrait up to the light and tilted it this way and that, to inspect the varnish. Having satisfied himself that it was smooth and even, he carefully set down the finished picture to dry. If he could snatch half an hour later, he would take it over to All Souls College that very day and hand it to the Sedleian Professor in person. First, though, he had a hue and cry to raise.

Chapter 47
Caraway Cake for Breakfast

Several times during a chilly night of at best occasional dozing sleep, Cate had been dimly aware of the men getting up and emptying their bladders in a corner of the enclosed yard. She thanked God she had thought to bring her shawl, which she wrapped tightly round her, and kept warm by drawing up her knees into her chest. Now, though, she too had to relieve herself. To the warbling accompaniment of a pre-dawn blackbird, she gingerly stretched her legs and sat forward, craning her neck to check the extent of slumber among her captors. Settle was slumped forward, but with a slight jump she noticed the whites of Francis's eyes fixed disconcertingly on her through the gloom. He half-rose as she straightened up, but – as she conveyed with a gesture her need for a private moment – the big fellow resumed his seat with a barely audible grunt.

Looking down in the corner the men had been using, she could just about make out a length of concave ceramic guttering that had been countersunk into the ground, leading down a slight incline to a hole in the far wall. There was even a half-full pail of water nearby, to wash away the waste. They were well prepared, indeed, to encamp themselves here. Having successfully squatted and sluiced, Cate found a bar of soap resting on a ledge, and used it to wash her hands in the remaining water. As she wiped them on her skirt, she felt a pang of hunger, though she knew they had finished all the provisions Francis had brought in the previous night.

Returning to her chair, her eyes alighted on her twin baskets. Of course – she still had a few caraway cakes that she never got

233

to sell. Her gratification rapidly gave way to calculation: if she was hungry, it followed that the others would be, too. Could she use this situation to sow division between them? Francis had grabbed her and carried her off with despatch and efficiency, but from what she had gleaned of the relationship and arrangement between them, he was merely fulfilling his part of a bargain struck for payment. That did not excuse his behaviour, but since then he had at least dealt with her impartially, so far as was compatible with maintaining the secrecy and security of her captivity – and his demeanour appeared relatively relaxed. Settle, who for the moment remained in uneasy slumber, was evidently motivated by a deeply felt hatred, compounded by the stress and strain of being on guard to avoid detection. There would be no possibility of plying him to softness.

Cate eased herself back into her chair and reached for the basket with the cakes in it, making just enough sound to attract the black man's attention, but – she hoped – not enough to rouse his paymaster; not yet, anyway. She made a show of pausing halfway through the act of reaching in to pull out a cake, and looking up to catch Francis's eye – which, as before, was turned on her. Deliberately, she extended the basket, and he leaned forward and took one of the cakes with an impassive expression, but a nod of gratitude. So far, so good: now for part two of her scheme. As she reclined, she simultaneously pulled the chair forward slightly, making a squeak on the wooden boards beneath. Sure enough, Settle gave a slight start, and looked around him as he blinked himself awake.

''Morning,' Francis pronounced indistinctly through a mouthful of cake.

'What the Devil...? What are you eating?' the thin man hissed.

'One of her cakes,' the other replied.

'What, you've taken food, from her?' He rose and dashed the

cake from Francis's hand. 'She's your prisoner, man, not your personal confectioner!'

The big man popped the last corner of cake left between his fingers into his mouth.

'You ought to calm down, Settle. We've a time to wait here yet.'

'Calm down? I'll give you "calm down"!' He drew his sword, turning to Cate. 'As for you, Papist trull, you'll sit there and keep quiet!'

'Indeed, I was quiet, sir,' Cate replied. 'I offered my basket to Master Francis without a word.' This seemed to inflame him even further, however.

'Silence!' Settle roared in her face – or rather, he would have roared, if he had not suddenly remembered that he, too, was supposed to be keeping quiet. As it was, the sound came out as a strangled half-yelp, half-whisper, the effort of which raised him on his toes and flushed his sallow complexion. Cate shrank from the uncontrolled animosity that raged in his eyes – but she was gratified, as she heard Settle's breathing slowly return to normal, that she had succeeded in giving the tensions between them a further twist. She could only hope for them eventually to yield some advantage that could help to get her out of her current predicament.

Chapter 48
Hue and Cry

Word had travelled fast that a young local woman had been abducted, apparently by two men from out of town: a situation that evidently gripped the city's imagination, as there was a good turnout for the search. Any man who'd beheld Cate in person for more than a fleeting moment, Luke thought, would need a heart of stone not to feel at least some stirrings of gallantry on her behalf.

Mayor Bowell mopped his brow and cleared his throat as he stood on the dais in front of the crowd, who'd been ushered into the Guildhall's main meeting chamber for the occasion.

'Now see here,' he began ineffectually.

Calvert piped up, 'Pray silence for the Mayor!' and the hubbub began to subside.

'This here's a hue and cry,' Bowell announced, 'to look for young Cate Napper from The Mitre, who's been missing since last night. Her father's here, and they're all sorely vexed, like: praying for her safe return.' Luke stood by his side, flanked by Jim Napper. The Mayor looked down at him, evidently in need of reminding what to say next.

'The London men, sir,' Luke whispered.

'Oh aye, 'tis reckoned she might've been taken by two London men. Dangerous characters, by all accounts. One's a blackamoor, if you can believe that. The same pair murdered Ged Unsworth, keeper of that there new tavern down the way. Stabbed him, so 'tis said.' He paused again as the men looked at him expectantly. 'Well, Luke Sandys here'll be in charge, as usual. You'll report to him. Do your best, sirs, 'tis all we can ask.' And, with that, he swept up Calvert and beat a hasty retreat.

It was gratifying to see such a large number of volunteers, including some of the city's well-known merchants and craftsmen. Whether they would be so keen tomorrow – Saturday, the main market day of the week – was debatable. For Cate's absence to extend through a second night was, however, something Luke devoutly wished to avoid in any case. Surely they would find her that day – and, if he was right about Settle's involvement, the trap he was planning to set for the pamphleteer should also lead him to Cate. He'd deployed two new constables to relieve Tim Blount on guard duty outside The Unicorn and Jacob's Well, but some time that afternoon he would slip back in and replace the wallet where they'd found it. Then, come nightfall, they'd stand the guard down, and, from a safe distance, watch and wait.

One notable absentee, as the Mayor was speaking, was Robshaw – but now, as Luke briefly filled in more details to go with Bowell's sketchy introduction, the deputy made his customary noisy entrance and stood at the back, puffing out his cheeks as he caught his master's eye.

'So, we'll divide into four teams,' Luke concluded, 'each one under a constable, who'll report to me. A team for each point of the compass – east along the High Street and into Holywell; north, to include St Giles; south, down Fish Street and the streets on the south side of the High, and west – Ronald Cox'll be in charge of that one, in St Ebbe's parish.' The so-named constable nodded. 'Ron, you might start by talking to your brother. I saw the two men we're looking for in his yard yesterday morning, looked as if they were buying a cartwheel off him.' Cox nodded again.

'I'll set up an office in here for the day, so if any of you get any information at all, please bring it here straight away.'

As the men dispersed, Robshaw bustled over to where Luke was standing.

'Where've you been?' the Chief Officer asked curtly.

'Sleepless night, sir.'

'Well, we all have those – but there's work to be done, man! You're liaison, you know that.'

Robshaw's role on these occasions was as a progress-chaser: roaming the streets and stopping the search teams as he met them, asking what they'd seen and heard, then getting them to report in to Luke if there was anything that might be significant. But he seemed more than usually agitated.

''Tis that there writing,' he said.

'You're not making sense, Robshaw. What writing?'

'In that wallet, what Settle dropped at The Unicorn.'

'Ah – I see. And?'

'Well, I knew I'd seen it somewhere before, like, and I was awake half the night trying to remember where.'

He had Luke's interest now, all right.

'And did you remember?'

'Aye – d'you mind that case we had the year before last, of the estate manager for Sir Thomas Spencer?'

'Yes – the forestalling case. Go on.' Spencer was a baronet with a splendid manor house at Yarnton, to the north of Oxford, and a generous swathe of valuable farmland that was, however, encumbered by inherited debt. His estate manager, a Paul Woolston, had been accused of 'forestalling': hoarding wheat and planning to release it on to the market later at an inflated price. Sir Thomas himself was suspected of masterminding the scheme; being, it was supposed, hungry for revenues to service his debts.

'Well, there was them two fellers what came up from London to write about it for the mercuries,' Robshaw went on. The affair had aroused keen political interest as one that might lead to Sir Thomas's downfall in public life and resignation from the House of Commons, where he stood out as a staunch supporter of the Crown.

'That's right. But the judge didn't like that, did he? Got us to remove them from the court.'

'Aye, and to confisticate their notebooks.'

'Confiscate, you mean.'

'Whatever. Anyhow, that's what they was writing, them there squiggles, same as Settle!' he finished triumphantly.

'Well that is interesting, Robshaw, well done. Anything else you remember?'

'Tacky graphy. That's what they called it. Tacky graphy.'

'Ah – tachygraphy. I've heard of it, of course. I don't know how to read it, but I can think of two men who probably can.'

'Who's that, then, sir?'

'The Bobs.'

'What – them clerks at the Bodleian?' Robshaw sounded doubtful.

'Yes, indeed. They're in charge of making transcripts of parliamentary debates, they'd deal with tachygraphy all the time. I'll take the wallet over there a bit later and have them take a look – thank you. Now, you'd best join in the search.'

'Yessir!'

Chapter 49
More Trouble on the Way

No sooner had Robshaw left to take up his roving brief for the day than Sandys received a deputation of Captain Sutherland, aide-de-camp to Colonel Russell, commander of the Royal Foot Guards, and – walking behind the officer and wearing his trademark sardonic half-smile – the intelligence-gatherer for the Lord Chancellor, whom Luke now knew as 'Tom'.

'I'll come straight to the point,' Sutherland began in characteristic clipped tones. 'You're to report to Christ Church this afternoon to represent the City at a command performance for His Majesty.'

As Luke made to demur – didn't these people realise he had a major operation on his hands? – the captain cut in.

'Colonel's orders. It's been agreed with the Mayor.' The tone was neutral, but Luke knew there was no way out of it.

'What does he want me there for?'

'Security, man! Can't take any risks – if the mob start to gather outside, we'll need some local knowledge on hand.'

'Very well. What is it this time, then – another drama?'

The officer drew a folded sheet of paper from inside his tunic and held it somewhat disdainfully up to the light.

'Says here, this one's a "dramatic opera". Theodosius, by a chap called Henry Purcell. Can't say I've heard of him.' He replaced the paper in his pocket. 'So, I'll come and call for you later.'

Luke nodded.

Tom watched in evident amusement as the captain turned

abruptly on his heel, tucked his cane under his arm and stalked off out of the Guildhall with a stiff military gait.

'Have to hand it to the Guards – they do a jolly impressive march-past,' he said. 'So – any progress with your murder?'

'Could be. We're looking for the pamphleteer of the Green Ribbon Club, Elkanah Settle, and a big fellow, a blackamoor, who was with him. We reckon they must've killed the innkeeper, Unsworth, to stop him telling us something that would have pointed to them as the men who killed Harbord as well.'

'I see,' the other replied. 'I wondered if the two could be connected.'

'So it looks as if they got wind of Harbord's treachery, as you were saying.'

Tom nodded silently to himself.

'Very well. Good luck with finding them. Meanwhile, there's something else you should know.'

'Oh, yes?' Were there to be yet more political twists and turns in the background?

'You have a troublemaker on the way. Chap called Stephen College, due to arrive in Oxford this evening, according to my source.'

'We've got plenty of troublemakers in town already, from what I've seen.'

'Not like this one. College is known as "The Protestant Joiner". Carpenter by trade, at least originally. These days he's a kind of all-purpose political agitator. Got a new cause with the Popish Plot. Writes songs, pamphlets, makes rabble-rousing speeches, that sort of thing. Goes about in full plate armour, like a medieval knight.' Luke's eyebrows rose in surprise. 'I know – but seeing is believing, as they say. He's quite a sight.'

'What does he want in Oxford, then?'

'Well... Put it like this. Parliament opens on Monday, so

this weekend is when the build-up to Parliament reaches a crescendo. If the Green Ribbons are going to try something, some kind of stunt, say, that's when they'll do it. And it could be connected with College.'

'Could be?'

'That's all I know at the moment. Of course, they're natural allies. I've got sources trying to find out more. If I get wind of anything that could affect the peace in Oxford, I'll let you know.'

'Thank you.' And, with that, the spy quietly slipped out.

Luke sat and pinched his lower lip, luxuriating in a rare opportunity for uninterrupted thought as the cavernous council chamber was suddenly empty. He was somewhat surprised at himself: he had intended to tell Tom about Settle's document wallet when he next showed up. Now the chance had come and gone, he had a nagging sense that he had failed in his duty by not doing so. Why hadn't he, then? Luke pulled absent-mindedly at a button of his jacket. If he was being honest: he needed the wallet as bait in the trap for Settle, because Settle probably had Cate. Once she was safe, that would be the time to render evidence of possible treason to the appropriate authorities. He stood, and began pacing around the perimeter of the capacious chamber. At the window, he paused and looked down on the street below. Within a couple of minutes, he had spotted two men he considered friends, and several others he knew by name. Wasn't this where his duty lay – to his own community and his own heart?

Moreover, the pamphleteer would likely prove a cunning and resourceful enemy. He was of a type Luke had rarely met: of no account physically, yet when he had spoken out from the back of The Unicorn and Jacob's Well, men had fallen silent to listen to him. The constables had already, that week, rescued one young woman from harm's way; but Gregory, though a thoroughly bad lot in Luke's opinion, at least wore his ill nature straightforwardly in his scowl and his impulsive rages. Settle, in contrast, was a subtle, calculating creature, whose intervention, at his and Robshaw's second encounter with the Green Ribbons, struck just the right note of innuendo to get under their skin. As long as only the two of them knew about the wallet and its contents, Luke had something that could potentially be held over him; something that might be needed to get Settle to cooperate.

Chapter 50
'Come back with the blades, once 'tis dark'

Settle at that moment was pacing up and down the confined space within the walled-in oubliette at the end of New Inn Yard, as Francis watched imperturbably and Cate looked down to avoid eye contact. Suddenly, there came a series of knocks at the door, in a rhythm she recognised as belonging to a popular patriotic song:

Here's a health unto His Majesty,
With a fa la la la la la la,
Confusion to his enemies,
With a fa la la la la la la.
And he who would not drink his health,
We wish him neither wit nor wealth,
Nor yet a rope to hang himself.
With a fal lal la la la la la la la la,
With a fal lal la la la la la.

Before the tattoo reached the last syllable of 'enemies', however, Settle had strode over to the door and started to turn the key in the lock. After he opened it, a hurried, whispered conversation followed, as she strained to hear.

'You're sure no one saw you?'

'Nay – take this, quickly, then we can get back. 'Tis a hue and cry: there's men out everywhere.'

'Tell Hawkins to come with the blades, once 'tis dark.'

'Aye, will do.' Whereupon the door shut and the key turned once more. Settle opened the box of provisions – for such it was – and set it down on the floorboards between his and Francis's chairs.

'Help yourself,' he growled to his henchman.

'What about her?' Francis inclined his head in Cate's direction.

'No point wasting good food and drink,' the pamphleteer sneered. Cate was not surprised. Anyway, it was not all that long since the caraway cake, and she still had one left in the basket: she could take a quick bite later, if necessary, while Settle was not looking.

Her mind turned to the whispered exchange at the doorway. Blades? Had she heard aright? And the reference to darkness: they obviously planned to stay in here for another night. Surely it would occur to one of the constables, or a volunteer in the hue and cry, to take a closer look at the bushes and ivy at the end of New Inn Yard? With a bit more luck, the men who'd brought the supplies would have been spotted. Perhaps 'Hawkins', whoever he was, would be careless, and give them away – although it would be dark by then, so less likely.

It occurred to her suddenly that her abduction was part of a plot involving the active participation of a considerable number of co-conspirators. The men apparently engaged in a noisy quarrel, who had distracted her at the crucial moment on Fish Street, were almost certainly in on it too. The realisation served only to sharpen her forebodings about what they could possibly have in store for her. What if she were to cry out for help? Her captors had made it abundantly clear that such a step would be met with violence – but how could that worsen the plight she was in already? Should she risk it? She might be lucky, and someone within earshot might raise the alarm: but then, on the other hand, she might not; and, every time she considered it, that possibility was, in the end, more than she could bear.

Chapter 51
Calling on the Professor

The search yielded early dividends with a snippet of information that seemed to support Luke's assumptions about what had happened the previous night. Robshaw's unmistakable heavy tread at the door of the Guildhall chamber pulled him out of the brown study into which he had lapsed over the matter of the wallet.

'Settle and his mate have gone missing,' the deputy announced excitedly. 'Ron Cox was told, by a landlady over in St Ebbe's – they never came back last night to their lodgings.'

'Ah, thank you, Robshaw. Well that confirms what we already thought: when they left The Unicorn, they went into hiding.'

'Perhaps they left town?'

'Unlikely. No one saw them from the city walls. No, they must be somewhere here.'

'And we got the black feller's name an' all – Jack Francis.'

'Right, thanks. Must have picked that up in England.' Thinking of Joan, he guessed: 'Perhaps descended from a freed slave, off a ship.'

'Jack Francis' – the name meant nothing, not to Luke at any rate. When – if – he saw Tom again, he could ask about him. The 'black feller' was a different proposition than Settle himself, for sure. Looked like he might be ex-military. Maybe he could ask Ed to come along – perhaps even with one of his fellow officers – when the moment came to apprehend the pair? If the show of force was sufficient to leave no doubt that any attempt at resistance was futile, it could save a lot of trouble. Yes: he would call in at Christ Church later and see his brother. For that to work, though, they had to catch the scoundrels. Where could they be?

'You take over here for a while, then,' he said to Robshaw.

'Where are you going?'

'I have to see Sir Thomas Millington, at All Souls. He's off to London any day now, I don't want to miss him. Anyway, it means you can sit in here for the rest of the day.'

'Very well – as long as I can nip over the road first, for coffee.'

'Coffee?'

'Or maybe a jug of ale. And a cake.'

An uneventful interval having elapsed, he duly returned from the New Inn with his half-eaten snack, and Luke set off along Blue Boar Street before turning left up Magpie Lane.

'That you, Luke? How's it going then?' Elizabeth called down as he crossed the threshold.

'Too soon to tell,' he replied. 'Plenty of men out, though.' His wife descended the staircase somewhat unsteadily, mopping at the corner of her mouth with a handkerchief.

'Have you been at the canary again, dear? 'Tis early for that, indeed.'

'Well, I've got no company here, till Celia comes this afternoon. What with you being out on constable duty all the time.' Luke's and Robshaw's wives, having met once at a civic function, had become firm friends, and met regularly to pore over their embroidery and take coffee. For now, though, she had evidently been indulging her appetite for stronger liquor.

'You've got those eyeglasses for her?' Luke had purchased a pair of spectacles some time back, and was impressed with the difference they made in his ability to discern the fine details of a picture frame; so he had arranged for the two ladies to receive a pair each as well, to help them follow their stitching.

'Aye, thank you, husband,' she assented, and – seeing that he was busy – left him to it.

Luke went through to his workshop, quickly ascertained that the varnish on his frame was dry, then wrapped a length of muslin around the picture and tied it in place with string. He let himself out of the house, and began whistling a jaunty air as he turned right towards the High Street. He pulled himself up short at the incongruity, with Cate still missing – only to resume as, he reasoned, he deserved half an hour away from his troubles and his duty, to enjoy a moment he had long antici-pated with pleasure.

He rashly nipped in front of an eastbound carriage on the way across the High, waving an apology at the driver as one of the horses shied, and stepped briskly up through the portico of All Souls. It was like entering a haven from the hustle and bustle outside. Greeting the porter, Luke paused to admire the carved stone ceiling of the lodge, with its symmetrically arranged intri-cate bosses, before entering the quadrangle and knocking on the first door to the right. The duck-egg blue half-moon of the college sundial – commissioned from Christopher Wren during his Fellowship, a quarter of a century earlier – glinted down from its perch, high on the wall of the medieval chapel. Presently, the door was opened by a young man who ushered Luke inside.

'Luke, dear boy. Greetings. You've just caught me.' Milling-ton's good-natured voice rang out from the far side of the room. How typical of the man that, through his rise to greatness, he had never forsaken old friends, or given himself airs and graces. He wore his eminence lightly.

'Thank you, Babbington,' the Sedleian Professor addressed the young man, 'you can finish packing those boxes, then you'd better get back to writing up results, eh?' Seeing Luke's quizzi-cal look, he explained: 'An undergraduate – taking a course in botany this term. Looks after me, God bless him, in between his studies: there's a task, d'you know?'

Sure enough, Millington's rooms were in some degree of chaos. Books had been taken down from his shelves and were piled up on several surfaces, as he prepared to remove himself for a season in London. But it was a stack of painted wooden panels, leaning against one wall, that caught Luke's attention. The topmost showed a figure that belonged, no doubt, in some biblical scene, only depicted in a state of undress that was, to say the least, unusual in devotional art. Millington followed his eye.

'Ah, you've found poor Fuller's panels.'

He walked over and showed Luke some of the others, which were in a similar style.

'Too much nudity, I'm afraid, for modern tastes,' the Professor said with a wry smile. 'Supposed to illustrate the Last Judgement. They were put up in the chapel less than twenty years ago, d'you know, but they've had to be taken down – some visitor said something to the Bishop, and the Bishop said something to the Warden.'

'And they've ended up in your chambers?' Luke could not help but feel amused.

'Aye, indeed, for the moment,' his host twinkled, evidently sharing the joke. 'It's probably assumed that, as a medical man, my interest in such forms is purely anatomical. And, at my time of life, the assumption is probably correct. D'you know?'

Millington's desk was strewn with plant samples, and he ushered Luke over to join him there.

'Now, if you'd care to look through here, Luke, you'll see something interesting.'

'A snake's head? There were some of them out in the meadow yesterday.'

'Aye, they're early this year, indeed. The part of the flower on that slide – d'you see? – that's the "attire" – or some men call it the stamen. It's the plant's male organ, d'you know?'

Luke peered down through the eyepiece of the Reeve microscope that held pride of place in the Professor's office. Sure enough, the portion of the flower Millington had cropped did look distinctly phallic.

'And this slide has the female part,' Millington told him, deftly exchanging one for the other.

'Fascinating – will you publish something on it, Tom?'

'Alas no, my dear chap – I'm far too busy these days. No, it's being written up by Nehemiah Grew – d'you know him?' Luke shook his head. 'Published The Anatomy of Plants, a few years ago – now he's putting out a second edition, so this'll be in it. But – forgive me – I haven't looked at your picture frame.' The Professor unwrapped the parcel and held the picture up to the light.

'A Lely frame, Tom, with oak leaf motif. In gold gilt, as we discussed.'

'Ah yes, a fine job, dear boy, a fine job. I'll get Babbington to wrap it back up. Just in time to take it with me to London. The Royal College will be delighted – thank you kindly.' He opened his desk drawer, removed a strongbox and unlocked it, and counted out the agreed price of twenty shillings.

'By the way,' Millington said, as Luke got up to leave. 'I heard our mutual friend Harbord came to grief the other day?'

'Why, yes, so he did – but I never realised you knew him.'

'I thought we both did. He was at Brasenose, if memory serves – he came to some of the Natural Philosophy meetings.'

Luke furrowed his brow.

'I'm pretty sure I never met him.'

'Ah well, perhaps before your time then, Luke. Always had a feeling he'd meet a sticky end, that one.'

'Come to think of it, I never knew he'd been at Oxford at all. His parliamentary file says he went to Leiden.'

'Why, I believe he did – but that was later. Left Oxford in a hurry, d'you know. Soon acquired a reputation as a philandering rogue, I'm afraid. Before long, he'd got some local girl into trouble, but didn't do the right thing by her, as you did. So he had to get his degree somewhere else, I suppose.'

There was a pause as Luke digested this new and surprising information.

'Do we know the girl?' he asked. He should surely find out as much from Millington, before the great man left for London, as he could.

The Professor squinted in thought.

'I seem to remember hearing she'd drowned, when the child was very young. So the boy was left without mother or father. It was all terribly tragic.'

Bidding the Professor farewell, Luke walked back home to deposit his fee – managing to slip in and out quietly enough to avoid another encounter with his wife – and strode off down Blue Boar Street deep in thought. Yes, he himself had 'done the right thing', as Millington put it. The consequences of any other course of action, especially for Elizabeth and the then-unborn Jane, would have been unthinkable. But he was left with a nagging sense of unfulfilled possibilities and potential – a sense that seemed to crystallise in the proximate yet frustratingly unreachable person of Catherine Weston, née Napper. Luke slowed his tread as he neared the Guildhall. Surely, now both his children had left home, he had met his family obligations? As Cate's image grew in his mind's eye, he was reminded that he, at least, had not yet reached the point where interest in such matters became purely academic, confined to observing the sexual organs of plants.

Then, so far as the investigation was concerned, did it change the picture at all, knowing that Harbord had an Oxford connection in his past – and one that was not to his credit? On balance, he was inclined to think not. If, in his record, all mention of his time at Brasenose had been suppressed, then it would be unlikely to play any part in his political activities or connections. Luke kicked a loose cobble against the wall, then intercepted it as it bounced back. The shady episode was not all that unusual, he reflected. Harbord was certainly not the only figure in public life who'd fathered a child on the wrong side of the sheets: from the King downwards, as it were.

No: the chief suspects in Harbord's killing, as in that of Unsworth, must surely still be Settle and his henchman – what was his name? – Francis. A shaft of light illuminated the threshold of the Guildhall as Luke approached it. The sun was nearing its zenith, as he had noted from Wren's turquoise sundial on leaving All Souls. The hours were counting down till he could put his theory to the test, that the pamphleteer would be so desperate for the return of his notes that he would risk returning to The Unicorn and Jacob's Well. And when he did that, he would walk straight into Luke's trap.

Chapter 52
An Unlikely Ally?

Cate spent much of the long span of daylight in silent prayer, as the men alternately dozed, or sharpened their swords on a small whetstone Francis produced from his pocket – truly, he seemed a resourceful character – or stood to pace restlessly back and forth. Always, they made sure at least one of them was awake and vigilant, lest she be tempted to cry out, or perhaps even try to scale the wall and escape: a notion she had briefly entertained early in her captivity, only to reject it as impractical.

At one point, there came a renewed rapping on the door: Here's-a-health-unto-His-Majesty. Settle strode hurriedly over and turned the key.

'What is it?' he hissed.

A lowered voice came from without, as Cate once more cocked an ear.

'College has arrived in Oxford. Wants a word with you.'

'Armstrong is supposed to be dealing with him.'

'Wants to meet up in person – says you need to be there when they plan how to coordinate, in the morning.' Settle let out an exasperated sigh.

'Where is he?'

'Back of the lodgings, just round the corner.' The pamphleteer turned to Francis.

'Well, there's nothing for it, I shall have to go out and speak to him; just hope no one sees. Don't let her out of your sight for a moment.' The other nodded assent, and Settle slipped away with his co-conspirator.

'Whence came you, sir?' Cate asked, on suddenly catching

Francis's eye after the passage of a lengthy interval. It was a question she had been weighing up for several hours: both out of a genuine curiosity, as to how someone so different from herself, and everyone she knew, came to be here; and out of calculation that – knowing nothing else about him – she must seek to draw out the man she'd identified as potentially the more pliable of her two captors by opening up the only subject she could think of.

'From Stepney. East London,' he replied, having observed her critically and seemingly decided there was no harm in answering, albeit in a manner that invited no follow-up enquiries.

'No, but... before?' the young woman persisted. Francis sighed, and she realised with a flush of self-reproach that he must have been subjected to many such interrogations.

'My father was out of Africa. A slave, captured and borne far away from home, to the New World, to work on a plantation.'

'I'm sorry to hear it.'

'Well, that's been and gone. This is a better place, I'll warrant.'

'So how did he come to be in England?'

The reply contained more than a hint of sarcasm.

'D'you not know, miss? The air of England is too pure to be breathed by slaves, so no man here can be owned by another – though plenty of Englishmen make money from the trade. Anyway, he escaped, stowed away on a ship, and came ashore in London town.' The account was matter of fact, but Cate's imagination strained to fill in the detail. Escape – in theory, it seemed so simple! If only it were so, for her now, in practice. She nerved herself to go on.

'I see. And your mother?'

'A washerwoman. English.'

'So you were brought up...?'

'As a Christian – and to not trust Papists.'

This was, she could tell, an attempt to deter further probing; but, rather than waste any of the time she had with him alone by falling silent, Cate changed tack.

'And what is your trade, sir?'

'Soldiering. I saw service with Monmouth, in Holland.' He added, as he saw her shape another question, 'Now, enough!'

Just then, Settle's return curtailed any further opportunity to keep him talking. The information Francis had divulged did, however, give her plenty to ponder. His father had been a slave. She racked her brains and dredged up a vague memory of one of Father Huddleston's lessons about the Crucifixion. Pontius Pilate, the Roman governor who'd washed his hands of responsibility while sending Christ to his death, was supposed to have been a descendant of freed slaves. Yes, that was it: slavery was a thing of ancient Rome. She had never heard of it in modern times, but, she supposed, there must be many wrongs in the modern world of which her upbringing had left her in blissful ignorance.

Slaves had first to be captured, of course – and they sometimes got away. Indeed, Francis seemingly owed his very existence to his father's successful flight from captivity. Would that make him still more vigilant, in preventing any attempt she might make to free herself? Or would it stay his hand at some crucial point, out of a residual fellow-feeling for her plight? Pilate, she recalled with a shudder, was disposed to show mercy, but proved powerless to stop the Crucifixion.

Chapter 53
A Special Kind of Cartwheel

Luke dropped back in at the Guildhall to find Robshaw in conclave with Ronald and Jethro Cox – the latter having, apparently, been fetched from his yard to give them some information in person.

''Tis about them two fellers, Master Sandys,' Ron began, in answer to Luke's raised eyebrow; but his brother cut in.

'They ordered a special kind of wheel, see – one with these here brackets on it.'

Luke took the wooden contraption from Jethro and examined it, admiring the precise craftsmanship with a practised eye. A thick, curved block, eight inches or so in length – one side had a broad groove cut into it, with edges slanted in a reverse diagonal, so the points faced inwards on the segment's end profile. Cut through the block were two round bolt-holes, with hexagonal countersinking for the heads on the cut side.

'So that part, it fits onto an extra ridge, all round the wheel, what has diagonals the other way, as a sliding dovetail joint,' Jethro explained.

'On a curve? How d'you do it?'

'With a chisel, and a steady hand.'

''Tis some carpentry, is that,' Luke said in admiration. 'What's its purpose?'

'Why, 'tis for attaching a roller on to the wheel of a cart, like.'

Seeing their puzzled looks, the wheelwright pulled a piece of paper and pencil from his apron pocket, and quickly sketched out the shape of the device.

'You have four of these blocks, see, and a crosspiece made

of iron, like this, what bolts on through them holes. Painted to keep off the rust. Then an axle attaches to the middle of the crosspiece, and through the middle of the roller.'

'What's that for, then?' Robshaw wondered.

''Tis for breaking up clumps of soil, before planting seeds in it.'

'But why not just use a longer axle through the cartwheels, and put the roller on the same one?' Luke enquired.

'Well, then the roller's like to lift off of the ground, and keep stopping,' Jethro replied. 'This way, it has its own axle, what turns independent of the cart. The wheel has a big iron block on the other side, round the axle, to balance it up. And the mechanism has a stop on it, if 'tis not needed – a chock what goes through the raised ridge.'

'Does it work?'

'I've never had no complaints. As long as you keep the surfaces smoothed and polished, 'twill run like water off a duck's back – if 'twas well-crafted in the first place.'

Luke snatched the sketch and turned it the other way up.

'We've seen a drawing like this recently!' he exclaimed, showing it to Robshaw.

'Why, aye – in that there folder.'

'Mind if I take this, Jethro?'

'Be my guest, Master Sandys.'

Halfway out of the room, Luke stopped and turned.

'How many of these do you make, by the way?'

The wheelwright sucked air in through his teeth.

'Not many! Not of that size, leastways. Last one was a couple of years back for Paul Woolston, from Sir Thomas Spencer's up at Yarnton. Mind, since the enclosure, his fields are that big, they're fit for giants. No wonder he wanted a big roller.'

'And are they expensive?'

'I charged them London fellers a pretty penny, I can tell you.

Said they'd pay me to stop all my other work for to give them this one right away. I keep the iron pieces ready, but joints take time, see. And there's a deal of wood in it.'

'I never took them Green Ribbons to be farming folk, that's for sure,' Robshaw remarked to Luke's retreating back, as he bounded away to his office to retrieve Settle's leather wallet from his desk drawer.

Back upstairs, on opening the folder, both he and Robshaw straight away spotted the similarity with Cox's drawing. What they had dismissed as mere 'doodles' included a rough likeness of the cartwheel Settle and his henchman had ordered, with its extra parts.

'Now, what can they possibly want that for?' Luke wondered aloud.

'Cussed if I know.'

'Maybe it's for some local landowner who supports their political aims?' Though neither constable could think of such a person among their acquaintance. Pawling, the tenant at Magdalen Farm, was no friend of the monarchy, and a supporter, in general, of efforts to thwart the Popish Plot and the Catholic succession; but he had no connections with London political clubs, so far as they knew. Luke tucked the leather binder under his arm and, reminding Robshaw to keep his ear to the ground for any clues as to Cate's whereabouts (though, in truth, the day's activity in the hue and cry had all but wound down), he set off to the Bodleian.

Chapter 54
'Tis treason, sir!'

As before, reaching the Bobs required him to negotiate a passage through the Foot Guards' ring of steel before climbing the stairs to the glorified cleaners' cupboard that had been pressed into service as temporary accommodation for the parliamentary clerks and past the stacks of files on the landing. He tapped on the door, which was ajar, though he could see no one inside among the maze of desks and boxes. Just as he was about to knock again, a pink face popped out from under one of the desks, and its owner rose from hands and knees through the not-so-very-great height to his feet, straightening his grey periwig as he did so.

'Good day to you, sir!'

'And to you, sir – Master Simkins, is it not?' At that moment, the other, paler-faced clerk emerged from a not-so-very-great distance away, in the far corner of the narrow room.

'I am Robert Simkins, sir,' this one said.

'And I am Robert Timpson. You are Master Sandys, from the Guildhall.'

'I beg your pardon, sirs – yes, indeed I am Luke Sandys. Thank you again for your help with the files the other day.'

'Think nothing of it, sir,' Bob Tim replied.

'Nothing at all, sir,' his colleague added. 'Now, how may we help you today, sir?'

Luke cleared a space on the nearest desk and opened up Settle's document wallet.

'I imagine you deal with tachygraphy, sirs, in keeping records of parliamentary debates?'

'Why yes, all the time, sir,' Bob Sim said.

'Well then, can you read this?' Luke showed them a double-page spread of the strange squiggles.

'Ah – Master Shelton's system,' Bob Tim said at once.

'Yes indeed, sir, Shelton's shorthand – a very good system, sir, very clear and useful,' the other Bob confirmed.

Together they pored over the pages as Luke pointed out specific passages which – he had deduced from the occasional longhand note in the margin, or set of initials – might be of particular interest. The Bobs alternately clicked their tongues and shook their heads as they read, their expressions becoming graver by the minute.

'Why – why, this is treason, sir,' Bob Sim pronounced at length, removing his eyeglasses as he looked up.

'The writer and his accomplices mean to assassinate His Majesty, sir.'

'And replace him on the throne of England…'

'…with James Scott, the Duke of Monmouth.'

''Tis treason, sir!' they chorused in unison.

Luke leafed through to the back page, from which – going by the initials, arrowheads and the drawing of the crown – he and Robshaw had formed the same impression. Now, as he explained to the Bobs, their reading of Settle's shorthand notes had confirmed it.

'And what of this section, sirs?' he went on, pointing to the lower half of the same sheet. ''Tis a mixture of numbers, initials and the same Shelton script, but – without knowing what the shorthand says – I can make neither head nor tail of it.'

The two bewigged heads bent obligingly back over the paper.

'Why, you should learn this one, sir, as an Oxford man, if you don't already know it,' Bob Tim said. 'There – a C, an L and a G – d'you see? College.'

'Does it say which one?'

'Well, sir,' Bob Sim began, then paused, mouthing silently. ''Tis not one that I've heard of. It begins with S–T... and that's an N at the end, I'm sure.'

'Could the S–T be the shortened form of "Saint" – as in St John's College?' Luke speculated.

'Hmm... unlikely, sir. Looks to be all one word. And that letter in the middle is a P, I'll warrant, not a J.'

'Looks like Stephen College,' Bob Tim said.

'That's it. Could be Stephen,' Bob Sim agreed.

'But... but that's not *a* college, that's the name of a person!' Bob Tim cried, in sudden alarm.

Of course: the warning that 'Tom', the intelligence officer for the Lord Chancellor, had given earlier. Stephen College was the troublemaker now reckoned to be on the way. And he was right in his surmise – the Green Ribbons obviously were in league with him. If College was planning to appear tomorrow – market day, the busiest of the week – then what did they have up their sleeve? 'Some kind of stunt,' the spy had guessed.

'The Protestant Joiner,' Luke said. 'I've been told he's coming to Oxford.'

The Bobs' demeanour turned, if anything, more serious still.

'Have nothing to do with that one, sir, I beg of you.'

'He's a rogue, sir. And a scoundrel!'

'Yes, I've been warned. But what of the section below that?'

'Well, sir, that word is said very often in Parliament these days: Papist.' Bob Sim traced the shorthand with his index finger. 'And the one next to it... here's a G, an R and an L. Grill?'

'Papist grill? Doesn't make sense, surely,' Luke said.

'Ah – possibly girl, in that case?' Bob Tim then took up the translation.

'Below that, we have the figure "3" – must be that, there's no such outline in Master Shelton's system. And that's "window". Plain as a pikestaff.'

'As a pikestaff, sir,' Bob Sim confirmed. 'And that's "Old"... then C-H, and a P, and an L – could be "Chapel", the vowel is an A.'

Luke followed the clerk's finger as he pointed out each letter. 'Third window of the Old Chapel?'

'Probably, sir.'

'That could be it, sir, yes.'

Lurching up at him from within, Luke felt a sickening access of insight.

'And what does it say below that?' he demanded, the new note of urgency in his voice raising the Bobs' eyebrows.

'Why, here's W-H-L,' Bob Tim began, 'and that squiggle above indicates the vowel-sound is an E – might be "wheel". Then, after it, 40s – almost certainly just as it looks, forty shillings. Mind, 'twould be an expensive wheel.'

'Expensive, indeed,' Luke murmured, his mouth suddenly dry. 'And the other word?' Now it was Bob Sim's turn to take up the work.

'It begins with a B, then L, D and S. The vowel is an A. 20s would be twenty shillings.'

'"Blades",' Luke said thickly. 'They've bought a wheel, and some blades, for sixty shillings.' He shook his head to clear it. 'Sirs, I must bid you good day. A matter has arisen that demands my immediate attention.' But Bob Tim put a hand on his arm.

'Someone should be told about this, sir.'

'The treason, sir,' Bob Sim added. Luke's mind raced. They were right, of course. But Settle's notes leant themselves to an interpretation he hardly dared formulate: one that would mean Cate was in deadly peril. He could go straight away to Lord Finch, the Lord Chancellor, lodged as he was in Christ Church College, and present his evidence – but he knew full well that, as soon as he did so, whatever leverage he might hold over the pamphleteer and his co-conspirators would be lost. Affairs of State would grind into motion, and what was the fate of one young woman compared with a seemingly well-developed plot to unseat the King of England? There would be arrests, and a crackdown – perhaps even a lockdown. But the danger in such a turn of events was surely that Cate, alive, would represent a 'loose end' to be tied off, before the Green Ribbons dispersed.

'May I prevail once more upon your assistance, sirs, and your understanding?' Luke began.

'If it lies within our compass, sir,' Bob Sim replied doubtfully.

'May I ask you to wait, before reporting this to anyone, and accept my assurance that the evidence will be presented to the proper authorities, at the proper time?'

'You're asking us to turn a blind eye, sir?' Bob Tim asked.

'Why, if 'tis too much to expect, sirs…' Well, now he was in a hole, and no mistake. Going to the Bobs had seemed the only way to find out what was in the notebook; but of course, as parliamentary clerks, they would be sworn to serve the Crown. If it came out later that they had known about the conspiracy, and kept quiet, they would be in trouble. He had let the cat out of the bag.

The Bobs looked meaningfully at one another.

'As long as you promise to report it later…'

'We can do that, sir.'

'Indeed, at Parliament, we have to turn blind eyes all the time.'

'There's just one condition, sir.'

'Yes?'

'A favour for a favour…'

'Get us out of this accursed room!' they cried, once more in unison. Inwardly, Luke breathed a sigh of relief. This, he could easily do, using his old Bodleian connections.

'Certainly, sirs – consider it done. You will be in more suit-able accommodation by the time Parliament opens. Now, I must go.' The Bobs' ecstatic good wishes ringing in his ears, he took the stone steps two at a time, scurried out of the library and off down the High Street back to the Guildhall, an inner frenzy of speculative dread lending wings to his feet.

Chapter 55
In Christ Church Cathedral

As Luke strode back into the chamber where reports had been coming in from the search, Robshaw hastily stuffed the last corner of a meat pasty into his mouth, wiped his hands on his coat front, and looked up expectantly.

'Come on!' Luke said. 'We're going to the cathedral.'

'What's the hurry?' the deputy protested, jogging along to keep up as his master set a brisk pace. 'You'll give us indigestion.'

The forced march stopped only when they reached the oldest corner of the building, the original Chapel of St Frideswide, onto which the much larger modern structure had been grafted. There, in the original north wall, were three medieval stained-glass windows. The first two, counting back from the shrine, depicted St Frideswide herself and St Mary the Virgin, cradling the infant Christ, respectively. And the third showed a crowned female figure in a white robe and blue skirts, holding, on the palm of her outstretched left hand, the unmistakable outline of a six-spoked wheel, with blades in the spaces between the spokes.

'God's body, it's what I thought,' Luke said, aghast. 'Saint Catherine the martyr: Catherine of Alexandria. The window must have given them the idea. Robshaw – they mean to Catherine-wheel her!'

The deputy had just recovered enough breath to try swallowing the corner of pasty, and now the horrified astonishment provoked by this news caused him to splutter, as Luke steadied himself by leaning on the back of a nearby wooden pew.

'How d'you know?' Robshaw asked, when he had recovered

– and Luke gave him a brief summary of the information he'd gleaned from the Bobs.

''Course, that's who she's named for,' he said, as they glumly contemplated the ancient image. 'Catherine of Alexandria, that is. When Cate was a girl, she'd come into the inn, and her Ma would say, "Catherine Alexandra Napper, I've told you not to play with them tankards" – or some such.'

Luke could scarcely bear to think about it, but he could not help visualising the way their 'stunt' would work.

'That's why they wanted that special wheel from Cox's yard: they'll shackle her hands and feet to the four blocks, and attach the blades to the wheel itself. The iron block on the other side will keep it upright. Then, when it rotates...' Now, however, the numbing effect of shock was beginning to give way to calculation. They were not finished yet. 'Wherever they are, my guess is, they'll try to coordinate it with some kind of speech by College.'

'College?'

'Aye – a fellow named Stephen College, an anti-Catholic extremist, and a rabble-rousing rogue, by all accounts. I saw that spy, "Tom" again earlier, and he told me College is heading to Oxford. Then the Bobs found mention of his name in Settle's notes, so they're obviously in cahoots.'

'Right, well we'll have to keep a dead sharp eye out for this College, then, tomorrow?'

'We will that. If we find him, we can assume Cate won't be far away. Then it'll be a case of getting to her in time.' Once more, he thought of the rotating blades.

'Unless we nab them at The Unicorn tonight,' Robshaw reminded him.

'Indeed – then we'd hopefully reach her before they have a chance to tie her on to that wheel.'

Chapter 56
A Desperate Realisation

'By God, man, must you make such a stink?' Settle exclaimed. Cate wrinkled her nose. They turned their backs to look the other way as Francis visited the 'corner of business', in order to – as he put it – 'nip one off'. He sluiced away the mess with water transferred to the pail from a rain-butt in the other corner.

'I suppose yours doesn't?' he retorted. Cate looked down to avoid eye contact during the long ensuing pall of mutual disgruntlement.

Settle broke the silence by opening what was, she realised straight away from his tone, another topic of contention.

'So, Hawkins'll be here with the blades and rope some time after dusk.'

'Aye, so you've said. But I'm taking no part in that, Settle, I've told you.'

'Well, we'll just have to dock your pay, then!'

'We'll see what Armstrong has to say about that!' Another angry pause ensued.

'You had no such qualms about killing Unsworth.'

Francis sighed. 'Unsworth was a bug. And a security risk. He knew too much, about all of us – and those two constables were leaning on him. This…' – he nodded in Cate's direction – 'this is different.' Cate listened intently, trying not to let the men see she was trembling. Was she about to find out what they were planning?

'All Papists are a security risk,' the other shot back. 'Or had you forgotten? Maybe just with the pretty ones, eh?'

'Look, Settle, I said I would help you to capture and hold her, and so I have. But I'm a soldier. Your "spectacular", as you call it – that's for you political fellows, leave me out of it.'

'Very well, then, we'll manage without you.'

Poor Cate was now in renewed agonies of conjecture, which she struggled to conceal. If she was to be involved in a 'spectacular', aimed at somehow drawing attention to her Roman Catholic faith, what could that possibly entail? She clutched at the crucifix through the fabric of her neck kerchief. That blades and rope were required left no room for doubt that Settle and his gang meant to harm her; and that she had, so far, been left untouched and unmolested – while a continuing source of relief in itself – added to the creeping dread that something uniquely vile now lay in store for her.

As she fretted, her eye strayed to the cartwheel propped against the wall at the far end of the enclosed yard. Every so often, she had idly wondered what it was doing there, but it scarcely merited any portion of her concern, given the circumstances. It was of an odd design, she now realised. There was a black-painted iron crosspiece attached to it, by means of four curved blocks, which fitted over a raised extra ring around its rim, at regular intervals. It was a big one: if she stood next to it, the top of her head would probably be about level with the top of the uppermost spokes. It must be about five-and-a-half feet in diameter.

Cate froze in sudden and awful insight, letting out an involuntary gasp that drew a look of suspicion from both men. She hurriedly covered her mouth with her hand, and turned away, lest they see the tears now starting from her eyes. The wheel, and the blades – surely that could only mean one thing? Settle knew, from the inscription in the prayer book he'd taken from her pocket, that she was named after St Catherine of Alexandria. They meant to re-enact the saint's martyrdom, in some twisted sectarian spectacle, calculated to impress the market-day crowds – she was to be Catherine-wheeled!

She clenched her fists. She would not let them see her crying; and, since preparations were clearly due to be completed overnight, she must bring forward a plan to escape. But how? Her ankle, tucked under one side of the chair as she hunched round to keep her face hidden, brushed against an obstacle. She felt down behind her skirt, and her hand closed around the neck of a ceramic bottle. Of course: it had contained the small beer she'd been given on the first evening, when Settle was preoccupied, and Francis evidently saw no reason to deprive her of whatever basic comfort might come their way. Could it somehow be of use?

Looking around now, the situation felt hopeless. The walls were high, and the door securely locked, with the only key in Settle's pocket. As the day's business in Oxford had worn on outside, the cries of commerce – and occasionally of anger, or merriment – had been faintly audible from Fish Street, at the far end of New Inn Yard. Many times Cate had considered calling for help, even at the risk of violent retribution – only to realise with dismal certainty that the likelihood of her cries being heard, let alone correctly interpreted, by a random passerby was so remote as to render the gesture worthless. No – the only chance must be when the door was opened, and her captors momentarily distracted. The bottle in her hand gave her an idea and, with it, the outline of a plan; a faint one, to be sure, but then her circumstances were desperate.

Chapter 57
A Dramatic Opera

The shadows were lengthening by the time they returned to Luke's office, only to find a waiting Captain Sutherland, cane tucked beneath his arm and his ginger moustache twitching.

'Ah, there you are, Sandys,' he said in evident relief. Curses! Luke had clean forgotten about the Royal command performance of Purcell's 'dramatic opera', and the requirement to attend in person.

Promising to present himself at the Christ Church College dining room, where the recital was to take place, in just a few minutes, Luke first led Robshaw across the road, where the pair re-entered The Unicorn and Jacob's Well. Getting down on hands and knees, he could still see the faint outline in the dust, on the floor under the bench on the far side from the street, where the wallet had lain when they initially found it. Making sure it was, so far as possible, in its original configuration of pages, with the calling cards sticking out of slots in its inside front cover as before, he carefully placed it back on to the exact same spot. The Chief Officer and deputy then shut the door of the inn behind them, and sent the two constables, who'd been on guard duty all day, home for the night.

'You settle yourself in behind the college doors, then,' Luke told Robshaw. Earlier, they had made the necessary arrangements with the porters, Greening and Hignett. Perched on a tall stool, the deputy was to keep watch, through a small hatch that opened in one of the tall oaken doors at eye level, for any movement around or into the tavern, more or less opposite on Fish

Street. 'When I get to Christ Church, I'll talk to Ed, and send him to join you.'

Luke found his brother keen to help. In truth, the Blues were becoming bored. They were, in effect, on standby whilst in Oxford, in case of any serious trouble. But Colonel Russell's Foot Guards were in charge of day-to-day security arrangements, and there were only so many drills they could do without feeling they would much rather be back in their respective barracks – either in London or elsewhere.

'We're not having this, Luke – not in Oxford. Young women being abducted? It won't stand.' Ed buckled on his scabbard. 'I'll get Tom Lucy to come along, too. He's spoiling for some action, we all are.' As the regiment had been on exercise that day, the officers were in full uniform, Luke noted with satisfaction: the more impressive the visual effect, the more likely their presence would be to deter trouble at a potentially crucial moment.

From the head of the high-ceilinged hall, the two progenitors-in-chief of Christ Church Cathedral and College – King Henry VIII and Cardinal Wolsey – glowered down in portrait on the assembled company. Did the present incumbent, Charles Stuart, shift uncomfortably on the throne in the middle of the floor, under their baleful eye? By now, Luke was virtually quivering with impatience. Members of the orchestra, the King's Players, chatted desultorily among themselves in between tuning up their instruments. College servants lit numerous candles against the incipient chill and gloom of the late afternoon, sending shadows across the painted paper backdrop: a vaguely sylvan tableau of blue sky, white fluffy clouds and green edging. How many hours did these people plan on taking? He swore to himself that, if this wretched 'dramatic opera' went on so long as to make him miss the chance to arrest Settle and his henchman in person, why, he'd convert to the republican cause on the spot. With another spasm of anxiety, he realised that, in the rush, he had omitted to tell the University Provost not to send his proctors to stand guard that night outside The Unicorn and Jacob's Well.

Finally, a stir at the door indicated that the conductor and singers had arrived, and the instrumentalists immediately sat up in their chairs, as if an invisible puppet-master had suddenly tightened their strings. Soprano singing evidently required the throat and chest to be free of constricting clothing, since the two young women who were to vocalise Purcell's libretto both wore gowns that were unusually low-cut at the front – the effect in no way diminished by their matching bejewelled necklaces. The King leant forward, propping an elbow on the arm of his gilded seat; the conductor tapped his music-stand with his baton, and, at last, the performance got under way. There was something ineffably soothing about the music and the deft movements of the players, as the trilling flageolet and dancing bows of the viols and cellos were enveloped in the harpsichord's metallic rustling caress. Then, it could not be denied that the talent of the two female singers brought the songs to vibrant life, causing even seasoned courtiers – for whom it was almost a point of honour to be unimpressed by artistic entertainments laid on for the King – to give their full attention.

For Luke, however, there was further annoyance as the piece unfolded, since it turned out that Purcell – or whoever had written the libretto to accompany his music – had got the story wrong. Who did these modern dramatists think they were, tampering with classical literature to suit themselves? He soon recognised the plot of the opera as based on the legend of Phyllis, which he had studied in Greek. A famous beauty, she married Demophon, King of Athens, and fell pregnant with his son – but the husband sailed away to war before the boy was born.

A grieving Phyllis visited the shore nine times in hopes of seeing his returning ship, but in vain; and on the last occasion she drowned herself in anguish, leaving her child motherless. Whereas, in this version, there was no child; her lover was called Philander – the name of her father in the original story – and Phyllis's suicide had been cast in more lurid terms, committed by stabbing herself. The candelabras guttered against the dusk beyond the dining hall windows as the lead soprano voiced the closing words with gusto:

Her ponyard then she took
And held it in her hand
And with a dying look
Cried, thus I fate command.

At this, the diva mimed the plunging of a knife into her heart, lest the image be lost on the audience, before continuing:

Philander! Ah my love I come
To meet thy shade below.
Ah, I come, she cried,
With a wound so wide
There needs no second blow.
In purple waves her blood
Ran streaming down the floor
Unmoved, she saw the flood
And blest the Dying hour.
Philander! Ah, Philander, still
The bleeding Phyllis cried
She wept a while
And she forced a smile
Then closed her eyes, and died.

As he clicked his tongue in irritation with the artistic liberties the composer had taken, and agitated over events that might – for all he knew, stuck in here – be unfolding even now at the tavern opposite, Luke felt a sudden and startling shift in his perspective on the week's events. Several puzzling details, which he'd up to now dismissed as inconsequential, suddenly began to make sense. Added together, they might even supply answers to several crucial questions.

Taking his leave of Captain Sutherland as the company quit the stage to rapturous applause, Luke walked along Fish Street in a fugue, his mind whirring and reeling over the insights now opening up, and their implications. By the time he had traversed the short distance to the main gates of Christ Church College, however, his dazed and befuddled condition was all but fully dispelled, and replaced by absolute clarity as to what they must do next.

Chapter 58
Back to the Abbey

'Robshaw!' Luke thrust open the great oaken door, causing his deputy and the two military officers to jump in alarm. 'You're coming with me.'

'Where to?'

'The abbey ruins. Come, let's knock up the duty ostler at the Guildhall and get a couple of horses. Ed and Tom, if you can stay here and keep watch – we'll be back later on.'

'What are you going to do there, Luke? 'Tis dark,' his brother asked.

'I'll explain later. No time to lose.' By the time they were mounted, the gibbous moon – which had waxed almost to fullness over the week – was high in the clear evening sky, so the horses could be trotted on their way out of the city to the west, slowing to a walk only as they reached more uncertain footing across the meadow, which gave Robshaw a chance to catch up.

'What we doing here then, Master Sandys?'

'We're going to see your ghost, Robshaw.'

'My ghost?'

'Yes – I thought at the time, even you couldn't be talking complete nonsense.'

'Why thank you, sir. I think…'

'So, what was it you reckon you saw?'

'Jiggered if I know.'

'Very well then, I'll tell you. Remember when we questioned Unsworth, what he said to us before we left him in that parlour?'

'A few things,' the deputy replied noncommittally.

'The man who called on Harbord earlier, on the day he was killed – said there was someone he should meet, now he was back in Oxford. That not strike you as odd?'

'Why, I suppose so.'

'Well it did me, but of course it went straight out of my mind. At that stage we didn't know Harbord had ever been here. But Thomas Millington told me, when I took his picture in today at All Souls, that Harbord had been a student at Brasenose.'

'But you was reading from that file what the Bobs gave us, and it said he went to Holland, or some such.'

'Indeed – but according to Millington, that was later. He fled Oxford when he got a girl pregnant.'

'The rogue!'

'That figure you saw, Robshaw, when we were at the abbey the other day, who looked like a younger version of Harbord – that wasn't his ghost; you just thought it was, because of the marsh fever. Nor was it his brother.'

'No?'

'No: I believe it was his son.'

There was a pause as this startling claim sank in.

'So what's Harbord's son doing at the abbey?' Robshaw queried.

'Why, 'tis as Silver told me – all those so-called vagabonds have a tragic tale to tell.'

'Aye – they would.'

'And Millington remembered that the mother drowned when the boy was an infant – like Phyllis.'

'Phyllis?'

'In the opera I've just seen, a character from Greek mythology. Only it got the story wrong, but never mind that now. Silver reckoned the vagabonds at the abbey were mostly orphaned, or abandoned in childhood.'

'So, who was that feller, then, as called on Harbord?'

'That's what we're here to find out,' Luke replied. 'This is the Old House; 'tis Friday, and well after dusk now – remember the note we found in Harbord's pocket. So, we're inviting ourselves to their fish supper.'

As the pair pushed their way through the bushes and around the tumbledown facing wall, someone shouted out 'Strangers!' and a row of faces – illuminated by the campfire in the middle of the old quadrangle – turned to them in unison, accompanied by the unmistakable swoosh of several blades being drawn from scabbards.

'Silver?' Luke called out – and was relieved at the answering call from the gloom at the far side of the hearth.

'Sandys, is that you? Welcome, old fellow.' Whereupon the assembled throng relaxed, conversation resumed, and the constables suddenly realised they were hungry, as the cooking aromas assailed their nostrils.

'So, what brings you back to the abbey?' the cleric enquired, as they cradled platters of grilled fish.

'We're looking for someone, who we think might be here,' Luke replied.

'What I thought was a ghost,' Robshaw added.

'Yes, it seemed a strange tale at the time. Well, come with me and you can have a look around.' At a discreet distance, they circled the campfire, scrutinising the faces of the 'vagabonds' – and others, well-wishers and friends who supported their efforts to create and sustain their own community here, and had come along as guests for the evening.

Luke and Robshaw exclaimed at the exact same moment: a face, caught in the dancing firelight, with the distinctive aquiline features they had last seen, drained of life, on the body of William Harbord.

'By God – that's him!'

'Silver, we need to speak to that man.' The priest followed the line of Luke's pointing finger.

'Ah! You'll do well to get much sense out of him, I'm afraid. That's poor Billy. A simpleton. I wonder...' He led them round to behind where the man was sitting; touched his shoulder and, when he turned, beckoned him to follow. As he rose, Luke noticed the older man he'd met on their previous visit to the abbey getting up as well. Seated a few yards away, he'd been watching the proceedings with interest.

Luke looked into Billy's face. He was about the right age – in his mid-twenties – to be Harbord's son, if the late MP's time at Oxford had come just before his own; and the physical resemblance was, indeed, striking. It was easy to see why the ailing Robshaw should think he'd seen a ghost. But, whereas the politician's eyes had gleamed with cunning when they'd met at The Unicorn and Jacob's Well, this unfortunate character's gaze reflected only dull, if amiable incomprehension.

Chapter 59
'You'd better tell us everything'

There was a sound of throat-clearing from behind the constables and Birch as they led Billy a little way away to a nook of the old ruins that was illuminated by a shaft of clear moonlight.

'Can I help you, sirs?' a voice from the shadows enquired, a little gruffly. Luke turned, and the owner of the voice stepped into the light.

'Ah – Master Fletcher, is it not?'

The man's face registered recognition, tinged with something else. Apprehension?

'Master Sandys. We met…'

'When we came with Kempster's men, yes.'

Luke stole a swift look at his friend, who signalled with a nod that Fletcher could be trusted.

'Do you know this man, sir?'

'I do indeed. What d'you want with him?'

Now he had renewed reason to size him up, Fletcher was, it seemed to Luke, perhaps in his sixties, and with a distinguished bearing, albeit having clearly seen better days. His coat, for instance, was of a good cut, but somewhat frayed around the collar.

'As you know, sir, we're looking into the murder of a Member of Parliament earlier this week in Oxford: William Harbord.' At the mention of Harbord's name, Billy issued an indeterminate noise, somewhere between a groan and a whimper, his face now contorted with what seemed like a conflict of emotions.

'It's all right, Billy,' Birch said, and the older man laid a hand on his arm in reassurance.

'We believe this man to be Harbord's son – can you confirm that?'

Fletcher let out a sigh that seemed to diminish him slightly in size, and left its mark in a perceptible deepening of the sad-looking wrinkles around his eyes.

'Aye, sirs, I can confirm that Billy here is indeed the son of William Harbord.' Robshaw gasped, but Luke was not to be delayed.

'Thank you, sir. And is he any relation of yours?'

'His full name is William Fletcher. He took our family name at birth, since Harbord had abandoned him by then.' He caught Robshaw's look of puzzled enquiry. 'My name is Martin Fletcher.'

The deputy looked meaningfully at Luke, clutching his arm.

'M. F., sir! The initials!'

'Yes, I'm coming to that.'

Luke turned his attention back to Fletcher. 'Did you write your initials on a note and give it to Harbord, asking him to come and meet you here this evening? "The Old House", Friday at dusk?'

'That I did.'

'Four magpies – four for a boy?'

'Aye. I thought I might have to leave the note at the inn, if he wasn't there. So I didn't spell it out – drew a picture he'd understand, instead, when it reached him.'

'So it was you who came to call on Harbord at The Unicorn and Jacob's Well on Monday, the day he was killed?'

There was a pause, as Fletcher evidently wrestled with some inner dilemma.

'That it was,' he said at last, in a subdued tone.

'I think you'd better tell us everything, Martin,' Birch said.

They sat down on a tumbledown portion of wall, and Fletcher began his tale.

'I'm retired now, sirs, but I made my career at sea. Rose to be a midshipman for the East India Company. So, I'd follow news from home in letters from my dear wife, Anne, God rest her soul.' The clergyman made a sympathetic murmur.

'So, anyway, one time, over twenty years ago now, I opened a letter urging me to hurry home. Our daughter, Marian, was in trouble. But I was unlucky: the note had been kept for me poste restante at Tangier, to pick up on our voyage east. Only we never put in there, on account of an outbreak of yellow fever on board. By the time I got the message, we were on the way back to England – but too late.'

'What happened?' Luke asked him.

'It was that Harbord,' he said, his voice thickening with anger and sorrow. 'He'd turned Marian's head with false promises and, by the time I got home, she'd had his child.'

'And where was Harbord himself?'

'Oh, he'd left in a hurry. Went back to his family estate in Norfolk, 'twas said. If I could've got a hold of him then, the scurvy knave!'

'He betrayed you?' Luke suggested gently. Fletcher turned to look at him eagerly, gratitude in his eyes mingling with concern that he was, perhaps, now all too well understood.

'Aye – he betrayed us.' He looked distantly into the cavorting flames.

Luke prompted Martin to continue.

'So, when you heard he was back in Oxford, you confronted him?'

'I wanted him to come and meet his son, to see the lives he'd ruined.'

'Lives?'

'When she realised Harbord was never coming back, poor

Marian tried to abort the pregnancy. It didn't work, as you've seen – she bore the child. But we always wondered if that was the reason why Billy wasn't quite right.'

'I heard she was drowned?'

'Drowned herself, more like. Stepped into the river at Osney in a flood that winter, and was carried off. We never found her.'

'I'm sorry to hear it, indeed.'

'Broke my wife's heart. I left her at home to bring up the boy.'

'And you stayed at sea?'

'I told myself I was helping, taking voyage after voyage, sending money for them – but in truth, I was running away.'

'When did you come back here, then?' Robshaw asked.

'Why, that would've been just over five years ago, when Anne died. I swore off seafaring, and came home to bury her, but, of Billy here, there was no sign. Then I agreed to help Reverend Birch collect goods for these poor folks, and I found him again, after all this time.' A tear rolled down Fletcher's cheek and glistened momentarily in the pale moonlight, before he brushed it away.

'You said before, he doesn't live with you,' Luke remembered.

Birch cleared his throat.

'Billy actually likes it here, Luke. It may not be much, but it's home – at least to him. The others tolerate his strange ways, and are kind to him.'

'And he's provided for?'

'As you've seen. And Martin chips in, when we need help.'

Luke pressed on with questioning Martin Fletcher.

'So, what happened, when you turned up at The Unicorn and Jacob's Well, and spoke to Harbord?'

'Why, of course, he got straight on his high horse. "I don't owe anybody anything" – they were his exact words.'

'The rogue!' Robshaw said again.

'But he took your note?'

'Had to, I reckon – only way to get rid of me. Raised voices were beginning to attract the attention of his "friends". I'll warrant they never knew about the family he'd abandoned.'

'And did you see him again, after that?'

Fletcher paused, evidently debating with himself, then rubbed his eyes before resuming his narrative.

'I'd walked out to call on an old shipmate, lately come to live at Kennington. He took a post as deputy keeper at the manor. Anyway, we got to jawing about old times, and took a drink or two,' he said, with a nervous glance at the vicar. Birch gestured at him to continue.

'So, by the time I set off back to town, it was late. Night watch waved me through at Bacon's, and I was walking up Fish Street, past the inn, when all of a sudden the door opens, and who should it be on the threshold but Harbord?'

'What was he doing, popping his head out at that time?' Robshaw cut in.

'Yes, I wonder... So – what happened next?' Luke asked.

Fletcher glanced at the young man, who had now resumed his seat with his back to them – content, apparently, to watch the fire and rest in the companionship of his fellow vagabonds – then again at Birch, who once more nodded at him to go on.

'Well, of course, my blood was up. I told him what for, didn't I?'

'Bet he loved that,' Robshaw said.

'Drew his dagger on me, so he did!'

'The rogue!' It was the deputy's favourite epithet all of a sudden, but Luke signalled him to be quiet, and leant forward.

'You're sure about that – he drew a weapon on you?'

'Sure as I'm sitting here talking to you.'

'And then?'

'Well, then it all got a bit confusing. He jabbed his blade toward me, and I caught hold of his wrist. Now, I'm not the man I was, but I always had a strong arm.'

'So...?'

'So, by the time I walked away...' Fletcher set his jaw before continuing. 'By the time I walked away that night, I'm pretty sure I'd turned his own dagger on him, still in his hand, and it skewered him through the vitals.'

All three of his listeners exhaled audibly at the same time.

'So it was you what killed him?' Robshaw cut to the chase.

'Well, steady on!' Birch said. 'From what we've heard, Martin acted in self-defence.'

'That would be for a jury to decide,' Luke said.

'You're arresting him?'

'We must, Silver, given what we've heard. But you're right, on Fletcher's own account, he acted in self-defence.'

'Under attack from a man who'd wronged his daughter. Surely no jury would convict him for that?'

'Maybe not. At least, it would be *in*voluntary manslaughter, not voluntary, since Harbord was the one who drew the weapon. But Fletcher, you'll have to come with us. One more thing – you didn't take Harbord's dagger?'

'No, indeed, sir – left it where it was.'

'That'll be why the blade was the wrong way up, an' all – if 'twas still in Harbord's own hand,' Robshaw said. Birch looked at him quizzically.

'When we examined the wound, it looked as though the blade had entered the body upside down,' Luke explained, 'with the sharp edge uppermost.'

At that, the constables turned to depart, leading their horses on foot as Fletcher trudged between them. As he showed no inclination to resist or try to escape, they left him unshackled – and, indeed, it was an uneventful walk to Oxford Castle, where they knocked up the gaolers, and had him committed to a cell for the night.

As they led their horses back towards the Guildhall, Robshaw asked:

'So what was it first put you on to him then?'

'I've been slow on the uptake, Robshaw. Distracted. I did wonder how Fletcher knew about Harbord, the first time I met him. There was clearly no love lost. But I put it out of my mind.'

'And then?'

'Millington remembered about Harbord being in Oxford and getting a girl pregnant. But of course I was worried about Cate by then.'

'So it was just now, then, that it all fell into place?'

'Yes. Watching the opera made me realise Harbord's son could still be around and, if he was orphaned, he might have ended up at the abbey. So he could have been your "ghost". Then when we saw Martin, I remembered his tale of woe that Silver had told me.'

'Good! Well, that's that.'

'Aye, well, now for the hard part – getting Cate back.'

Chapter 60
The Chimes of Great Tom

Ed fished in his pocket for his silver hip-flask, took a swig, and passed it wordlessly to Tom Lucy. The officers had kept The Unicorn and Jacob's Well under surveillance for three hours or so when the mighty bell suspended high in the cathedral next door tolled the nine o'clock student curfew. Ed started forward on his stool. What was this? Two men were walking towards the entrance of the inn. He turned to his fellow captain and saw that he, too, had noticed it: the first such incident of any importance since they took up their vigil.

'That could be them,' Ed whispered. Would they go inside? He loosened his sabre in its scabbard and slipped off the stool. Strangely, however, the pair merely came to a halt outside the front door of the tavern, and stood there.

'Bold, are they not?' Ed remarked. 'I mean, not bothering to hide themselves.'

A couple of minutes passed by, and they realised something was amiss.

'The men we're looking for – I thought one was supposed to be big, and the other small,' Lucy said. 'These fellows both look about the same size.'

'You're right,' Ed replied. He strained to see to the other side of the road. 'And I don't think one's a blackamoor, either.' At that point, a cloud that had scudded across the moon suddenly cleared, and they could pick out more detail.

'Ah, no! They're University proctors.'
'Really?'
'Yes – look at their uniforms.'

'This could ruin everything, Sandys.'

Ed decided on a policy of direct action.

'I'll have to go and tell them to get lost.'

'Right. I'll hold the fort,' Lucy replied.

'Good evening to you, sirs,' the captain called out, as he crossed the road towards the proctors. The pair nodded warily in response. 'Captain Edwin Sandys, at your service. Did my brother not tell you? There's to be no guard posted outside the inn tonight. We're watching it from behind the college gates instead.'

'No sir, they did not tell us,' one of them said.

'I wondered why there was no constables here, like, when we arrived,' the other remarked.

As the chimes of Great Tom died away, Francis stood up.

'I'll go and take another look at the inn. Surely the night watch won't be guarding it again tonight?'

'Yes, you'd think the constables would have everything they need from there, by now,' Settle replied thoughtfully. 'If they are still there, it'll be a sign that something's up.'

As usual, Cate pretended not to listen to the men's conversation, but she stored this away as another sign of the pamphleteer's nervousness. As he opened the door to let Francis out, her fingers closed around the bottle underneath her chair and hidden by her skirt – but this was not, in truth, the opportunity she had been waiting for, since, of itself, the departure of the big fellow created insufficient distraction. She had begun seriously considering an attempt to catch Settle unawares and wrest the key from him, but on this occasion he caught her eye on the way back to his seat, fixed a hostile glare in her direction, and placed his sword across his knee.

Here's-a-health-unto-His-Majesty – Francis had scarcely set

off when there came a knock at the door. Surely he could not be back already? Settle crossed rapidly to the door and opened it, sheathing his blade as he went.

'Hawkins! About time.'

Cate coiled like a cat ready to spring, her fingers clasping the neck of the bottle. The newcomer was a tall, heavily built fellow who briefly turned towards her one of the cruellest faces, Cate thought, that she had ever seen. He handed in a square wooden box.

'Take hold of this, Settle, there's a good chap.'

'The blades?'

'Aye. Francis not with you?'

'No, he's… stepped out.'

'"Stepped out"? You know he can't be seen, man, else he'll give us away! How many blackamoors are there, abroad on the streets of Oxford?'

'I'm well aware of that, Hawkins,' Settle snapped.

The pamphleteer turned to stow the box on the ground at the far end of the walled-in area, next to the cartwheel; but without closing the door, since Hawkins then slipped out for a second item: a coil of rope. For a brief moment as he came back in, the door swung open, and both men were facing away from it – and from Cate. This was her chance. She swung the bottle up in one motion from underneath her chair, and lobbed it in a perfect arc over the far wall, where it fell with a distinctive crash-and-tinkle on some hard surface beyond.

'What the Devil?' Hawkins cried, reaching for the hilt of his sword. 'Someone's spying on us back there! Give us a leg-up.' As he placed his foot in Settle's cupped hands and lifted himself up to peer over the wall, Cate moved as quickly and quietly as she could towards the still-open door. This was working better than she had dared hope. She shifted her weight from right to left foot, then to the right again, to jink around the door without touching it, lest its hinges creak – she had thought of everything. With a backward glance to see she was not being followed, she sprang through the gap and into the undergrowth outside – she was free!

It was with a jarring thump that Cate, turning to face forwards, ran headfirst into the barrel chest of the man moving in the opposite direction and pulling a low cart, up the path of New Inn Yard towards the hidey-hole.

'Whoa, there,' said a deep voice – and, in an instant, her hopes and spirits were dashed, as she was seized in an implacable grip.

'Let me go, sir!' she cried. 'Let me go, I beg of you!'

'Not so fast. 'Tis not so often a young lady rushes into my arms. Seems I got here in the nick of time.'

By now, Hawkins and Settle had come tumbling out, drawn by the commotion. With a foul oath, Hawkins cuffed her across the face with the back of a heavy hand, and she fell to her knees.

'Try and trick us, would you, Papist trull?' He reached again for his sword, then returned his hand to his side, seething. 'Only to think what's coming to you – you'll wish I'd finished you off now, by tomorrow morn!'

'Settle, what's this?' Francis came jogging back up the yard. 'Get back inside, all of you. The streets are not empty – we must keep our heads down.' Cate sobbed in despair. She had come so close to escape. Why, oh why had this other man had to come along at that precise moment? Lifted and propelled back into the yard, she sank into a heap in the corner, shoulders heaving in impotent rage and frustration, along with dread at the fate that awaited her.

Chapter 61
Recriminations

'How the deuce did you come to let her out?' Francis was demanding. 'If it hadn't been for Armstrong here, turning up at the right moment, you'd have lost her – and she'd be calling down the night watch!'

'Why, we was short-handed, 'cause you decided to go walk-about,' Hawkins shot back, his eyes flashing with temper.

Recriminations did not end with the departure of Armstrong and Hawkins for the night, now they had delivered their contributions to the plan for Cate's execution.

'Did you get the wallet?' Settle demanded, once the others had gone.

'Nay,' the other answered shortly.

'You're not telling me those constables are still there?'

'Worse. Two proctors – and a captain of the Blues. Even in this light, I reckon I recognised him – could only be from Maastricht. And if he was there, God knows he'd recognise me.'

'Well, maybe you'll have to do for him as you did for Unsworth.'

'You're not paying me enough to cross swords with a Horse Guards officer.'

'I'd say you're turning yellow, though, to look at you, 'tis impossible to tell,' Settle returned with a sneer.

Francis took a step and loomed over the smaller man, who backed off, though without lowering his gaze.

'I'll let the insult go, Settle, this once,' the ex-soldier said, releasing the sword-hilt from his grasp. 'Though you should know there's men now dead who took that liberty with me in the past. I'd chance my arm with him in a duel, if the proctors weren't there to raise the alarm. But then we'd have the whole regiment down on us.'

'They'd have to find us first.'

'You don't get it, do you? Think it's difficult to carry out this plan of yours amid a hue and cry, run by the local constables? Why, a Guards regiment could lock this city down like that' – and he snapped his fingers.

'Very well,' the pamphleteer replied. 'We'll just have to fetch it in the morn, while all eyes are on College.'

Back at The Unicorn and Jacob's Well, after some minutes of indecision, the two night watchmen set off to report on the unexpected development to the head proctor. Feeling greatly relieved, Ed returned to his post, with no means of knowing that the encounter had been witnessed – and misconstrued – by their quarry, who had, of course, turned away just before the men dispersed.

Chapter 62
A Plan is Formed

Luke and Robshaw were handing their horses back in to the ostler when, out of the shadows, came a now familiar voice:

'Sandys! A word, if you please.' It was 'Tom'. He did have a knack of appearing as if from nowhere. Luke waved his deputy off to join the Guards captains at Christ Church College, and ushered the spy into his office, where he lit a candle and they sat down. This time, he had some news of his own to impart.

Both men started to talk at once.

'No – you first,' Luke said.

'Very well. Stephen College is here in Oxford,' Tom announced, sitting back to savour the effect of this news. Luke felt a chill through his – what was the word Fletcher had used? – his 'vitals'.

'He's going to make a speech tomorrow morning, to the market crowds.'

'I see.'

'I should tell you, the Green Ribbons are planning to build a stage for him outside The New Inn.'

'But – but that's opposite us here, at the Guildhall.'

'Quite so. Can you think of any reason why?' Luke shook his head.

'Well... I told you he was a rabble-rouser. I'm afraid he might be planning to rouse a rabble against you.'

'Against me?' This was, indeed, an alarming prospect.

'Well – against the City. He's likely to pick up on this business about Harbord – you know, "MP stands for Murdered by

Papists", while the constables do nothing; Oxford is complacent about the threat from Rome, that sort of thing.'

Now it was Luke's turn. He found it was a moment he'd been looking forward to.

'Well, his information is out of date. We know who killed Harbord.'

Tom leant forward.

'Really?'

Luke recounted Martin Fletcher's story, with its antecedents in Harbord's wrongful treatment of his daughter, and abandonment of their child. The spy listened intently, then, at the conclusion of the narrative, asked eagerly:

'How many people know about this?'

'Well, there's Birch, and Robshaw – and he's probably told my brother by now. The gaolers at the Castle have Fletcher's company for tonight, at least, but they ask no questions.'

'Then we'll have to make sure the story reaches a wider audience, won't we?' Tom said, with a smile that would be chilling, were it not for the mutual interests that put them on the same side.

'And how can we do that?'

'I've spent the week building up a number of local assets. As things stand, they're primed to heckle College at his speech tomorrow. When he talks about Harbord, they're to shout out about the man's treachery with the French.'

'Will that work?'

'Probably not, by itself. It's too far removed from what people think they know about him, as you pointed out. But now we have something much better to go on.'

'And what shall I do?'

Tom paused, pinching his lower lip.

'Your sidekick, Robshaw. He's well known in the town?'

'Very.'

'Get him to stand in the middle of the crowd when College gets on his hind legs. Tell him to confirm what people say about Harbord.'

'Very well.'

'It'll sink Harbord's reputation, 'tis certain – posthumously, of course. More to the point, if it's timed right, it'll blow a great big hole in College's, as well. And that, my dear fellow, will make this whole trip to Oxford worthwhile. Now, I must get to work.' And, with that, he was gone.

Chapter 63
A Night of Tension

The Sandys brothers exchanged glances as Robshaw noisily finished off the snacks Tom Lucy had spirited out of the officers' mess at Christ Church – the captain's last contribution to the night's endeavours before turning in for some rest. The sky was now lightening.

'Where in God's name are they?'

'You're quite sure they're still in Oxford, Luke?' Ed asked for what felt like the twentieth time.

'Have to be. No one saw them leave – the city gates are guarded round the clock. And Settle will have to get that wallet back.' It had become an article of faith.

'Can't see us in here, can they?' Robshaw asked, between mouthfuls. As dawn was breaking, they checked the lines of sight from their hide.

'We'd see them first, I'm sure.' Ed rested his fists on his angled thighs, while Robshaw picked his teeth, and Luke – unable to sit still any longer – got up from the high stool and peered through the crack made by the little door in the great oaken gates, as if looking hard enough would cause the quarry to materialise before his eyes.

Slumped in the corner of her walled-in prison at the end of New Inn Yard, Cate passed an interminable night. Through the miasma of despair and dread, the men's occasional movements registered but dimly. Over and over, she upbraided herself. What if she had not looked back at the very moment of escape? Surely then, she could have sidestepped Armstrong as he advanced, and relied on her nimble feet to keep her out of reach? Why hadn't she simply bitten the hand that clamped itself around her upper arm, and shocked him into letting go? Her penitence mingled with bitter recollections of Father Morris's scolding, and the scorn of Lady Weston. Surely, it seemed now, they were right about her shortcomings. If only she could have seen them for herself.

Cate had often looked at the framed picture on her windowsill and wondered what it must have been like for poor St Catherine, all those centuries ago, to be slain in that cruel and agonising way. She clamped her hands on the sides of the chair in an effort to control her shivering. Would men really, truly do that, now, in England? Surely they would be unable to bring themselves to follow through on the purpose she had attributed to them? Francis had called it a 'spectacular' – a sectarian ritual too grisly and perverted for him to be a willing participant, at any rate; though that had not prevented him from snatching and holding her in the first place.

Did she dream it, or did the ex-military man get up, at some point when clouds were scudding across the moon; step, with that surprising delicacy of his, around the snoring Settle, and make his way to the other end of the yard to kneel by her chair?

'You know, don't you?' he seemed to say – to which she responded by nodding in mute despair. 'Well, keep your chin up and your wits about you. It might never happen.' In this dream, she must have looked at him in wonderment, for she could recall saying nothing, but he seemed to go on to explain.

'A lot still has to go according to plan if they're to pull this off.' Her most vivid memory, which went furthest to suggest the exchange might have been real, was of his lips brushing her ear, so close were they as he spoke. 'I've done my part by bringing you here and guarding you. I follow orders. But if

something goes wrong, I'll look for a chance to stop them.'
With that, he receded – was it into the fog of her unconscious,
whence he had come – or in reality, back to his seat? She could
not tell. As the darkness began to lift, however, she redoubled
her silent prayers, and clung to a glimmer of hope that might –
just might – be slightly brighter than before.

Chapter 64
A Political Rally

The first market traders were beginning to assemble the wooden frames of their stalls towards the top end of Fish Street, and unloading boxes of produce from horse-drawn carts. It would soon be time for the porters to open the Christ Church College gates. The return of Captain Lucy, suitably refreshed by a couple of hours' sleep, felt to Luke like the moment to change things.

'Ed and Tom, can you stay here?' he asked. 'When the gates are opened, you can keep out of sight behind the wall.'

'Surely. And you?'

'I need to be able to see what's going on outside The New Inn. That's where College is supposed to be making his speech.'

'What about me?' Robshaw enquired.

'I have a special role for you, Robshaw. Come with me.'

As the pair strode up the gentle gradient towards the Guild-hall, Luke explained.

'College will try to make mischief over Harbord's murder – why haven't we caught the killer, it's a conspiracy of Papists and so forth.'

'Want me to give him some stick?' the deputy growled, fingering his stave. 'I feel like a bit of a barney, after a night like that.'

'Nay, leave your weapon alone. Your job is more subtle.'

'Not sure I'm in the mood for "subtle".'

'When College starts up about Harbord, people in the crowd will shout out about the wrong he did to that girl, and his abandoned bastard son.'

'How will they know about that, then? We only just found out ourselves.'

'All the work of the other "Tom", the spy for the Lord Chancellor. He turned up last night, remember, as we were stabling the horses. I brought him up to speed. Anyway, when they say those things, you're to confirm them. Loudly. People will believe it, coming from you.' The man was not too fuddled or fatigued to swell a little with pride at this rare compliment.

'Aye – will do. You can count on me, Master Sandys.'

'Good fellow.' With that, Luke slipped round the back of the Guildhall, in through the door of his office and up the stairs, to a mezzanine landing with a narrow window that faced directly on to the street below, propping it slightly ajar so he could hear, as well as see, events as they unfolded.

The foot traffic was thickening now, with market-goers eager to get business under way on a day when bigger crowds were expected than Oxford had seen in many a year. Then, suddenly, there was a commotion, and some movement from the corner of Queen Street, away to the right. Four men were pushing their way through the pedestrians, carrying heavy wooden objects that were clearly designed to fit together into a makeshift platform or dais. And they all wore green ribbons, either on the breast of their jackets, or round their hats, or both. Robshaw turned to look up from his position at street level, and caught Luke's eye. As they constructed the stage, another two Green Ribbon men arrived. One of them, he recognised as the MP, Edward Norton, who'd addressed the mob in the High Street. The planks, struts and trestles having now been levered and slotted into place, Norton turned to his friends, nodded and stepped up. One of the men who'd carried the stage whistled loudly through his fingers, while the others cried: 'Pray quiet! Pray quiet!'

'Friends,' Norton began, when a degree of hush had

descended. 'We meet in grave danger, on this market day.' An ominous answering growl rose from his audience. Where were the other Green Ribbon men now? A couple were making their way back up Fish Street – presumably to fetch College. Norton was clearly the warm-up man. And was that a glimpse of another one, or even two, disappearing up the narrow yard running along the side of the New Inn? But the MP was now ramping up his rhetoric.

'You know me, sirs, as a Member of Parliament. And proud to serve with some of the best men of England. One such was William Harbord. William Harbord, MP.' The hush deepened, as if in respect for the dead. 'It stands for Member of Parliament. It could stand for "Man of the People". For William Harbord was a man of the people. And this week, sirs – this week in Oxford – it stands for something else.'

'Murdered by Papists!' a voice cried from amid the crowd, to loud acclaim.

'Aye, sir! You have it right,' Norton continued. 'Murdered by Papists, indeed.' While the attention of the audience was on the speaker, Robshaw stole a glance up at the window, raising an eyebrow. Luke frowned and shook his head, making a hand gesture he hoped would signal the deputy to wait. His interventions would be needed for when College took to the podium.

Chapter 65
'Please, sirs, no!'

The familiar rhythm at the door – Here's-a-health-unto-His-Majesty – roused Cate from her indeterminate condition of exhaustion, wretchedness and sheer, limp resignation. Hawkins entered, with another Green Ribbon man whom she had not previously seen.

''Tis time,' this one said. 'Armstrong has gone to fetch College. Better tie her up,' – with a nod in Cate's direction.

First, Hawkins and Settle pushed the low cart, which Armstrong had been bringing when she'd run headlong into him the previous night, over to the cartwheel, lifted it on and settled it between two wooden spars secured in place on the trolley. Then, Hawkins and the newcomer turned in her direction.

'P–please, sirs, no,' she whimpered.

'Silence, Papist hussy!' Settle snapped in his nasal tones. Francis sat in the chair at the far end of the covered area, elbow resting on one of its arms and chin cupped in his hand – looking away from her.

Strong hands grabbed Cate roughly by the shoulder, and the fabric of her dress at the nape of her neck, and carried her over to the cart. She vainly struggled for a moment as Hawkins held her left wrist, and the other man tied it tightly on to one of the wooden blocks with a length of rope pre-cut for the purpose. Her breath coming in short gasps and a nauseous feeling rising in her throat, Cate looked frantically from side to side, espying out of the corner of her eye a thick wooden chock, set to the perpendicular from the wheel's rim. Could it be… yes, she was sure, it was holding the apparatus of the four blocks and iron

313

crosspiece – on to which she was now being shackled – and the wheel, together. When it was removed, the one would be free to rotate relative to the other.

'Now we can put on the blades,' the new man grunted. 'Settle – that's your job, since Francis won't join in.' With a curse, the pamphleteer now went to the box Hawkins had brought, and pulled out what looked like a dagger, only with an attachment added to the hilt to enable it to fit on to a spoke of the wheel. One by one, he secured six of these in position between Cate's outstretched limbs. As the last one clicked on, Hawkins was bending down to knot a length of rope around her right ankle, when the rhythmic knock at the door came again. The other Green Ribbon man turned the key in the lock and opened it a crack. An excited voice spoke from outside:

'Make haste! College is taking the stand!'

Chapter 66
What if he had miscalculated?

A gasp rippled through the market-day crowd at a spectacular sight: what looked for all the world like a medieval knight, astride a white charger – decked out with the cross of St George – and apparently wearing full plate armour. With a flourish, the rider doffed his helmet and slid down from his mount, handing the headgear, along with his black leather gauntlets, to one of the Green Ribbons, as he strode purposefully towards the pop-up stage. Norton led the audience in a loud cheer.

'Now, gentlemen!' The MP turned his palms outwards and downwards to appeal for calm. "Tis mine honour, indeed, to present our next speaker. A doughty defender of our liberties, sirs. A fearless witness to the truth. Here to tell us more, about the perils of Popery – the Protestant Joiner himself, Stephen College!' The announcement, and College's ascent to the dais, were greeted with tumultuous applause from market traders and customers alike.

'Sirs,' College began, when the noise had subsided. 'I am come to warn you of the Antichrist in your midst, here in Oxford.' There was the noise, discernible to Luke from his elevated position, of a sharp intake of breath among many in the crowd. 'Opposite us is the Guildhall. Seat of the authorities in Oxford – authorities who sit idle, sirs. The mayor, the bailiffs and constables – all have pawned their very souls. They take no action to protect the City, or its God-fearing people, against this Antichrist!'

Luke took a step back from the window as irate expressions turned towards the building.

315

'Before the morn is out, sirs,' College continued, 'we will demonstrate how Papists should be dealt with.'

Where was Cate? Where was Settle? What if he had mis-calculated – that the wallet was of lesser consequence than he thought; or that others in the group would press ahead regard-less, with College's 'demonstration'? For the moment, though, the speaker was concentrating on the issue of the succession to the throne.

'The King sits just down the road, sirs, in Christ Church. Still abed, no doubt, with his Catholic whore.' There was a growl of disapproval. 'Then he'll spend the day plotting with his ministers to thwart the will of our elected Parliament, and impose a Popish successor on us.' Another growl. 'And who will stand against this infamy, sirs? Why, none other than our good friends, Members of Parliament among 'em – the Green Rib-bon Club.' Heads were nodded, and the noise was now one of approbation. 'Men of the people indeed. And none better, sirs, than the late William Harbord.' College now adopted a more subdued tone. 'What was William Harbord's "crime"? Why, to defend us, sirs, and our liberties. And his "punishment"? To be viciously stabbed, by Papists!'

This time, however, a piercing voice from the other side of the street – directly below where Luke was standing – cut through the general hubbub.

'No, he wasn't!'

College's head lifted sharply as he surveyed the sea of faces in front of him. Before he could respond, however, another speaker piped up.

'Harbord's killer is locked up in the Castle, right now.' A few of Robshaw's neighbours turned towards him, and the deputy confirmed the news.

'Aye, 'tis true. He confessed, last night. 'Twas in self-defence, when Harbord drew a dagger on him.' As the mood on the street tilted towards confusion at these unexpected tidings, another of Tom's 'local assets' took up the chorus.

''Twas in a quarrel over Harbord's bastard son, from when he was in Oxford.'

'He got a young maid in trouble, then abandoned her, the rogue!' the first voice chimed in contemptuously, as the focus of anger shifted among the crowd.

'Then she drowned herself, poor thing,' yet another added, from the far edge of the throng around the podium.

As Robshaw straight away verified these statements to those around him, College tried to reclaim the initiative.

'Be that as it may, sirs,' – but he was struggling to wrest back the attention of the gathering. Suddenly, a thin figure, clad all in black, emerged from the end of New Inn Yard, over the Protestant Joiner's right shoulder. Settle – at last! Luke glimpsed the pamphleteer turn right to make his way down Fish Street towards The Unicorn and Jacob's Well, before flying down the Guildhall stairs two at a time and bursting out on to the packed thoroughfare in pursuit.

'Make way, sirs. Make way there, please.' Luke unhitched the wooden stave from his belt and used it to push his way through, ignoring the cost his progress exacted in bruises and lost tempers. At the edge of his field of vision, some kind of missile, thrown from the crowd – perhaps a coin, or a small pebble – hit College a glancing blow on the side of his breastplate; but it did not make quite the sound he expected. A heartbeat later, he realised. Of course: it was not made of metal after all, but wood, painted with silver gilt, like a picture frame. 'Seeing is believing,' Tom had said, referring to the armour – a cornerstone, Luke reflected briefly in his haste, of his own world view. But evidence could be misleading, as the episode with Gregory's coat had shown him. Sometimes, to discern the truth, you had to know what you were looking for. Now he was clear of the mob, the view down Fish Street opened up, and he was just in time to see Settle try the front door of The Unicorn and Jacob's Well and – finding that it swung open – enter the premises. Luke lengthened his stride, and loped away down the incline.

Peeking out from their perch behind the open lower gate of Christ Church College, Ed and Tom Lucy spotted Settle as he hastened along the pavement opposite. Conspicuous because their section of the road was virtually deserted – with all attention concentrated on the area around the impromptu speaking stage – the scurrying pamphleteer looked back over his shoulder to check no one was following, and approached the inn.

'See that?'

'Aye – looks like it might be one of our pair. No idea what's happened to the other one, but still.'

The captains buttoned up their tunics to the neck, attached their scabbards to their belts, and set out across the road, immediately seeing Luke's converging figure to their right. The Sandys brothers greeted each other with a wave, and – without words passing between them – the Guards followed Luke across the threshold.

'Stop right there!' Luke cried. At the far side of the room, Settle was in the very act of straightening up from bending down to retrieve the document wallet – which he stuffed hastily into his inside pocket. He flinched, but quickly recovered his poise.

'You've no business with me. I'm retrieving some personal property, is all. Now you'd better get out of my way, and let me get back to the meeting.' There was a rustle, as Ed and Tom Lucy both drew their sabres, and Settle gulped and shrank back.

'I'm arresting you for the murder of the landlord here, Ged Unsworth, for one,' Luke said, advancing on him with the captains behind him on either side. 'And I demand you tell me what you've done with Catherine Napper! Where is she?'

A sly look came over the face of the Green Ribbon man.

'Friend of yours, is she? You know she's a Papist, yet you do nothing about it!' Luke seized Settle by his lapels, and pinned him against the back wall.

'If I don't get her back safe and sound, it'll go ill with you, I swear.'

'Let me go! You've no evidence against me.'

'Oh, haven't I just?'

Chapter 67
A Small Chink of Hope?

'What the Devil's going on out there?' Hawkins cursed. Armstrong, whom Cate in her dejection recognised as the man whose untimely arrival had stymied her escape, pushed open the unlocked door without the usual knock, entering with another Green Ribbon in a state of agitation.

'College has lost them!'

'What d'you mean, "lost them"?'

'A man's been arrested for killing Harbord.'

'That's happened before.'

'Aye, but this one's confessed. Men in the crowd knew about it – we didn't.'

'He's supposed to get their blood up for the spectacular!' Hawkins spat in disgust. 'You were supposed to fix the crowd, you and Norton.'

'Norton's taking a turn on stage now, trying to get the thing back on course.'

As the four Green Ribbons glared at each other, Francis stood up and took a pace forward from the far end of the enclosed space.

'No point going through with it now, then.'

'When we want your opinion, Francis, we'll ask for it,' Hawkins shot back. Cate pricked up her ears, feeling the tiniest lift in the near-unbearable weariness that had descended on her as she stood, manacled to the deadly wood-and-iron apparatus that articulated with the giant cartwheel. Maybe, as she'd been hoping, her captors would not all turn out to be on the same side, at least not on the matter of the 'spectacular'. But surely it was too late to make any difference? For what seemed like the hundredth time, she was scourged by conflicting feelings of injustice, and of self-reproach for her own part in her predicament. If only she had not looked back, as she slipped through the door! Or was this, perhaps, even a punishment for her sin, of entertaining thoughts of a married man? Thank God she had confessed and sought absolution through Father Morris.

She was getting pins and needles in her right ankle, since the cord Hawkins had attached there had also bound in a fold of her skirt, and trapped it at an odd angle; so she jiggled her leg, as unobtrusively as she could. Might as well try to relieve that trivial discomfort, at least. As she looked down, the fabric pulled clear of the rope, and she felt a distinct loosening of the restraint. What was this? Checking that she was not being watched, she flexed the ankle experimentally, finding that there was some leeway in the knot – enough, perhaps, to allow her to free her foot. It was the last of her limbs to be fastened, she remembered – and Hawkins had been interrupted while tying it. He must have missed a loop.

To be able to extricate herself from one of four fetters was of little practical use, to be sure, even if she could – as long as the other three were all tight – but this, too, was a minor chink of hope. She would keep the foot where it was for now, but she might be able lift it out if the need arose.

'We'll just have to wait,' Armstrong was saying, 'and hope College can get back on his legs and rouse them again. I'll come back when they're ready.' He slipped out of the door, leaving Hawkins and the two others with her, as well as Francis, who stayed at the far end of the enclosure.

Chapter 68
A Bargain is Struck

Luke turned to the two Guards captains.

'Master Settle and I need a word in private.' So, Ed and Tom Lucy waited in the main bar while Luke seized the Green Ribbon man by the arm and propelled him through to the back parlour: the very parlour, in fact, where Unsworth had met his doom. He pushed the pamphleteer into the corner, drew his dagger and held it to the man's throat.

'I know what's in that wallet, and why you came back for it. I had the shorthand translated. And we both know it would send you to the Tower. They'd surely hang you, but they'd have to scrape up what was left of you, first.'

Settle gulped again, but still seemed in no way cowed. 'I know what goes on in the vaults under that inn, The Mitre – and I know you've turned a blind eye to it. That makes you a Papist collaborator.'

Luke stepped back, and sheathed his blade.

'Very well. It seems we both have something on the other. You'll give me that wallet, before we leave this place. And you'll take me to where Cate's being held. And as long as she and her family are safe, I'll not take it across the road, as I should, to give to Lord Finch.'

The other stood scowling, it seemed for an age. Finally, he sighed, and his shoulders slumped.

'Know that I do it not for myself, but for the other men named in here, who have England's best interests at heart,' he said, drawing the wallet from beneath his jacket, and handing it over. Luke transferred it to his own pocket.

'Now – Cate!' Picking up the two captains, they hurried out through the inn and up Fish Street towards the Guildhall. College was now back on the platform. As they drew near, snatches of his invective, directed against the Duke of York, were just audible – though many in the crowd seemed to be arguing volubly among themselves at the same time.

Chapter 69
Blades

Armstrong had returned.

''Tis no good – there's a fight broken out now in the mob. Some are saying Harbord was being paid by the French.'

'How can that be?' one of the other Green Ribbons demanded, sharply. Hawkins turned to look at Cate, with an expression so full of hatred and malice that, as she caught his eye, a massive sob rose irresistibly within her.

'We should wheel her out and set her off, just the same.'

'Don't be so damn stupid, man!' Armstrong spat. 'How's that going to look, without College telling the crowd what we're doing, and why? They've stopped listening to him.'

'It'd be one less Papist in Oxford,' the other replied, his eyes glittering, and took a step towards her. Cate nearly fainted in terror.

At that moment, a shadow flitted across her field of vision, and a deep voice cut through the palpable air of menace.

'I think not.' It was Francis! His movement was so quick and fluid – his sabre seeming to materialise in his hand as if from nowhere – that he managed to interpose himself between Cate and the other three Green Ribbons, as Armstrong, the fourth, stood off to one side, an agonised expression on his face. 'I told you before, Hawkins, there's no point going through with it.'

With a fearful oath, Hawkins drew his own sword, and sprang forward – but in one almost graceful motion, Francis swatted his blade aside, and brought his own up on the back-swing to nick the big man below the ear. Hawkins sank to one knee and pressed his hand to his neck. Now, though, the ex-soldier had to face the two others, with Armstrong seemingly immobilised by panic at the disintegration of their scheme. Francis easily evaded a wild slash from one of them, repositioning with more difficulty just in time to fend off the other. As the pair circled, Hawkins recovered his weapon, blood trickling over his collar. Cate panted with the tension: now it was three on to one. Surely even Francis could not take on all of them at once?

His movement was a blur. A great 'zing!' rang out as first he parried to his left, then just about deflected a thrust from the man in the centre. Hawkins' attack from the other side, however, came just too quickly – and, while he managed to divert the blow, twisting the blade as it flew towards him, the heavy hand-guard on the big man's sword-hilt caught Francis a mighty buffet to the side of the head. He fell to his knees, the sabre jolting out of his hand and skittering off across the enclosed yard.

Pushing one of the other Green Ribbons aside, Hawkins now lifted his weapon, and made to strike what would surely be a mortal blow to the black man's prostrate form. Desperate at seeing her last defender thus exposed, Cate wriggled her right ankle – and, sure enough, her foot was free. Immediately, she reached out with it and prodded Hawkins' backside as hard as she could. With the weight of the sword in his raised hand already pitching him forwards as he swung, the touch was enough to overbalance him, and he stumbled over the unconscious Francis and went crashing down.

Cate's flash of triumph, as the other two Green Ribbons stood momentarily nonplussed, was followed immediately by a vertiginous moment of terror: the momentum from her kick was starting to topple the whole assemblage forwards. She was going to plunge to the ground! The huge wheel would crush her, and, with hands bound, she would not even be able to break her fall. Frantically, she thrust her body mass backwards as hard as she could, somehow arresting and reversing the impetus. The iron counterweight tilted it backwards, but it did not have far to go, the trolley on which it rested having been placed hard up against the wall. As she felt it make contact with the vertical surface, Cate was suffused with relief – but only for an instant. The chock, holding the rim and the dovetailed apparatus together, dislodged, and fell with an ominous thump.

The wheel lurched alarmingly on its footing, and Cate felt the X-shaped structure start to swing round; the blades, gleaming and jutting from their positions on the spokes, waiting to cut into her as she rotated. With all her might, she strained the other way, just managing to counter the motion. But how long could she go on doing it, as the now independently spinning circles propelled her this way and that? As she looked up, Hawkins had scrambled to his feet and was reaching for his sword from where it had come to rest, a murderous expression on his face.

Chapter 70
'You never know where a door will open'

With the two Horse Guards captains, Luke padded up Fish Street behind Settle, urging them on as they ran. At the junction with New Inn Yard, the pamphleteer suddenly stopped, turned round to face them, and began to back away.

'She's down there,' he panted, gesturing towards the narrow opening, an unaccustomed look of panic on his face. 'I'll go no further with you.' With that, he turned again, and ran off into the crowd, which was now reduced to chaos and confusion as multiple brawls and quarrels raged – the speakers having apparently abandoned their improvised stage altogether.

'Shouldn't we go after him?' Ed demanded. 'You have him under arrest, don't you? Can't let him get away.'

If Luke hesitated, however, it was only for a split second.

'Nay – let's find Cate first, we'll worry about Settle later.' He felt the reassuring bulk of the wallet under his coat. Surely it would be straightforward from here, to reach her and make her safe? The pamphleteer would surely not risk any harm coming to her, out of fear for his own skin? A fear mingled, Luke suddenly realised, with a different terror – at the prospect of Settle's own comrades witnessing him arrive on the scene of her captivity in the company of a City constable and two officers of the Blues. He would look like a traitor to their cause. That must be why he had run off.

The captains drew their sabres, and they set off down New Inn Yard at a brisk walk, looking this way and that. It took but a few seconds to traverse the length of the alleyway, but felt far longer, as one nook or recess after another proved blank.

'What the Devil did he mean, "she's down there"?' Tom Lucy demanded. They were staring at a patch of tangled vegetation, in front of a wall, which was covered with evergreen ivy.

'Whatever we're looking for, it can't just be a wood-shed or something,' Ed said, stepping to one side to look back the way they had come. 'Must be a big enough space to have held three people for two days and nights.'

Three people: Cate, Settle – and Francis, the blackamoor, whom they had not yet seen. He must be here somewhere. Joan was not the only one in Oxford any more. A tiny worm of rec-ollection burrowed its way towards the surface of Luke's mem-ory. Joan: what was it Joan had said, when he complained about the lack of progress in the investigation?

'You never know where a door will open,' he said out loud. The others looked at him blankly. A sudden intuition now quickening his stride, Luke grabbed his stave and hacked back the undergrowth, stepping through it to take a closer look at the wall.

'The door – it's here!' he exclaimed, turning to the others – but they were now right behind him. The three of them burst in, to be confronted by the Green Ribbon men, brandishing their swords. Armstrong was slumped on the floor to one side, breathing heavily, and Francis had seemingly passed out – lying face down towards the far corner.

A pitiable cry came from over by the right-hand wall.

'Luke!' At last! She was alive. He had begun to fear they had killed her, as their plot failed. But he registered in an instant that something was very wrong: Cate was at a diagonal angle. And – Christ! – bound to Jethro Cox's terrible wheel! Luke sprang towards her just as the momentum accelerated her towards the blades that were sticking out from the spokes. A whisker above the first of the razor-sharp edges, he caught her in his arms, righted her, and clasped her to his chest, her chin resting on his shoulder.

Suddenly, he felt her tense through the huge sobs now racking her slight frame. As best he could without releasing his grip, he looked round, then braced for a blow as the biggest of the three swordsmen – Hawkins – made to strike. But the contortion of fury on the man's reddened face abruptly gave way to an expression of astonishment, and he looked down at a thin metal object suddenly protruding from alongside his sternum.

'No you don't.' It was Tom Lucy, whose reflexes and skill at arms had won his promotion, despite his youth. The officer drew his blade back out, and Hawkins crumpled to the ground.

'Drop it,' Ed was saying to the others, in a warning tone, as his fellow captain turned round to face them. The remaining pair let their swords fall, and placed their hands behind their heads.

'Who's that in there? That you, Master Sandys?' There was no mistaking those gruff, bumptious tones.

'Robshaw! In here, quick!' The door was thrust open, but the first to enter was Settle, his arms manacled behind his back and his ear clasped in Robshaw's meaty fist, a grimace of pain on his rodent-like features.

'Found this one trying to slip away,' the deputy said, with a triumphant grin. 'Got hold of him, clapped him in irons, and boxed his ears till he told us where you was. See, my way's best for making them talk.'

Settle let out a whimper, as two other constables followed them into the now very crowded walled-in space, and restrained the other Green Ribbon men under the captains' watchful eyes. As they were led out, Cate finally found enough breath to speak.

'You'd better untie me, Luke.' As he cradled her waist with

one arm to steady her, and reached up with his other hand to loosen the bond around her wrist, their eyes met, and she smiled for the first time. Even through her tears, there was an unmistakable light of recognition, which passed between them like incandescence from a taper to a candle.

Chapter 71
One Last Mystery

'Against thee, thee only, have I sinned,' Settle intoned, his sardonic expression back in place; 'and done this evil in thy sight: that thou mightest be justified when thou speakest, and be clear when thou judgest.'

'You plan to plead Benefit of Clergy?' Luke exclaimed. 'But murder's not been a clergyable offence for a hundred years.' The 'benefit' was to avoid punishment under criminal law: instead, an offender had merely to convince a bishop of genuine repentance. To qualify, a convicted man had to prove he could read aloud the words of the 51st psalm, from a written text put in front of him in court – which would present no difficulty for Settle, especially as he evidently knew the relevant passage by heart. But the recourse had been abolished for murderers under Queen Elizabeth, over a century earlier.

'Ah, but Unsworth was not murdered – he died in a chance medley, with no pre-pensed malice. 'Twas manslaughter, at most.'

'I see you know the letter of the law, as well as the Psalter.'

Confined though he was in a cell at Oxford Castle, the pamphleteer's customary self-assurance had returned.

'The gaolers here will let one have access to legal texts – for a consideration. And it never does to sit idle.'

'Anyway, that's rot, about Unsworth, and you know it.'

'What I know or don't know is neither here nor there. 'Tis what you can prove – in front of the right judge, of course,' he added, smirking. 'Anyway, even if that doesn't work, I'm sure Old Rowley will give me a pardon.'

'The King? Why would he do that?'

'Well – I've heard there were treasonous mutterings in that tavern. Unsworth, as the innkeeper, must have been aware. And yet he didn't report them. Maybe we just took the law into our own hands.'

Luke let his breath out with a 'pfff'. 'You've got some nerve, I'll give you that. And Royal pardons don't come cheap.' But he could already guess the answer.

'Money's no object to the people I work for.'

The chief gaoler jingled his bunch of keys to signal to Luke that it was time to wrap up the interview.

'At least let me ask you about one thing that's been puzzling me.'

'You can ask.'

'Harbord's dagger. We found it on the ground at New Inn Yard. You – or someone – removed it from his body.' The other gave a cautious nod. 'Why?'

'Well... we found him about a minute before the night watch turned up. We had no idea who'd killed him. But it did look odd, that his own dagger had been used. A single-edged Scotch dirk – very distinctive. So we undid his belt, grabbed the knife, sheath and all, and made ourselves scarce.'

'Might have interfered with the tale you wanted to tell, that he'd been attacked by "Papists"?'

By way of reply, Settle simply gave a shrug and sat back in his chair, a complacent expression on his rodent-like face.

Luke felt a tension relax within him as he was escorted back towards the daylight. A dangerous enemy was to go free: surely it was just a matter of time before Settle's friends arranged for his release. But at least he had proved Harbord's murder was not a political killing – in the nick of time to save Cate. He would have to satisfy himself with that. As he approached the Castle's open front gate, a familiar figure was limned on the threshold against the morning sky. There was no mistaking that tapered upper body, and the slightly convex curvature of a tall capotaine hat.

'Francis?'

The big fellow turned, a half-smile on his face, and touched his brim with an index finger. 'Master Sandys! At your service, sir.' Another man, who was standing slightly off to one side, let out an impatient sigh.

'Aren't you due back in court for the committal hearing?'

'It seems I'm wanted elsewhere.'

The newcomer waved a piece of paper, retrieved from an inside pocket of his coat.

'Order from the magistrate for his release,' he said. ''Tis all above board.'

Luke briefly scanned the document, which was counter-signed at the bottom by a Colonel Gerard, commanding officer of Gerard's Regiment of Horse.

'So you've got off the charges through "Benefit of Service". You're to go to Tangier, it says?'

'Aye, with Captain Coy here. We're to reinforce the garrison. Can't let a bunch of heathens get their hands on the King's wedding present.'

The port city, Luke remembered, had been transferred to English rule when Charles married Catherine of Braganza, decades earlier.

'Come, Francis,' Coy snapped. 'We sail on the night tide.' The castle ostler had brought out two horses, saddled up for the journey to London.

'You'll have to make haste.'

Francis finished pulling on a pair of fine leather gloves, and mounted a strong-looking bay mare. 'Don't worry. 'Tis a fast road from Oxford. As long as there are no cattle on it.' And with that, he winked, clicked his tongue to gee up his mount, and they were off.

Chapter 72
Happy Couple

Oxford was returning to normal. Parliament had been dismissed after a single week in session, when MPs presented another Exclusion Bill from the Commons, and it was duly voted down by the Lords. Rumour had it that Charles would now rule alone, with financial support from his cousin, Louis XIV of France – obviating the grubby business of bargaining with Parliament for supply. So, politicians and their hangers-on set off back for London, and the city's taverners, merchants and traders put away their surplus stock in disappointment.

There had been joyous scenes at The Mitre when Cate arrived after walking the short distance from New Inn Yard, leaning on Luke's arm as her legs were weak and unsteady after her ordeal. He was giving a daughter back to her parents, which was no doubt where she belonged – for now. Would she ever belong by his side? The couple met, days later, for another confidential chat over coffee, in their favourite corner overlooking Turl Street.

'So poor old Martin Fletcher is the only one who'll stand trial, after all that.' He watched her carefully as she digested his news. The expression of dismay, as she heard about Settle's manoeuvrings, soon passed, however.

'They'll never convict Martin, though, surely? After what his family have been through?'

'I doubt it. He might get off with a warning. After all, Harbord's name is mud. Any local jury would know all about that.' They settled back in companionable silence, watching the steam from their coffee cups gradually subside.

'I do love you, dear Cate,' he finally declared, catching her eye.

'I know, Luke. But it can never be.' She took out a handkerchief, and discreetly dabbed her eyes, as her other hand briefly entwined in his, across the table.

'I could leave Elizabeth,' he began. But she cut him off.

'Could you, Luke? Really? You'd miss her, after all these years. And what would become of her? You're not that heartless, God knows – and I am not, anyway.' She withdrew the hand and, for a tense moment, they held each other's eye. She could see he felt thwarted, and her heart went out to him; he could see she was adamant, if regretful. Then they both subsided, and chuckled.

'And there's Father Morris, I presume?' he said, taking a sip of coffee.

'Aye – and there's Father Morris. He wants to spirit me away to a convent, in France!'

'Well, we can't have that.'

'Indeed we can't. I love my home. No one can take me away from here.'

Luke thought of Settle's document wallet, now locked safely in a strongbox at Magpie Lane. Somehow, he had never got round to reporting it. The Green Ribbon Club had left Oxford – for now. But events of the past week had shown the lengths to which men could be driven by political fervour and fanaticism. It felt right to keep the evidence as an insurance policy against any threat to Cate and her family in the future. If he could not embrace her as he would wish to, he could at least do something to keep her safe. Even so, Luke left The Mitre with a heavy tread, feeling that a door had, this time, decisively closed. Head throbbing, he turned towards Simon Gibson's for solace. Perhaps he would get a phial of that new medicine the apothecary was so keen on. What was it called? 'Laudanum'. What harm could it do, after all?

A week after that, the sun was streaming through the plain glass windows of St Andrew's Church, at Marston. The pews set aside for the families from Magdalen Farm were full to bursting, and a goodly crowd of well-wishers had swollen the usual congregation. John Davies, the farrier, had recovered his twinkle, and even old Greening, the porter from Christ Church, who'd known Emily since childhood, twisted his features into what he fondly imagined was a beneficent smile.

'...To have and to hold, as long as you both shall live?' old Reverend Fairclough wheezed. Emily gazed at Richard adoringly.

'I will.'

'I now pronounce you husband and wife. You may kiss the bride.'

Standing by the church door, Robshaw raised a flask to the couple, and took a deep draught. Luke recognised it from somewhere – didn't it belong to Ed? The captain must have given it to him, as a souvenir from their exploits.

Richard and Emily stepped out into a perfect spring morning, as Farmer Pawling and Jacob held either end of a green bough that arched over the newlyweds. A little too loudly, Robshaw said:

'Fertility symbol, that is. Mind, they don't need one of them, this pair, do they?' Emily's cheeks flushed as she walked past, pretending she hadn't heard. Liza beamed with a mixture of pride and relief that her youngest daughter was finally off her hands. Elizabeth squeezed Luke's elbow, and he looked fondly down into her familiar face.

'Emily's a buxom bride, and no mistake,' she said softly, with a knowing and slightly wistful smile.

'Aye – that she is.' And the couple walked arm in arm along the path out of the churchyard, to the carriage that was to take them to the wedding feast at the farmstead and, later, back to the quiet house on Magpie Lane.

THE END

Historical Note

The English Parliament under King Charles II sat at Oxford in March 1681. Elected members reached the Convocation Room of the University by passing through the Bodleian Library courtyard and the medieval Divinity School. His Majesty was escorted from Windsor by the Horse Guards under their Colonel, Aubrey de Vere, the 20th Earl of Oxford, and his security upon arrival in the city was the responsibility of the Foot Guards under their commander, Colonel Russell. Officers in the latter of those illustrious regiments included a Captain Sutherland; and, in the former, Captains Thomas Lucy, Henry Slingsby and Edwin Sandys.

The Unicorn and Jacob's Well opened on St Aldate's – then called Fish Street – no doubt to capitalise on the influx of trade as MPs and their hangers-on came to town. One of the elected members of the House of Commons was William Harbord, of Thetford in Norfolk, who was notable for his record as an agitator on the subject of the so-called Popish Plot.

In general, I have tried to bring seventeenth-century Oxford to life by building into the novel, as settings, minor characters and asides, some of the notable figures and controversies of the time, drawn from the historical record. That record mentions no such person as Luke Sandys. Citizens were expected to take a turn on duty as one of twenty or so constables in Oxford, under the elected officials: the bailiffs and – above them – the councillors and the mayor. But the practice among freemen of paying a fine to avoid this inconvenient hiatus in craft or commerce was already well established; thus opening the possibility for other men to perform contiguous terms in their stead.

While there was no formal role of 'detective' in the law

enforcement apparatus of the time, constables were expected to gather information and evidence to render to magistrates, judges and juries, who would determine the guilt or otherwise of an accused person. Rules of evidence were observed by the courts with varying degrees of fidelity, but the attitude I have attributed to my chief protagonist – of taking pains to avoid hanging the wrong man – was certainly shared by some of those involved in dispensing justice, if not all.

In *Blood on the Stone*, Luke is a graduate in his early forties. By early modern times, the sons of well-to-do merchants and successful craftsmen – people of the 'middling sort', as they were known – had begun to receive formal education, up to and including university study, if they could afford it. He would have entered Christ Church College as an undergraduate in his middle teens, so his student days would have spanned some of the 1650s, with Christopher Wren and Richard Jones among his illustrious contemporaries.

At that time, Oxford was a crucible of what later became known as the Scientific Revolution: a transformation of knowledge and ideas about the natural world bookended by publication of the 'heliocentric' theory of Nicolaus Copernicus (the earth orbiting the sun, not the other way round) in 1543, and Isaac Newton's *Principia Mathematica* in 1687. John Wilkins, Warden of Wadham College in the mid-seventeenth century, convened regular meetings of a 'Natural Philosophy circle', at which scientific breakthroughs were demonstrated, among them Boyle's law of gases, and the cellular structure of living tissue. The latter was enabled by the development of powerful microscopes, such as those manufactured by Richard Reeve to specifications by Robert Hooke – a luminary of Wilkins' meetings and prime mover in a group which then set up the Royal Society in London. (Its motto, *nullius in verba* – take no one's word for it – is said to have been suggested by the King himself.)

The Mayors of Oxford were Robert Pawling in 1679–80 and John Bowell in 1680–81. Pawling ran a mercer's shop at 126 High Street (where some of the ornate frontage he installed can still be seen to this day). He oversaw the granting of the Freedom of the City to Titus Oates, accuser-in-chief of the Popish Plot, and to James Scott, Duke of Monmouth, the latter of which occasions was satirised in a popular verse. Evidently a man of considerable energies, Pawling's deeds in commercial and public life overlapped with his tenancy of Magdalen Farm, whose lands extended across the lower slopes of Headington at least as far as the old London road. John Fell was Bishop of Oxford from 1676 to his death, a decade later; under him, the Reverend Peter Birch was Vicar of St Thomas's, in Osney. Sir Thomas Millington was both Sedleian Professor of Natural Philosophy and a Fellow of the Royal College of Physicians.

The story incorporates several real episodes of the time – or, at least, episodes oft-recounted as real. Dr John Radcliffe – who in his will endowed the Radcliffe Library – was said to be reluctant ever to leave a convivial company, and on one occasion had to be forcibly removed from such a gathering by a military man under the false pretences of being wanted to render medical assistance to his colonel – who turned out, instead, to be his 'comrade', lodged in a narrow alleyway. I have taken minor liberties with the timeline of Radcliffe's career. He qualified as a doctor a year after the events of *Blood on the Stone*, but to have him treating patients, and for that to play a part in the plot, was irresistible – especially given his enduring renown in Oxford, where the local hospital is named after him.

Nell Gwynn, it is said, pacified an angry mob by looking out of her carriage window, whilst in Oxford to accompany the King for the parliament, and identifying herself as 'the Protestant whore' – rather than the Catholic one, the Duchess of Portsmouth – whereupon the crowd cheered and let her pass by. The Royal party was entertained by a performance of Charles Saunders' play, *Tamerlane the Great*: a drama only distantly related, it seems, to the much better-known *Tamburlaine the Great*, written by Christopher Marlowe nearly a century earlier. The description at the start of Chapter Nine of the welcome laid on by the dignitaries of Oxford, for the formal entry of the Royal party into the city, draws on contemporary accounts. And Captain John Coy, who appears in the penultimate chapter, was one of the officers and men of Gerard's Regiment of Horse (later renamed The Royal Dragoons) who went to reinforce the English garrison at Tangier in 1680.

Looming large in the political context for the novel are the Exclusion Crisis and the Popish Plot. England had gone so far as to execute a king and undergo nearly a decade of military dictatorship, all in the name of protecting the liberties of its people from the depredations of the Crown. So there was widespread alarm that a 'Papist' could once again sit on the English throne and re-impose absolute rule, after the manner of continental monarchs such as the reigning King Louis XIV of France. The House of Commons wanted to exclude King Charles II's brother, the Roman Catholic James, Duke of York, from the line of succession, but its will was thwarted by the House of Lords.

The Country party, or Whigs, then seized on the Popish Plot, claimed to be a conspiracy by Jesuits to assassinate Charles, and used it as a pretext to persecute England's remaining Catholic clergy and laity alike. Public opinion was inflamed through such means as the increased circulation of newsletters, or 'mercuries', and political pamphlets, including those quoted in Chapters Six and Eight; and weaponised by provoking or procuring political unrest on the streets, of which 'rioting' by City of London apprentices represented the iconic form. The decision by King Charles and his advisers to bring Parliament to Oxford was calculated to isolate political process from this fraught atmosphere. But of course the pamphleteers, propagandists and provocateurs – among them, the 'Protestant Joiner', Stephen College – then descended on the city themselves.

As for Emily: there was always some agricultural work for women in England, albeit reduced, by early modern times, due to the enclosures of the previous two centuries. So a young woman could well be a cowherd as a contribution to her family's keep as sub-tenants on a big farm. March is early in the year, certainly, for cattle to be grazing out of doors, but in a warm spring the growth in some fields is just about sufficient – though the beasts would have to be taken in for the night. She could also be involved in such tasks as making cheese, and soap.

Neither was it all that uncommon for a courting couple to 'get carried away', as happened to Emily and Richard (and, before them, Luke and Elizabeth). The general response of the local clergy in such cases, it seems, was to read the banns of marriage as quickly as possible, to minimise the perceived offence to public decency. Above all, a child must be born into wedlock, or face the lifelong stigma of bastardy; and a father must do right by a woman he had impregnated. Parish officials would be charged with exacting maintenance payments for an illegitimate child, if in need of support – and if paternity could be established.

The real 'hero' of the novel is arguably Oxford itself. By 1681, major building work in the area of the city dominated by the University was largely completed. The interregnum proved but a temporary hiatus in the growth under the Stuart Kings. Notable additions of the seventeenth century include Wadham and Pembroke Colleges; the Ashmolean Museum; the Botanical Gardens; the Sheldonian Theatre; and Bishop Fell's improvements to the Quadrangles of Christ Church. The building of Tom Tower, Christopher Wren's neo-Gothic masterpiece which completed today's college frontage on St Aldate's, commenced a few months after the Parliament and would have been, at the time of the novel, one of only two significant missing elements from the classic Oxford skyline immortalised in Matthew Arnold's later image of 'dreaming spires' (the other being the Radcliffe Camera, completed in 1749).

Today's visitors can still enjoy the view, through all points of the compass, from the top of Carfax Tower. At street level, they can wander down Magpie Lane and turn right on to Blue Boar Street; then, if they so wish, return to the High Street by way of either Wheatsheaf Yard or Alfred Street, which in those days was called Bear Lane. They can even still refresh themselves with a drink or a meal in The Mitre. The medieval Guildhall was replaced by a purpose-built Town Hall in 1752, then again by today's imposing structure in the 1890s – but each has occupied the same site.

The influence of the Scientific Revolution was far reaching, and underpinned the European Enlightenment. For rigorously assembled evidence – available to all through sensory perception and processed by critical reasoning and debate – to be the basis for conclusions and judgement, not only in the laboratory but also in society at large, is a principle over which many have struggled. For that principle to be confronted by prejudice and bombast on behalf of sectional interests is, arguably, as familiar a syndrome in our own time as in that of the Popish Plot. Perhaps it is not too much of an exaggeration to identify the period of *Blood on the Stone* as a time when Oxford, through the power of its ideas and the experience of its people, began to move decisively towards one of those two modes of engagement with the wider world, and away from the other.

Jake Lynch
Oxford, 2019

Acknowledgements

Thanks to Annabel, Rosemary and Mark for gallantry in reading my first draft. Thanks to all friends at West Oxford Pantomime Association for good times and comradeship, and for unleashing my creative side. Thanks to Steve Jones, for sharp eyes and sound advice. Thanks to the Oxfordshire County Library Service, and its dedicated professional staff. And to students, staff and supporters of the Centre for Peace and Conflict Studies at the University of Sydney, for inspiring my commitment to, and interest in the origins of, human rights as the organising principle for a good society.

Unbound is the world's first crowdfunding publisher, established in 2011.

We believe that wonderful things can happen when you clear a path for people who share a passion. That's why we've built a platform that brings together readers and authors to crowdfund books they believe in – and give fresh ideas that don't fit the traditional mould the chance they deserve.

This book is in your hands because readers made it possible. Everyone who pledged their support is listed at the front of the book and below. Join them by visiting unbound.com and supporting a book today.

Sveinung Kiplesund
Anne Kocek
Antony Loewenstein
Kathryn Logan
Kosta Lucas
Jason MacLeod
Ken Macnab
Melissa Martin
Grace Mathew
Ingrid Matthews
Eyal Mayroz
Helen McCue
Jad Melki
Lindsay Mell
Stewart Mills
Bonaventure Mkandawire
Kim Morris
Chris Nash
Carlo Navato
Anne Noonan
Ciarán O'Raighne
Sahar Okhovat
Ana Pararajasingham
Hannah Patchett
Sabrina Patrick-Urrutia
Marianne Perez de Fransius
Cathy Peters

Vivienne Porzsolt
Sanjay Ramesh
John Read
Charlie Rose
Aime Saba
Phoebe Saintilan
Nan San
Paul Scott
Priya Shaw
Ibrahim Sorie Kamara
Frank Stilwell
Neal Sussman
The Revd Graham T G Sykes
Elizabeth Symonds
Oren Thaler
Sayara Thurston
Elissa Tivona
Alma Torlakovic
Camellia Webb-Gannon
Thordis Weber
Hannah Whelan
Ron Witton
Punam Yadav
Yasmine Yakushova
Steven Youngblood
Tingting Zhang